EMERGENCE
Book 1

Ian McKinley

EMERGENCE

DOUBLE DRAGON

A DOUBLE DRAGON PAPERBACK

ISBN 978-1-78695-536-4

Double Dragon
is an imprint of
Fiction4All

This Edition Published 2021
Fiction4All
www.fiction4all.com

Cover art by Deron Douglas
www.derondouglas.ca

Prologue

"There's a difference between you and me," I said calmly, trying to ignore the 12-inch hunting knife being waved in my face. "A real serious difference." I could hear adrenalin morph my accent towards its Glasgow roots.

"You young guys all go for big weapons. With the ultrasharp ceramic edges on the chibs of today, you just don't need all that bloody size and mass. And it's all for show, to frighten me. You've probably got a neat wee laser in your pocket that'd do a much better job than your stupid big fucking blade." The nutcase actually unconsciously tapped his left pocket with his free hand. Transparent as a window.

"Me, however, I'm just a poor, helpless, old cunt." My God, did he look disturbed by me swearing? Happy enough to slash me to death, but embarrassed by a slang term for the female sexual organ. Fucking fundamentalist God-bothers! His accent, as he crashed into my office and demanded that I *take the posture,* immediately nailed down his nationality and I had already started to have suspicions about his Weltblick, based on his scarred but well-scrubbed, monolithic, football-quarterback appearance. A bit like a hard-used Mormon missionary on steroids.

"You've got that big fucking blade and all I've got is this fuckin' pencil!" I took it from my shirt pocket and brandished it in his direction. "A pencil!" I screamed at the top of my voice - which is, if I say so myself, much louder than you would expect from my diminutive stature. "A fuckin', cuntin' pencil! Everyone else has biros or fountain pens or fuckin' styluses bluetoothed to their cuntin' palmtops! But what do I get? This shitty pencil! What the fuck was God thinking about? Is She out of her fucking tiny little mind?"

The poor bastard was squirming now, which looked completely incongruous given his size and shape. It must be like one of his nightmares where he finds himself getting a hard-on in the locker room or an irresistible urge to wear a pink tutu to his Sunday church service. I was betting that he was wondering if he had missed CERN and strayed into the local loony bin. "But professor,... " he started, managing to look surprised as I rammed the pencil into his left eye.

... and he spoke no more.

Chapter 1

The club was dimly lit, loud and packed with sweaty, gyrating bodies. I'm cool, however: calm and in my zone. The top predator. The entire club is my Serengeti. I'm the alpha male lion, basking under a tree while my harem is out on the hunt. I peer past the bottles behind the bar and catch a view of myself in a mirror. I don't look like anything special - spiky ginger hair, thin face and deep brown eyes that have been described as having an evil sparkle. I prefer to think of them gleaming with intelligence but, in any case, they certainly don't seem to discourage the fairer sex.

Of course, nothing is what it seems: my expert system is hard at work ripping the guts out of poor defenseless databases while I play about with a synthchem cocktail at the bar. It might look like the same fluorescent shit that the proles around me were quaffing, but this was serious kit. Not illegal, of course, because there is no point running the risk of being screwed about by the Polizei, who always have narks in places like this. But the latest good gear, nevertheless. It takes ten minutes to produce a new super-stimulant and a decade to get it licensed or banned. So there is a ton of ace stuff floating around, if you know where to go to beta test it. Some, obviously, would just totally fuck you up. If you have the inside gen, however, you can actually get paid to have a really outrageously good time. Not that I need the money, it's just the principle that makes it extra fun.

Access to inside knowledge: that's what it's actually all about. That's what puts me right at the top of the food chain. I sip my drink and feel the chemical enhancements kicking in. I'm faster, smarter, better looking - even my balls are bigger! But that's not what puts me on the top.

Look at the competition! Designer sculpted bodies, designer animated tattoos, designer clothing ...everything tailored by someone else to ensure that they radiate *today*. Nobody even slightly yesterday would try to chance their arm in this place. These are the hunters, male, female and other, making a living from the low-hanging fruit. Fruit? Well, much of the prey is fruity enough. The 12-year old rich-bitches, augmented to 17 or so with hacked IDs to match. The techno-crumblies, who you couldn't prove to be a couple - or many - decades past their sell-by-date without radiocarbon dating. Or the sad types of no specific gender: just looking for anyone to accept them for what they are, even if they haven't the foggiest idea what that might be. No challenge in that arena, not for me!

I'm following it all with a neural link to Babe. My slave lioness pride leader is what keeps me ahead of the competition. Everyone entering this dive is scanned in a dozen different ways: video, audio, IR, UV, terahertz, who knows what? I've no idea what all that shit is about, but Babe does. She rips databases... and not in a gentle way. Everything that can be extracted from the global knowledge base about any target is torn into shreds by state-of-the-art software, with the single aim of determining their potential interest to me and exposing their vulnerabilities. One simple cost-benefit analysis later and I've identified my victims and sketched the optimum route to their downfall.

"Overkill! Overkill!" my mental image of a prole screams. "Why bother?" A very good question, I concede to myself.

I look around the club, with its self-selected subset of humanity - a sexier, richer, more dynamic cohort - and smile. This is what makes me the only real alpha here. I take what I want because I can. It isn't that I actually need to do things this way. I sit at the top of a very big heap in the biggest pharmaceutical concern in the world. Of course, a pleb like my mental sparring partner would have no idea that it is so very big. According to norm-accessible info, it appears as just one of the *Big Six*. But there is no *Six*. There is only one. And only someone at stratospheric management level, or their ace Knowledge Engineer, would know this.

In the real world I have power. I am the ubergeek who makes the hoi polloi salarymen shit blood and ice-queen exec assistants wet their knickers on the basis of a raised eyebrow. I know this. I've seen the stains. But, for me, that isn't real power. That's just management hierarchy: a weak and insipid substitute for the finesse of fingertip manipulation. This you get only when taking control of someone who has no idea of who or what you are.

I was toying with my lurid drink, brushing the glass against my lower lip and coasting on almost-illicit pheromones, when Babe hooked a big one. With the computational power that I have at my fingertips - or, more accurately, supporting my mid-brain - I could have my evil way with almost anyone that I choose. The expert system usually gives probabilities in the upper 90% range. Rarely, however, a victim emerges that would fit my profile in terms of desirable attributes, but would probably not fall for one of the pre-programmed seduction routines: 50%, 40%, lower. These were the ones where the chase was justified. I checked the vid that was uploading directly to the visual centers of my brain, bypassing all the usual optical stuff that the unenhanced depended on. Yes, she definitely looked my type.

All the hacked and restructured info was streaming through the uplink in parallel, but my attention was focused on the simple vid. The woman strolled confidently into the club, apparently oblivious to the surgically enhanced stereotypes packing the place. Short, tight-muscled, small breasts; all presented in a leotard that covered her like a coat of paint. She passed an Amazon lurking at the entrance, 2 meters of tailored six-pack, gleaming skin tones and triple X tits, and didn't bat an eyelid. Natural, her body screamed, the real kit here!

The background was seeping in... name, address, education and employment history. Age: she was forty and looked a very tight thirty-two, -three, something thereabouts. It really was natural, though! I wasn't drooling, but could certainly feel the first twinges of a hard-on.

No doubt about it, this was my target for the evening. Separate from the herd and pounce. The smart systems had already spotted my interest and modified the lighting and sound profiles to present an invisible, yet unavoidable, track from the entrance to the vacant seat beside me. I don't run the club, but I own the company that does, so I can pretty well fuck with things any way I please. The sheep on the dance floor, and the wolves prowling around it, wouldn't notice anyway, even if the guiding pathway had been walled with bricks.

While my victim wends her way towards me, the rest of my seduction kit kicks in. The woman is wearing dynamic fabric, some kind of Escher sort of pattern. I don't have to even make a subliminal demand, but already feel my t-shirt tighten and can be sure that I am now sporting a matching pattern. Amazing how easy that makes the first intro! I'm forced to exhale as my trousers tighten, giving me a more sculpted profile. I could get this from surgery or, perish the thought, exercise, but why bother when smart fabrics can do the work for you?

I can now see my prey in the flesh as a gap opens up in the heaving crowd. The 3D pattern of ultrasonics leaves no choice in the matter and the raven-haired vision clicks towards me on high stiletto heels. The lead-in is set, but I need to make a move within the next few seconds. The intro should have been with me ages ago; several seconds, at least. But my expert system is dumb. I double check. There is nothing my seduction toolkit can offer that has more than a 25% chance of success. Now I really have a hard-on. This is a woman that I must have.

As she approaches the bar, I catch her eye. She raises an eyebrow in an incredibly cute manner and I merely nod like an imbecile to indicate that the stool beside me is free. On the surface, I am cool, calm and collected. Below this, I'm screaming though my neural link for any background that will let me get into this nymph's pants. She is absolutely gorgeous.

Not beautiful, I suppose, by conventional standards. But beauty is now a simple commodity available to anyone with enough cash and, as such, has lost all of its pulling power. Certainly for me. Devastatingly, gob-smackingly cute: that's something that you don't get on the pharm- or surgical-enhancement menu. You can't define what it is, so it can't be faked. It's natural and this dream is the epitome of what it can be.

She drops inelegantly onto the stool and swivels back and forth, allowing me to admire her profile. Black, unfashionably curly hair, cut to shoulder length, perfectly frames her visage. Her face seems small, surrounded by the mass of curls, but the glint in her eyes and the smile on her scarlet lips hint at a vivacious character that makes simple physical description inadequate. She radiates hot! But not in a brassy, obvious way. Sultry, deep heat, which can only be spotted by someone who knows where to look. Somebody like me.

I still don't have any help from my expert system as she turns towards me, making me painfully aware that my tight trousers have exposed a growing erection to any glance below belt level. My arms drop onto my lap just in time, a millisecond before I am clocked from head to toe in a completely unabashed manner.

"Snap!" she says. It indicates how much that she has thrown me off balance that my link has to remind me that this is because our smart fabrics are showing the same pattern. I have, at least, enough forethought to set up a trace routine, to ensure that the dynamic fabric patters gradually synchronize, before I answer.

"Shit! I was assured that this sequence was unique! Look at it, it's exactly the bloody same. We must look like twins - or a really sad couple. Anyway, I'm really sorry. This looks much better on you. Actually, it looks a hell of a lot better. I'll download something else."

Rabbiting like this presented the perfect opportunity for me to examine her in real life. The terahertz scans captured nothing that could be hidden by her skin-tight clothing. Small, but perfectly formed breasts were topped by nipples like acorns. These fought for my attention with the clear evidence that, not only was she not wearing underwear, but was also an aficionado of *landing strip* pubic topiary. A dream! If someone had programmed a catch for me, it would have been this woman. It wouldn't have been me doing the programming, I had to concede. I would never have guessed that this particular combination of appearance and attitude could hit me so hard.

So now Babe finally comes up with something useful. Her body movements are mirroring the music. A dancer! Now I'm cooking with gas!

"Do you know how well that pattern goes with the music?" I sound like a total dick, but I'm running without ES support. "Do you dance? I don't want to push, but this Escher stuff would be fantastic with movement. I was actually looking for someone... "

"... to download this, so you could dance with her." Her grin was so natural that Babe went mute again. I have all the completely predictable moves of the host of normal club actors and wanabees pre-programmed. Innocent naive fucks up the system, apparently.

"... well, yes, but that sounds a bit manipulative. Really, all I want to do is dance." Christ! I sounded like one of the Travolta clones who were making the dance floor a danger zone for unenhanced humans. *"Give me an edge!"* I screamed silently through the neural link.

"You're on your own, big boy!" Neural links are sub-vocal, conceptual. But I'd swear that was the voice of my primary school maths teacher. Totally useless teacher, but female in a school for Catholic boys. Subliminal message: take whatever crap input is provided by the software with a very big pinch of salt.

All this high tech subterfuge was burning teraflops, but to no avail. "OK, let's dance," she responded before I resorted to any of the nested patter lines that Babe was, finally, beginning to generate for me.

Again I was caught out like a smash-and-grab lobotomy victim. So busy getting the tactical chat-up planned, it hadn't occurred to me, or my fucking increasingly annoyingly inefficient software, that the first line would work.

"Dance? Dance, indeed! You don't mind the tacky twin outfits?"

"Not at all," she smiled wickedly, "as long as they're a challenge rather than a crutch!"

Wow! Pulling my chain! Kid gloves are off here! "*Sort music and lights*," I commanded - just to establish who was in charge of this operation. Despite all of my previous complaints, I knew that this was exactly the job that Babe excelled in. The analysis had been running since this woman had entered the club and sparked my interest. A subtle variation in the heavily sampled house/grunge dance beat was enough to nail down her tastes in music. A rip-off of an ancient Dire Straits number, tuned in to her body's micro-movements, was enough. SHE pulled ME up onto the dance floor.

Now it's sorted. Coast to bedroom!

But it wasn't moving that way! The woman just loved dancing! We were working-out on the floor in a way that would grind the hard core aerobics set to a greasy spot in no time. I was keeping up, thanks to chemical enhancements, but you get nought for nought. I was sweating like a pig as my neurally-linked mistress controlled the sound; melding it to our movements to make even the crappiest input from my side seem natural. No matter how often I screwed up, Babe was ahead of me, making my stumbling appear to be completely in synch with the jungle rhythms.

We weren't having sex, but it was close enough to bring me right up to the edge. Babe was running the entire club entertainment system: sound, sub-sonics, lights, pheromones. The resulting dance environment blended our movements and, wherever possible, encouraged close physical contact. Initially this was just the twists and blocks of techno-jive but, as the tempo slowed, easily moved into close grinds and pelvic thrusts. It was auto-catalytic in a strange kind of way. This bar was run primarily to support my individual pick-ups, but there was enough overflow in this case to bring on a feeding frenzy of the other hungry predators, supported by their willing victims. Artificial pheromones set up the initial ambience, but they were rapidly being drowned out by the real thing. It was heading towards a flashmob orgy: a focus of the gutter media. Been there, done that, but never actually started one before.

I was torn. I didn't want to break this flow, but I knew that the dance floor wasn't going to get me to where I really wanted to go. We were dancing as if we had practiced for a decade. Her natural ability was perfectly complemented by my supporting technology. But it had to stop before the inevitable chaos broke loose - these excess pheromones weren't being generated on their own - or I had a heart attack.

So, time to stop for a drink and then move on to dirty tricks time. Not date rape, just a little suggestion-enhancer that might facilitate an escape from disco hell. As my dance partner dashed off for a quick toilet visit, I realized that, formally, we hadn't even exchanged names. I had a downloaded precis of the entire history of Andrea Meier since birth, but we hadn't introduced ourselves so far. "*Run this!*" I left the tricky bits to Babe: all I had to do was identify the problem and the smart software would solve it.

Now we were back on course! Back from the loo, the delectable Andrea glugged the drink I offered her and immediately attempted to share most of it with me in a very messy kiss. No problems! A bit of enhanced suggestion wasn't going to slow me down at all!

"How about... " was as far as I got before I was grabbed in a most intimate fashion, making it clear that my state of arousal had been noted.

"Now! On the floor if you want!" Andrea was straining against me and cramming her tongue into my mouth. Of course! She was falling for the top predator: she can't resist it. All of the technological support that got me to this point was immaterial to the final success. This was me! Couldn't possible fail!

***

I woke up naked, face down on my bed, with a very sore head and an intense pain in my bum. The former was not, by any manner of means, unusual after a night on the prowl. The latter scared me shitless.

The life of a top predator is not without risks. I know that. It's exactly why I work under the umbrella of my ES support. Could someone have sneaked under my firewall? Was Andrea a bloke?

I strained to remember what had happened. We danced. We got really physical. We came upstairs. This is why I bought the club in the first place: not only have I my own personalized hunting ground, but a comfortable pad for the kill lies immediately above.

Then what? She was like a ferret in heat and certainly had no concealed pieces of male anatomy! We were groping around and ripping off items of clothing before we got the door of the apartment closed. But then things got cloudy. I was ready to go, no doubt about it, but seem to have collapsed just after things started to get interesting. A blank thereafter.

Fucking smart drugs! Must be an interaction between the shit I was sampling and the enhancer that Andrea spat into my mouth. Could that be it?

I almost started to relax as I rolled over to grab a clear-up patch from the emergency supply by the side of the bed. Then I realized that, no matter what knocked me out, it didn't explain my painful arse.

"Fuck! Fuck, Fuck, Fuck! Fuckity fuck for fuck's sake!" I screamed aloud. My anal virginity was gone; without even knowing how or to whom. "Fuck, Fuck, Fuck!" Even though bashing my skull against pillows was having no direct physical effect, the effort of moving my head was enough to hammer nails of pain through my cranium.

As if to intensify my misery, exactly then my phone cut in with a high-pitched scream. Normally, a noise like this would be reason enough to simply throw the fucking thing out of the window. But my phone doesn't scream: it has an awful tacky disco version of *Scotland the Brave*. Truly fucking awful, I agree, but I can be sure that nobody would ever consider using the same tune. It does not scream with a sound like an anally-abused banshee, I grimaced as this simile came to mind, it simply can't. Worse than that, there're only about five people on the planet with the ability to call me on this piece of shit. I use such low-tech crap only to demonstrate my contempt for underlings when I call them and other lowlife.

Regardless, it was doing my very fragile head in. "What?" I shouted, falling back with a sigh as I finally managed to slap the dermal analgesic onto the side of my neck.

The message was clearly artificially generated, but top-range audio that allowed enough definition to bring back a memory of the nymph that I had attempted to bed. It was definitely my nemesis. "Tom, sorry about this, but you really do deserve it. Trying to use your smart computer systems and chemicals to seduce a poor, defenseless girl. Shame on you!" Even through the voice synthesis interface, her snigger, or snort, came through clearly. She was taking the piss... and enjoying it.

"Anyway, as you know by now, I've left you a little present. It might smart a little but, I can assure you, there're loads of guys who'd pay hard-earned cash to get even bigger things shoved up their asses. So, now we come to the good and bad news. The good news is that, if you do what we tell you to, you'll never even know that you have a capsule of neurotoxin stuffed up your jacksy. The bad news is that, if you don't play, you won't live long enough to worry about it. All you need to know is that the capsule is tailored with every anti-tampering trigger known to man, so don't fuck about with it! Just wait for instructions. I suggest that you have a bit of a kip now: you're going to be a bloody busy little bee tomorrow."

There was a pause, then the message continued "... but I've got to say you've got a tight bum on you! Shame that we couldn't have gone to your room under other circumstances. Then I'd have really given you a run for your money!" The artificially generated laugh sounded more like a witch's cackle, so was probably added for effect. My head had now cleared enough to have Babe analyze the call in real time. Her synthesis was short but cruel. "*Downloaded here, so no tracing possible. It looks like the fucker has become the fuckee!*" I couldn't have put it better myself.

Chapter 2

Now I was really scared. Bad enough to be anally raped, but I worked for Big Pharm. I knew exactly how bad a tailored neurotoxin could be. We had an entire division that worked on such shit: superficially developing biowarfare defenses, but with a healthy income from military and intelligence black-ops applications. You could choose from an entire palette of irreversible agents, depending on how much you wanted your victim to suffer before they finally kicked the bucket. I have never been accused of being squeamish, but one glance at product testing video documentation was enough to give me nightmares.

I can't remember the last time I felt this emotion. Sometime in school, I guess, when the psycho gangs preyed on geeks and anybody else who appeared to be weak and defenseless. I was weak in those days, but I rapidly learned how to defend myself without body-building and martial arts. The bullies who picked on me got expelled, had unfortunate accidents, their parents got jailed, their houses burned down. Nobody could possibly prove that I had anything to do with it, but the message quickly spread through the school. Fuck with this geek and something really terrible would happen to you. I had become an ubergeek before I had even heard of the term.

I shook my head to try to physically pull myself together. This was just not on! Nobody fucks about with me! Fuckee? Fuckee? I'll show them fuckee!

"Babe, move on this. All scans since this bitch arrived: strip and analyze. Backtracks on ... where the fuck did she come from? Forward runs ... how far can we go? Then extrapolate further. Everything that you can find on this Andrea. What is she doing and why me?"

My head was now completely clear. Whatever Andrea's mouthful had contained was now chemically cleansed from my system.

Now the more intrusive bit. "*What scanning options will nail down what was done to me?*"

Babe responded immediately, as if my ES toolkit had already been working on this question. Probably it had. "*Blood work to test the drug used, then an anal swab to check what you might be carrying. Considering the message, scanning is probably not a good idea.*"

"*Dead bloody right; although how I can avoid being scanned in this day and age is a bit trickier. Going to the office is definitely out of the question.*"

"*You can use the STD analyzer in the toilet here for the samples: it's currently set up for saliva samples, but the reprogramming is running now.*"

As I complied with Babe's instructions, my fear was increasingly transmogrified into rage. No way! No way! Someone was trying to play me. This was not going to happen!

***

Emerging from the toilet, the results of Babe's work were already summarized in slick, color-coded

3D. Neural links are great, but there are some things easier viewed in a real live hologram. If interfering lasers can be considered real life, that is.

Babe had taken over the questions that I had posed into an argumentation model, summarizing petabytes of purloined information. It was all shown in an interlinked network. The back-tracks: Andrea had emerged from Zurich Kloten airport and taken a taxi directly to the club. Hacking into security cameras in a Swiss airport is tricky, but doable. I sent Babe off on this track, with a feeling that it wouldn't get anywhere. Cab records were also ripped: seemed she paid cash.

This was clearly linked in the matrix to the forward tracks. Taxi straight back to the airport. Not even a call, just hailed one of the cabs that lurk around the Niederdorf 24-7. Paid cash.

The airline records were linked to both threads and much easier to rip. No Andrea Meier on any incoming or leaving flight within a 24 hour window. This didn't surprise me at all.

Now the link to the gen on Andrea herself. All the background was solid. The woman lived in Lengnau, a village just outside Zurich. The resemblance was close: however the real Andrea was the happy mother of a couple of kids and kept in shape as an aerobics instructress. She certainly was not my nemesis. It was the retinal scan that had made the link: match was over 95%. All the rest of the physical measurements were roughly consistent, so worked well with the fuzzy systems that you need to handle such a barrage of imprecise data. I expanded the real Andrea's image and rotated it slowly. Yes, very nice. I could see me being physically attracted to this woman. But the sparkle, the evil grin, it wasn't there.

It wasn't so obvious in a static image. I switched to the video record from the bar and the vivacity of *my Andrea* was palpable. Easy to do, I realized. Wear smart contacts and the retinal scan will dominate all other input. Nevertheless, a lot of background work would have been needed to fit the attacker to a local fall guy ... or is it fall gal in this case? "*Get on it,* I commanded, almost annoyed as the "*Running, boss,"* response overlapped with it.

Now the main block of video that I had been tap dancing around. It formed the center of the argumentation model, with links like neurons spreading in all directions. I inhaled, remembering some yoga shit from my early geek-looking-for-females days, and then slowly exhaled as I gave the play command. As 3D video, not a direct neural link. I wasn't going to relish replaying my humiliation.

My apartment is designed for seduction. Every possible monitor to help me on my way and, more importantly, record my inevitable success, was set up for this. Would my opponent know this?

Babe had, with usual efficiency, trimmed down vast quantities of multi-spectral input to the critical bits. I sat down to view the holographic replay of myself entering the apartment, already a bit unsteady on my feet. The vixen was all over me, ripping off clothes, climbing on my body, licking and biting anywhere in reach. I knew that I was viewing my rape, but I was getting hot and sweaty regardless. Whoever set me up, chose the right woman for the job!

As I was pushed towards the bedroom, I could already see that the drug she must have slipped me was cutting in. I was staggering, but meekly moving in any direction that I was pushed. High-grade date rape kit. I shouldn't have held back with this bitch!

Now I was on the bed, rapidly and efficiently having my last items of clothing stripped off. I was grinning like a moron, clearly on another planet. The view was from the hi-res camera behind the ceiling mirror; a point of view that I've spent many happy hours replaying. Then Andrea turned and looked directly at the mirror. She knew the camera was there! She rummaged about in a small handbag and then slowly donned surgical gloves. After smearing the gloves with a gel of some kind, she extracted a device that looked a lot like a large caliber bullet and whispered into my ear. I saw myself turn onto my stomach and spread the cheeks of my bum.

"What are you doing, you stupid bastard?" I screamed, forgetting for the moment that this was a record of times past.

I watched the rest of the procedure, but couldn't concentrate on anything other than the way in which I had been violated.

***

The rest of the scanned material played for about a quarter of an hour. My beautiful assailant finished her work on my body, mucked about with my phone, then stripped off and strolled into the shower. Her few items of clothing were chucked into the recycler and then she soaped down comprehensively with something that she took from her handbag. The 3D coverage of the shower was crystal clear, as it was designed to be. She was doing a very comprehensive job with the bar of soap. My erection was beginning to recover.

"*Fuck! Analysis of this - is it what I think it is?*"

Babe was able, as I expected, to make sense of even such a cryptic command.

"*DNA scrub: we can do the analysis, but it is likely that everything that we can recover prior to this point would be matched with Andrea Meier of Lengnau.*"

I groaned in agreement as I watched the vision of loveliness blow dry and then pull on a diaphanous full-body suit that expanded from a small pouch like the costume out of the Flash's ring. One second it was totally transparent, then it was so intensely jet black that all that could be seen were the places that she wasn't.

All the supporting scans were running in parallel to the vid feed when everything suddenly went white - or black - as the default mode of the system might be.

"*Was that...* "

"*... a focused emp blast? Seems to be.*"

"*Can't I even finish...* "

"... a fucking sentence around here? Apparently not, boss. Here's some of the good stuff."

I was ready for one of my regular fights with my Expert System, or Artificial Intelligence as it preferred to be called, when the new nodes emerging in the argumentation model grabbed my attention.

"*Class, Babe!*" I murmured subconsciously. There was no verbal reply, but the simulated warmth in my cortex was unmistakable. "*AI, AI - you're a fucking AI!*" I conceded as I saw the threads peeled from the persona of my Andrea.

The first branch of the analysis was linguistic. Andrea's English was, to my untutored ear, inseparable from the typical Swiss polyglot ability that I had begun to take for granted. Babe's tools were much more sophisticated. Certainly native English speaking with a lot of time spent in Scotland or Ireland, but probably an ex-pat brought up somewhere with an American influence. Highest probability Japan, Guam or somewhere similar.

Then the pubes. "*Babe, I just can't believe how good you are!*" A smug response registered as a shiver that ran up my spine. The combination of that particular trimmed profile and the smartware suit that showed it off to its maximum effect was the signature of a very small, but extremely select, outfit in Shibuya, Tokyo. Not only that, but the link snaked to a network of dance clubs in Shibuya and neighboring Roppongi, Akasaka and Shinjuku. There was a lot of fluff obscuring the direct link: goth lolitas and Elvis impersonators with expensive designer pubes, proclivity to dress up in weird kit and interest in dancing. Nevertheless, a cosplay group stood out. Before I could even think about an order, an ancient youtube video fast-forwarded to freeze on a grainy still, which blurred further as the enhancement tools worked over it. The optimized image focused on a girl of about 18, clad only in body paint, representing the manga character Carol from a story called *Chirality* according to the background info.

I couldn't tear my eyes from this crappy 2D image. There was no doubt about it. This was the girl who would become the woman that would screw me over. She was gorgeous, cute, enigmatic, sexy. I would have pounced on her in an instant if she had wandered into the club. But, somehow, not quite as totally devastating as she would be in a couple of decades.

"Get yourself sorted out man!" I commanded myself, as if vocalization would make it more probable. I know what I'm doing. I'm the master of deep semantic analysis, which forms the basis of the knowledge web and all its associated applications. Like high-tech seduction. "Don't fixate!" I'm sure that this heartfelt plea doesn't make a blind bit of difference to Babe, who must be running with all of this mixed input.

"*There are two things that you need to sort out...*" Babe's neural link had the texture of ice-crusted snow, indicating that this was serious. As if I needed reminding. "*...the immediate threat and the long term threat.*" This had the feeling of an old physics lecturer. It meant that I was supposed to solve the riddle on my own. The AI had an idea, but its confidence was so low that I was being put on the front line.

The immediate threat was clear: whatever had been rammed up my backside. The long term threat had to be those responsible because, given my work situation, there would be no way that they would mess with me unless there was something huge to be gained. For the first time since I woke up, I had the feeling of being in charge of things. So, I had two clear problems to solve very quickly. This is what I do. I'm back in my zone!

Intermezzo 1

A known terrorist, tied to various Christian fundamentalist cults, simply waltzes into a CERN office and attacks a senior staff member. The enquiry by the Swiss police is focusing on how someone on Interpol's new Class 1a list managed to gain access to the building, although I'm sure that this will prove to involve a simple cloned ID. CERN security has improved a lot since the Large Hadron Collider became a focus for protest by a wide range of anti-scientific nutcases a couple of decades ago: but this is focused on the main labs, not an overspill admin office on the outskirts of Geneva. The actual incident was clear, caught in real time by a webcam in my office. The fact that a knife-wielding attacker was taken down by an aging professor's pencil was simply accepted as a fact demonstrating self-defense. Probably regarded as the inevitable consequence of me being foreign: a Swiss professor would have presumably been expected to have used the corkscrew of his obligatory Sackmesser.

The CIA, however, was much less sanguine. Within four hours of the incident, three grim looking heavies accompanied by an Interpol liaison guy arrived at my office. Only the leader of the group, Chuck, introduced himself. My scanners had, however, identified the entire team as they clambered out of their limo in the car park. After my last unexpected visitor, I had over-ridden the standard security software with some smarter additions of my own.

Chuck quickly summed up their problem in a concise, if rather brusque, manner. "Now Professor O'Neil, let's see if you can help me here. We have one Charlie Mullins comes to see you armed with a serious hunting knife. There are the questions of why he targeted you and how he got in, but this Charlie has a hellova record. He spent years training Christian survivalists in post-apocalyptic urban warfare and, for at least the last decade, has been up to his neck planning and implementing right-wing terrorist actions in the US of A, Europe and the Middle East. He's thirty eight years old, six-two, built like a brick outhouse and has black belts in a half dozen real martial arts, not sports things like karate and judo. My two guys here, together, would have great deal of difficulty taking him down." The two guys mentioned seemed rather unhappy about this criticism of their fighting abilities, but did not raise any objection to their boss's summary of Mullins' martial skill-set.

"Now you... " he looked me up and down with a distinct scowl, "... are sixty-four years old, five-eight, rather skinny and, as far as we can find out, without any form of combat training whatsoever. How did you manage to take this guy down, armed only with an icepick?"

"Actually, it was a pencil," I corrected him, eager to break into this analysis before it led into areas where I didn't want to go. "In fact, if you look at it the right way, you'll see that there's no problem here at all. If I had been a black-belt shithouse like your guys, rather than the runty academic that I am, I would certainly have come off worse in this encounter. But, as you have pointed out, I was clearly no physical threat, so an attack was not expected. What young Mister Mullins failed to appreciate was that my job, which I'm very good at by the way, involves innovative problem solving. As soon as I recognized that he considered me neutralized by his knife, all I needed to do was select an appropriate tool to solve this problem."

"You pushed the pencil through his eye and into his brain. He was dead by the time the police arrived."

"Yes, death was almost instantaneous. Of course, the difference in height helped me to get the angle right."

"So you cold-bloodedly calculated how to kill this guy and then just did it."

"You don't expect me to have attempted something non-lethal?" I glowered at him with my best look of professorial scorn, usually reserved for particularly thick undergraduates. "This was obviously someone far too dangerous for anything like that."

"But you did this without any combat training!"

"No formal training, as you're certainly aware, but I grew up at the end of last century in a very rough suburb of Glasgow, so I have enough combat experience to last a lifetime."

Chuck had no answer for that.

Chapter 3

Babe - or BABE - is a biologically accessed bio-computer ensemble. This is just geek-speak for a neural link to an organic-quantum supercomputer. BABE is a generic term, but Babe is my very own tailored system. As far as I'm aware, it's the most advanced that currently exists. Of course, even with the search resources that I have, I can never be sure: the military or another top industrial Knowledge Engineering outfit might have something similar. I, of course, have made sure that nobody else has any inkling of my Babe's full capabilities, including my employers. To be brutally honest, I'm not sure that even I know how far Babe has evolved to date.

My tailoring has focused on expert system optimization and smart search engines, so Babe's own claim that she is an Artificial Intelligence may well be justified. Emergence is a sensitive area and I'm certainly not going to get another geek in for a second opinion. The thing about Babe - whether she is really an AI or not - is that she autonomically runs a work program that constantly upgrades both her hardware and software. She identifies any new developments that could be useful, purchases them and incorporates them into her core. She even does the creative accounting that allows costs to be hidden within the discretionary R&D budget that I have at my disposal.

My neural link is probably the most extreme example of Babe's abilities to integrate developments from disparate technical fields.

Conventional biological access involves skull electrodes or a cap capable of producing and reading magnetic fields. Babe spotted that cutting-edge Pharm research on implants for control of neurological disorders like Parkinson's, organic wires for wearable electronics, nano-machines for focused cancer treatment and synthetic organism production for bioreactor synthesis of specialist organic chemicals could be combined to grow a bio-interface within my skull. As the components required were all well-established, the only novelty was in the way in which they were combined and the entire installation process had less risk than any normal surgical intervention. Again I can't prove that nobody else has done the same thing, but it is unlikely that they could without access to a knowledge base equivalent to mine.

Of course, helping me seduce young ladies is not Babe's only, or even main, role. That really would be overkill. In knowledge engineering speak, she - or it - would be called a general, creative problem-solving machine. We are partners with a relationship closer than most married couples. I specify the problems and Babe solves them.

The creative part, I think, is clearly specifying the problem. This is what I had to do now - and very quickly. As far as I could see, the job done by my opponents, whoever they might be, was extremely professional and carried out in an almost flawless manner. Despite all my resources, they had, literally, caught me with my trousers down. Almost flawless, but two big slips: underestimation of the search capacity that Babe provided me with and granting me time to gain the initiative. I had to make the most of these.

"Job one," I vocalized, as speaking the problem aloud helps me ensure that it is clearly defined, "find the lady." That was the easy one.

"Job two, identify possible explanations for this entire operation." A lot trickier. Even Babe would need a bit of help here. "This can be broken down into a who and a why. These must be closely related. I certainly must be a carefully chosen victim: this job would have required a hell of a lot of advance preparation tailored towards yours truly. So it has got to be someone with a lot of resources... or power, which is much the same thing. So, that should be at least 99.99% of global population ruled out. Unfortunately, that still leaves a lot of possibilities."

"*Somewhat over a million,*" interrupted Babe, just to show she was still following me.

"Well, the who is coupled to the why. Why me? Now, I might not be the most pleasant of guys... "

A burst of virtual laughter showed just how well software could represent sarcasm.

"... but the people that I piss-off on a regular basis don't have the neurons, or the cojones, for a caper like this. OK, I get up the noses of some of the big bosses of powerful divisions: HR, legal offence, PR. So what? They know that they can't do without me. They would be delighted to see me nuked by an arse-delivered neurotoxin, but they'd lose dosh if I kicked it. If there had been a credible alternative to me, they'd have taken me out years ago. And they'd do it directly, not pissing about like this."

I stopped, spotting that I was drifting a bit off topic. "Look at possibilities in-house anyway," I finished. I really didn't think there was a chance that anyone working directly for Big Pharm or any of its multitude of spin-offs, partners and suppliers could be up to anything this big without leaving a trace on Babe's radar, but a double-check would do no harm.

"OK, outside, in the real world. Who might hate me?"

"*That only cuts it down to anybody who's ever met you!*"

I was beginning to think that I needed to have a look at generation of humor in AIs, but I dragged my thoughts back on track. "Well, I suppose there have been some of my encounters at the club that haven't finished so well. But they're definitely the exception rather than the rule."

"*Could be because I handle all the Dear Joan communication?*" my virtual scribe pointed out. "*Then again, some of them might have seen the kind of footage that you circulate to your even sadder friends.*"

"Mmm, good point!" I conceded. "I have sent some juicy stuff about, but only to good pals."

"*And you'd trust them not to pass it about*?"

"OK, point made. Run checks on everything that's ever gone out and run traces on all the girls involved."

I thought in silence for a moment, but couldn't really think of anyone else that I'd pissed off enough to warrant a toxin suppository. "Right, the other line would be someone who has targeted me, not because of what I have done in the past, but because of what I could do in the future. The most obvious would be somebody who could benefit from my access to the entire Pharm knowledge base."

"That would be just about every major multinational and most governments."

"I suppose so," I agreed. "Get onto that as well." Seconds of silence ticked by, but I my brain had gone blank. "Right, and anything else I haven't thought of," I added, lamely.

***

I was beginning to feel tired and thought about fake-Andrea's recommendation of a nap. Definitely not! This would lose vital time to prepare for the next bout of this battle. I have often claimed not to be competitive and will go out of my way to avoid most games and all sports. When I do end up in a game, however, coming second is not an option for me. "Optimum stimulant!" I mumbled as I wandered over to the espresso machine and punched up a triple. By the time that this Heath Robinson monster had finished pouring, a pink capsule had dropped into my hand from the drug synthesizer.

Thirty seconds after washing down the capsule with a sip of scalding coffee, the drug hit like a dive into a pool of glacier melt water. I felt bright-eyed and bushy-tailed and could feel a rush of optimism. This was, however, not the flush of over-confidence or well-nigh omnipotence that can be engendered by off-the-shelf stimulants and enhancers. It was just that, as soon as I moved into the familiar realm of chemically-enhanced cogitation, the full benefits of my link to Babe were realized.

My need for vocalization disappeared and the holographic information model that floated in front of my eyes seemed to expand and contract of its own volition, responding to some subliminal interest on my part.

I decided to go back and nail down the easy bits first. Pseudo-Andrea was quickly identified as a certain Cindy Green, whose life history was being assembled from diverse open sources and hacked databases as quickly as I could develop questions to ask about her. Hundreds of megabytes of files from her childhood and early teens were scanned and quickly dropped into bins providing background fodder for the personality profiling tools. All I needed to know for now was that she was the daughter of an economics professor who shuttled between Nagoya and Stanford Universities and who had managed to pick a Japanese wife from amongst his students during his first visit to Nippon. The American professor was a naturalized Englishman and his wife had a Japanese father and Irish mother: this mixed race heritage maybe helping to explain their daughter's exotic beauty.

Cindy was completely bilingual and graduated in '10 from Tokyo University with a degree in economics. Clearly pre-ordained for a high-flying position in academia or, more likely, a multinational of her choice. There, however, my smart search engine ran into treacle. The branching information tree, which had been expanding like a starburst firework, froze and only minor twiglets continued to grow from the major branches defining Cindy's life. This is, of course, anomalous in the extreme. Moore's Law and its various corollaries ensure that information about any topic expands exponentially with time, in parallel to global growth in computing power.

The breathing space provided by the reduced barrage of material defining Cindy's world allowed further anomalies in the details of her late teens and twenties to come to the fore. A carefully orchestrated attack on a high profile target like myself should have been carried out by a ninja, someone with an extensive background in the military: intelligence black ops, something like that. OK, the seduction part might be a bit more Mata Hari. Maybe a smart girl gone bad, with a background of rebellion and a bit of cash-raising by casual prostitution, the latter certainly not uncommon among students in the Tokyo of the early 21st century. But there was not the slightest inkling of this in her profile, nothing at all that was even slightly dubious.

The fastest-filling files post-graduation were all unavoidable background shit that defines existence: bank statements, tax records, payments for rent and utilities. It was far too flimsy, however; not enough for a real person. Where were the logs of telephone calls, internet use, travel, purchases? It looked like Cindy was a phantom: maybe the real person died in 2010 and her shade was maintained entirely as a cloak for future activities like the assault on me. I knew of several government agencies that did this and even stranger things all the time.

I was just about to scrap this line of investigation when we had a serendipitous hit on a remote link that was so peripheral that it wasn't even visible on the summary model. I say *we* because, by now, it was hard to tell where my meat cortex ended and Babe's artificial neural network commenced. In any case, the brainwave was to search image records, despite the fact that no CCTV anywhere near the address that we had obtained had been archived - a fact that was strange in itself. A stray correlation dredged up the original Google street view recordings from Akasaka and stripped off the anonymizing function for the faces of anybody inadvertently caught during videoing. The software image match was rated at over 90%, but as soon as the enhanced image appeared I could see it was a hit alright. Cindy had obviously turned to look straight at the camera and, despite a rather strange hairstyle that put me immediately in mind of Betty Page, it was clearly my elusive nemesis.

That was all we needed: confirmation that this was a real person and not an identity shell. With an exact date and location of this hit, along with analysis of clothing and haircut, we were able to focus hacks on security camera archives and private online photo albums. It was slow work but, nevertheless, the argumentation model was expanding again. Despite sophisticated management routines, this was mainly computational grunt work that was burning petaflops. Even for a machine as fast as Babe, this meant shoving normal day work down the list of priorities, giving a drop in performance that would become noticeable even to my staff, who I didn't consider to be the sharpest knifes in the drawer. Nevertheless, I really didn't give a damn: this search was not only critical for my continuing health, it was also becoming increasingly fascinating.

I closed my eyes and diverted the input from my neural link to a buffer. There were layers upon layers to this Cindy, but how much had I been expected to find out? Of course, someone without the tools that I had at my disposal would never have identified the woman's real identity in the first place. Nevertheless, I had been specifically targeted by someone who had carried out a fairly comprehensive background search, right down to details of my den here and my taste in women. Having never felt threatened, I had never gone out of my way to hide my private life. That was going to change, anyway. "*Got that?*" I checked.

"*On the to-do list, once we get these priority jobs out of the way,*" Babe responded instantly, confirming that this action was diverted to the bin containing lower priority work.

"OK, let's assume that whoever planned all this expected me to get at least as far as Cindy, although maybe not as quickly as I did..."

"...as quickly as we did" slipped into my mind as a seeming afterthought.

"Whatever! Anyway, don't interrupt until I ask for your input!" A fleeting image of a long-suffering servant tugging a forelock vanished before I could properly latch onto it. Bloody smart-arse machine!

"So we have somebody that can live with me identifying the girl and probably assumes that, even with the search machines that I can access, I won't get much more than ancient history. Does that make sense?"

"Could indicate a lot of confidence in their digital security, or else a much more sophisticated play..."

"...because the material that I can easily dig up looks so artificial!" I completed the thought, recalling my previous discomfort at the early search output. *"This seems a bit far-fetched, though. Someone starting to plan this caper twenty years ago..."*

"...or doing a bit of digital history rewriting to produce the same effect." Babe pointed out as the same thought came to me.

"In which case, it's head-to-head, love. Someone thinks they're good enough to hide stuff from us. They'll have focused on net-accessible, but can't possibly have gotten to a fraction of the stuff

that's offline. Spend cash on meat-bots and see what we can dig up."

"On it, boss. But, in the interim, you may want to have a look at some of the stuff you're buffering. You'll love it: prime geek-porn."

Well, I couldn't fail to rise to bait like that. I opened my eyes as the buffer content flashed onto the information hologram and highlighted links between different branches in the tree representing everything we had been able to extract on Miss Green. The pubes again: who would have believed it! Some sad Japanese collector of antique 2D porn had a huge file of images of pubic topiary, which seemed to come from an old voyeur web site. These were all captured from a hidden camera in a select spa in Roppongi and were cross-linked to snaps taken of women entering and leaving the premises. There was Cindy again, along with hundreds of images of the pubic topiary process accumulated over about seven years. Most of the photos and video clips were blurry, but the sight of my nemesis having her pussy pruned in what looked like a gynecological examination chair caused a distinct pressure build-up in my groin, reminding me that I was still clad only in my birthday suit.

More links expanded. The spa was still in business, but security seemed much tighter. Certainly no further spy-cam stuff that we could find. *"OK, that's a good start for meat. Get someone to put a monitor on that place and get a girl make an appointment with the beaver-trimmer. Anything else from that locale?"*

"Nothing openly available. That area's full of celebs and politicos, so security is tight. Hacking is ongoing, but may take a bit."

"Anything else in the vicinity? Dubious government agencies or corporations?"

*"Mainly banks..."*a new branch appeared on my hologram, *"...and some prime penthouse space that originally belonged to Mitsubishi Re, but gets impossible to trace ownership of after 2017..."*

"...after the big mergers with Hong Kong-Shanghai, Zurich, Munich and God-knows how many other re-insurers," I finished, watching the network flesh-out before my eyes. *"So, is this just a coincidence?"*

"We'll know a bit more when I get some local meat onto it," Babe responded in a confident manner, confirming my suspicion that a sensible story was finally beginning to emerge. *"Should I hack the Re?"*

This was the big question that was already tasking me. I wasn't sure but, from my experience in the pharmaceutical industry, I suspected strongly that if I scraped about I'd find that there were a lot fewer independent reinsurers, or even insurers, than you would be told by a Wiki. If I was facing a megacorp, then a hack from someone in my position would be effectively a declaration of corporate war. It would be different if I could prove that they had initiated hostilities, but I had nothing solid. Indeed, the more I thought about it, the less sense it made. Insurers might war with banks or other financial institutions, but not pharm conglomerates.

"*Unless...*" I started, but hadn't even framed the question before Babe had the answer.

"*Nope, no past big claims that look dodgy or anything what might develop in the near future. So our employer has done nothing to provoke anything like this.*"

Right, I was on my own. I pushed the envelope with what was covered by my job remit, but had never even contemplated an action as crazy as this. Just gut feeling - and a pain in the arse, I reminded myself. "*OK, do it. Just make fucking sure that we're not caught. If this gets traced back to me, I'll wish that the fucking neurotoxin bomb in my bum had gone off immediately.*"

Intermezzo 2

Interpol and the CIA had, independently and probably unknown to each other, both bugged my office. As I had expected this development, I had already established the tools to intercept their back-links and apply automatic censoring that removed anything that I might want to keep to myself. I was tempted, just out of badness, to add in some material tailored to send them off on wild goose chases, but I resisted. Better to keep this option for some time when it could be of direct benefit to me.

Before I started earning my salary from CERN for the day ahead, I had a quick hack into the CIA case files. Very thin indeed. The main highlight was their recognition that I definitely wasn't what I seemed to be. I sighed, but acknowledged that this was inevitable. On paper, I was a division head with overall responsibility for information and knowledge management. The overall budget of my division was apparently some 2% of CERN's humungous total but, when you stripped away all the double accounting chaff, in reality we provided a net contribution that covered almost 18% of the organization's running costs. And this was just the profit made from selling CERN knowledge to third parties. The reduction to the cost of CERN's operations resulting from the tools that we supplied was of a similar order of magnitude.

All of this was causing some consternation. How did the most abstruse and ivory-towered of all R&D organizations manage to make money in the dog-eat-dog world of commerce? There was now a team of a dozen agents trying to find an answer; one that, presumably, might explain why I might be a terrorist target.

Well, it was a shame that I was such a center of attention, but at least I could focus on maintaining the bigger secret. There was certainly a division, but nobody in it actually worked on anything to do with knowledge engineering apart from myself. The rest of my nominal employees were actually just part of CERN's huge administration infrastructure, predominantly human resource support. I paid myself as much as I needed and spent the rest of my budget on computing. The Director General knew this but, as far as I was aware, nobody else - and I wanted to keep it that way. That's what worried me most about the attack, was there someone else who knew my secret?

Chapter 4

In order to divert myself from thinking too much about the potential consequences of being caught hacking a megacorp, I moved to a completely different part of my problem network. "*So, what do we have on the little present that this Cindy rammed up my back passage?*"

"On the capsule itself, nothing: there's not a trace from your swab and, of course, any kind of scanning is out of the question."

"Definitely no scanning, I'm not risking this bloody thing going off. But, not a trace of anything? That seems strange."

"Nothing from the capsule. It's probably ceramic or coated in something completely inert such as diamond-like carbon or titanium carbide. There is, however, something interesting in the traces of the gel."

I vividly remembered the vixen rubbing something on her surgical gloves and felt a distinct twinge in my anal sphincter. "*The lubricant?*" I guessed.

"There are traces of a silicone-based lubricant, but the interesting bit involves the bio-adhesive, which is now bonding the device to the wall of your rectum. It's a fairly standard biodegradable glue that acts for about a week. After that, you will simply pass the capsule naturally."

"That's interesting enough on its own. It gives us a timescale for whatever it's been planned that I

am supposed to do. Is there any way that we can speed things up?"

"We could certainly feed you something that would accelerate degradation of the adhesive when it got that far, but this would take a while. A suppository would be faster..."

"But would risk setting off some kind of anti-tampering device! I really do not want to go there! Are there any non-invasive options?"

Babe appeared to hesitate, as if trying to break something to me gently. Wired though I was, I recognized that this was taking my anthropomorphization of a software package to extremes. Nevertheless, the response seemed to fit in with this interpretation, presented in a way that brought an image to mind of a kind old family doctor. *"Yes, there does seem to be an option for introducing a reagent that shouldn't risk being picked up as tampering. We could, for example, reverse the natural peristalsis of the colon."*

"Wouldn't the drugs needed act as possible triggers? It seems dodgy enough introducing an agent that degrades the adhesive."

"Any novel chemical could certainly be a trigger, which is why the reagent would contain only the enzymes that cause the normal biodegradation of the adhesive, but in concentrations above those normally present. A drug that reversed peristalsis would certainly be a risk, so the safe option would be for you to use the yoga basti method. All it needs is muscle control." An associated link provided background and images

of skinny young men with apparently deformed stomachs.

"*You have got to be kidding!*" I objected. "*That kind of shit takes years to learn, even if you are good at yoga, which I definitely ain't. We'd be quicker letting the bloody glue break down as planned.*"

My mental image of the doctor strengthened. "*It would definitely take a while if you had to do it by yourself, but there seems to be no reason why I can't help you there.*"

"Can you do that? I've never heard of anything like that before."

"While we've been discussing this, I've accessed everything recent on man-machine interfaces..." A new information model appeared before my eyes and links associated with biofeedback exploded into fine detail. "*As you can see, the principle is well established; it just hasn't been tried for this particular application.*"

"But this is research with all kinds of different interfaces..."

"...none of which is as sophisticated as ours, or linked to an AI as smart as me," Babe finished with a distinctly smug tone. *"All I need to confirm that it'll work is for you to relax and open our link for unrestricted two-way communication."*

"Can't harm, I suppose - in for a penny..." I mumbled out loud as I closed my eyes and ramped up my interface to maximum bandwidth. Although my nano-engineered implant was powered by mutant mitochondria and thus avoided the restrictions of normal battery-powered devices, I could maintain this level of power drain for short periods only. After fifteen seconds, I let the bandwidth drop back to normal. *"Was that enough?"*

"More than: all functionality confirmed and routines set up for your colonic rinse, if you want to try it."

"How can you be so sure?" I inquired, curious to know details despite my complete trust of my clever software.

The biofeedback model expanded to show the results of Babe's tests. Initial pings to map neural links to muscles and then a ten second demonstration of control of autonomous nervous system, increasing resting heart rate to exactly 100 and holding it there.

"Fuck it, Babe!" I gasped. "You were fucking about with my heart. That's a bit fucking extreme for a demonstration of principle. You could have killed me."

The reply seemed to hide a smirk. *"Well, would you rather the big test involved fucking about with a toxic timebomb?"*

There was no answer to that, so I didn't even attempt one.

***

While Babe was presenting this option for solving the problem of my booby-trapped bottom, parallel routines were organizing all the practical details for implementing it. As these appeared on the hologram, I realized for the first time that I had been awakened at five o′clock on a Sunday morning and it was now almost seven. Even in a large 21st century city, there were limits to the speed at which meat agents could be mobilized to get a hold of materials not available in my apartment.

Two hours I'd been at this already. Time certainly flies when you're enjoying yourself, I thought, realizing that I was actually having fun in an extremely weird, masochistic manner. It was the challenge: so much trickier than most of the stuff that made up my normal working day. The challenge and the fact that we were making progress. I could feel in my water that I was pulling ahead. I was going to win this game.

I dismissed the bum-disposal file, as Babe had labeled it, with typically warped humor. Back to the enigmatic Cindy. The hack of Mitsubishi Re was moving at a glacial rate, but this was OK with me. Better slow and silent than crash in and get caught in the act. I scanned through other branches of the argumentation model, looking at the answers emerging to the big questions.

Who was my assailant? Cindy was slowly fleshing out as a real person but, without the search power at my disposal - and a bit of luck, I acknowledged - I'd probably have discounted this trace. It led also to her apparent employer, which should be confirmed soon and should also help nail down the associated questions of why me and why now. Somewhat separate was the more detailed question of why give me breathing space before letting me know exactly what I was expected to do within the next week. Of the options to answer this, I highlighted a chain focused on making me receptive to the demands that would certainly come.

The logic seemed convincing. Wake me with a chemical hangover, threaten me to put me in a panic and demonstrate that I was completely outclassed. Then let me stew for a couple of hours. This would work if my hidden opponents were convinced that I would make no significant progress in this period. They then make a demand with a tight deadline and I would be forced to give in. This would be more effective than waking me at eight and making the same demand cold. I'd be much more likely to attempt to screw about with them in such a case.

This gelled with the entire choreographed attack of the previous night, indicating very intimate knowledge of my personality and lifestyle. Other cross-links to supporting evidence had emerged over the last couple of hours. Tracing distribution of videos of my conquests came up with Bucky, an acquaintance that I considered a bit of a wanker. I couldn't quite remember why I had sent him anything in the first place, but probably just me strutting my stuff and trying to piss him off. In any case, last month he'd forwarded all the images that I'd sent him as a single package to an untraceable auto-burn address. He'd also received a payment of 10,000 euro on the same day by direct bank transfer from an anonymous source.

"Bastard!" I cursed aloud. "Burn this cunt!"

"Didn't I tell you that your unpleasant nature would catch you out someday," Babe responded, sounding very much like my mum. Nevertheless, a Trojan immediately diverted the entire contents of Bucky's bank account to Oxfam. My AI had clearly anticipated my response here and set up everything in advance. Certainly knew me better than my own mother ever did, I conceded.

A further cross-link was then highlighted, showing a deep hack of the transfer that provided my Judas with his pieces of silver. The source was impossible to trace, but the transfer confirmation contained an embedded currency conversion rate. This payment had been provided from an account in Japanese Yen. It was certainly coming together.

I was just about to leave the model breaking down details of how this attack could have been planned when a flash and Babe's simultaneous *ping* alerted me to first results from the Mitsubishi hack. This input had established a red-highlighted thread directly to a branch on this hologram.

I followed the link and was initially confused. This wasn't even stuff from the hack proper, just a sophisticated analysis of low-security communication flows indicating that at least a half-dozen seemingly independent reinsurers were actually a single organization, a finding that didn't surprise me in the slightest. Most of these Res were based in Bermuda, but the information pathways showed a central node that appeared to act as a coordination link. As yet, this node was associated with only an internal identification code, but its location was clear - the Caribbean island of Saint Martin.

Now the back-link appeared. Less than forty minutes after pseudo Andrea was dropped off at Kloten, a private jet took off with destination logged as SXM. The code was for the international airport on the Dutch side of the island, I was further informed.

"Yes!" I jumped to my feet and punched above my head. "Has that plane landed yet?"

"ETA in about two hours, around three am local time. Hacks into airport security already initiated, but the main terminal is closed at night. Must be a specially organized private landing. Trying to get some meat organized, but it's very early Sunday morning in the middle of nowhere. No pharm facilities on island, so it will have to be a private detective or something similar. It's not a 24-7 kind of place, so it's tricky."

"Whatever. Better get some professional muscle out there anyway."

"Order is already sent. A hard team is being assembled in Curacao and will be helicoptered over at first light, about five am local."

"Let's just hope this isn't a false alarm," I muttered under my breath but, in my core, I was certain that it wasn't.

Intermezzo 3

The software package I was running could trace its heritage back to a primordial code dating to the end of the 20th century that implemented TIPS - the Theory of Innovative Problem Solving. Of course, the capabilities of my program compared to its ancestor would be like comparing 3D holographic e-pads to tin cans connected by string. Nevertheless, the basic principles were the same: define the problem in terms of specific conflicts and then search a knowledge base for approaches that have been used in the past to solve similar conflicts, even if these have been in completely different technical areas.

I could easily define my goals: to identify who was responsible for sending a fundamentalist hitman to visit me and to ensure that they didn't attempt anything of the sort again. The conflicts were that both goals required clarification of the intention of the visit and how that led to me being targeted in the first place. All of this I could input in plain language and then simply sit at my work station and see how things develop, refining the goals and conflicts in dialogue mode.

I really wasn't expecting anything earth-shattering from this tool, however. In most cases it simply acted to reinforce my own deductions and flesh them out in detail. It was also handicapped by having access only to information that was accessible to others. Possession of rather awesome hacking abilities meant that this was just about anything available in electronic format, which covers almost everything these days. The few exceptions are important, though, as these include the secrets that I hoard in my head. As I firmly believe that anything shared between two or more people is no longer a secret, I am extremely careful in this regard, even when it comes to my own personal and highly secure computer. If I can access the files of others without leaving a trace, it would be stupid of me to assume that nobody else could do the same.

The first iteration of the conflicts was obvious enough. Most probable reasons for my visitation could be either to pressurize me into doing something for a third party or to stop me doing something that I had already started or was expected to start in the near future. The records available on the deceased made it clear that he was not the most subtle of men and hence it seemed probable that he was intended to block something and would not have stopped short of homicide, if that had been required.

It's not possible to make money without making enemies and my commercial successes were linked to a huge file of potentially disgruntled competitors. Again, the software assessment matched my own gut feelings: some cases might have been serious enough for a personal attack on me to be considered, but none of them would fit with the fundamentalist religious nutcase link.

So this left my hobby, the games I played with the tools that I needed for my day job. In my youth I'd been a *White Hat*, an informatics expert who worked against computer criminals. I had coordinated an informal team of geeks who specialized in trace-backs of spam and phishing, frying the source computers and ripping-off any associated bank accounts. We worked under the group identity of *Robin Hood* and did, indeed, pass our swag back to victims; after deduction of a handling fee that covered our costs and encouraged mugs not to be so stupid in the future. At one time we had bounties on our heads from organized crime ogroups in Russia, Japan, Italy, the USA and Mexico, but nipped these in the bud by countering with raids on bank accounts held by those involved. We ripped off the amount of the announced bounty: initially once a day, then once an hour, then once a minute. We could have gone further, but nobody held out long enough. There must be a number of gangsters who would have happily crucified every member of Robin, but there was never an indication of anyone getting close two decades ago and the trail was well cold by now.

Although all such information was buried deep behind multiple firewalls, it was accessible to the problem-solving program and hence picked up as a potential solution to the attack, but with very low assessed probability. Too old, too unlikely, too little benefit for the organizer and, again, no explanation of the fundamentalist link. I agreed completely.

So the program was narrowing-in to things I had been up to more recently. This was based on my own records of private searches over the last decade, something I sincerely hoped would not be available to others. My extensive hacks into corporate databases of every major multinational corporation and into confidential files of governments and political parties produced a list of aggrieved parties that looked like a Who's Who of international power. Although correlations were still running to rank individuals and organizations in terms of links to fundamentalist Christians, pattern recognition didn't pull anything significant out of my treatment of these targets. In all cases, confidential policy documents were mapped against stated policy and then compared to continuous trend analysis of actions in key environmental areas.

I smiled; there were no clear patterns. This is the really tricky part. Hiding your actions by swamping your real work in a mass of related material is straightforward enough. Doing it in a manner that ensures ultra-smart pattern recognition doesn't spot traces that allow the chaff to be stripped away: that is hard. Even harder when you're doing it without computer help. The problem with camouflaging software is that, no matter how good it is, it can always be reverse-engineered. Human creativity is better: if you are rigorous enough, I reminded myself.

To prove the point to myself, I left the search running in the background and called up simultaneous summaries of all main categories of global environmental hazards. A dozen holograms sprang into existence forming a semi-circle over the worktop that surrounded my huge swivel chair. I was studying only one of these, whimsically labeled the Population Bomb Disposal Team, but nobody could possibly know this. My workspace is separate from my main office and rigorously excludes any imaging devices. Any hack of my work records would show exactly the same analysis being carried out on all impact groups. In each of these, movers and shakers with particular long-term interests were displayed along with summaries of actual, possible and potential future alliances. Opponents to the actions were also noted in a similar manner. For the PBDT, and I was certain in most of the environmental preservation actions, different fundamentalist groups appeared on both pro and anti sides, indications again of the fundamentally illogical, if not downright perverse, nature of organized religion. There appeared to be no action, no matter how fucked-up, that was not supported by someone's idea of God - and usual several different God variants that disagreed with respect to everything else. Basically, the PBDT included those who recognized over-population as a major, if not the major, threat to the well-being of the planet. Their aim, whenever openly stated, was to reduce growth rates and, as rapidly as possible, move to a situation where global population was at a sustainable level. This was usually stated to be somewhere around a couple of billion or less: in some cases, a lot less. God-bothering nutters on the pro side often espoused extreme solutions, such as engineered plagues tailored for the fasted growing population groups. Although some anti groups focused on simplistic anti-contraception messages, there were also a number who simply considered a population-driven catastrophe as part of God's plan, which they were quite happy to help on its way by extolling the virtues of large families and limiting education of women.

I overlaid this information with the output from analysis of possible justifications for dispatching my unfortunate assassin. All group summaries showed red trace-back links, inevitable cases when security breaches had been spotted and attempts made to follow these back to source. Again, my attention was only on the PBDT and, in particular, the trace initiated by Internat Re. The software had put no special weighting on this as, like all the others, it had come nowhere near identifying the host server. The closest it got was a botnet that I ran in the monolithic computer complex of Swiss Pharmaceuticals. Like all of my zombie proxies, it used spare resources in organizations that I had already targeted, so didn't really introduce further risks. Even better, in this case company Knowledge Management ran under that tosser Tom Fallon. That arrogant young bastard was a credible source of any hack attack and the resulting shitstorm that could descend on him as a result of it would be well deserved.

Chapter 5

The little drug synthesizer in my apartment was good, but not nearly up to natural enzymes, so I had to wait on a rush dispatch from a pharm-sponsored lab at the ETH, Zurich's world-class university. Babe had also wakened one of my minions who lived nearby and sent him on a shopping trip. When young Andreas appeared at my door, I could see that he looked fit to burst from a mixture of fear and curiosity. Although I never mentioned it directly, I knew that salacious rumors about this apartment circulated amongst my underlings. Being commanded to go shopping early on a Sunday for a plastic basin, a container of insect repellent, a sealable plastic food container and a Stanley knife must really have set his brain on fire, although I didn't think much out of the ordinary was needed to overheat that somewhat limited organ. I buzzed him up and dragged on a robe, but made no effort to tidy either the mess of clothes strewn about the room or the disheveled bed.

I opened the door of my pad before he could knock and took the garish blue basin that contained the other items while he stuttered "Herr Fallon..., Chef... this is the stuff..."

"Fine, now beat it!" I replied, ungraciously.

"*No wonder your staff like you so much,*" Babe commented facetiously, before adding, *"...but good timing, as that's the enzymes arriving now."*

Good timing indeed. I released the outer door lock again and a young woman rushed in, still wearing a white lab coat, passing an even more bemused Andreas on the top of the stairs.

I smiled warmly as I took the proffered capsule. "Thanks a lot, love. I'll see you get a bonus for this." "*Set that up,*" I commanded as, with another smile and a slightly raised eyebrow, I closed the apartment door on the breathless girl.

"*It's amazing how much better you treat pretty young women,*" Babe observed in parallel to a flash of an account transfer of 5000 CHF from my R&D budget to a certain Gabi Supersaxo.

"Not just pretty, there's also the fact that she doesn't work for me, so I don't need to keep up the tough act that is needed to maintain discipline."

"Act? Act? You're just a natural-born bastard," the link contained the essence of a delightful giggle. *"The fact that she doesn't work for you means only that she's a target that doesn't involve shitting on your own doorstep."*

"I presume that this lecture confirms that you've logged all her details for further use."

"Of course, although some of these details may not please you much."

"Why would that be?"

"Young Gabi was married only two months ago and is already expecting her first child." Now the accompanying giggle seemed more annoying than delightful.

***

It took only a few minutes to set up things for Babe's biofeedback trick. The basin was filled with warm water and the enzyme added to it. We needed only the cap of the bug spray which, after a quick slice with the box-cutter, produced a smoothly tapered cylinder.

Convinced though I am that a software package cannot be claimed to show emotions, I couldn't help feeling that Babe was enjoying every second of my humiliation as I entered the bathroom, stripped off the robe, shoved the plastic cylinder up my arse, squatted with my backside in the water and fully opened my neural interface.

"*If you're sitting comfortably, now I'll begin.*" The completely superfluous commentary brought to mind the narrator in some otherwise long-forgotten TV program for kids. "*The cylinder to hold the sphincter open is probably not completely necessary as I could probably over-ride the autonomic closing reflex, but it simplifies things.*"

"And adds to my misery!" I grunted as my abdominal muscles cramped in a most unnatural manner.

"*These muscle contractions induce a partial vacuum, which will draw in the enzyme-containing solution.*" The sensation was bizarre and, although not painful, distinctly uncomfortable. "*You are aware, of course, that lots of sad buggers do this for kicks,*" the AI added unnecessarily. "*Anyway, we've flooded the rectum and sigmoid colon now, so I'll seal the sphincter after you withdraw the plastic support.*"

"What now?"

"It should take about forty-five minutes to an hour to work and then you can simply eliminate the offending object in the time-honored meat manner."

"So I just settle down on the bog here?"

"No reason to - I can certainly keep you tight with minimum effort. In any case, it would probably be easiest to void into the basin: we will want forensics on the device and its contents."

"...which you have already organized!"

"...pick up scheduled in seventy-five minutes!"

I quickly showered, toweled myself dry and drew on a pair of loose cotton shorts and a plain white t-shirt. For some reason, the thought of the reactions going on in my gut made me want to be clothed, rather than wandering around naked, as I usually did when alone.

The information model had expanded considerably in my absence, with input from the Mitsubishi hack now extended to cover all the linked members of what was internally referred to as Internat Re. The really good news was that Cindy was now fully exposed as a real person. Indeed a high flyer: the Director of External Security, no less. Very interesting and a piece of knowledge that helped explain the extremely high levels of data protection on her personal life since she entered this firm. The new problem was explaining how someone at such a level got involved in dirty, hands-on actions like this. People at director level gave the orders that were carried out by grunts much further down the food chain.

Babe had hacked in via Human Resources and the holo presented an outline of Cindy's career profile. Truly impressive! Recruited directly into Mitsubishi Security Division and fast-tracked to head of external operations. The fusion of the Re-insurers was apparent from a sequence of management restructures and the creation of two new coordination divisions - Threat Assessment and External Security. Cindy had been head of the latter since its formation.

As was to be expected, it was proving a much harder job to hack into anything from the security divisions, so I had nothing to explain this woman's meteoric rise in the time after her recruitment. It would have been remarkable enough under any circumstances, but for a woman in a Tokyo-based company it was even more amazing.

All of a sudden, my mind was made up. I wasn't consciously aware that I had even been considering this option and so it seemed like someone else was announcing "Set me up with a jet - I want to go to this Saint Martin place."

"What?" I chuckled at the response; was it possible to surprise software? If so, it seems that I had.

"I want to go visit this Cindy," I enunciated slowly and clearly as if talking to a child. "We should keep it quiet as I don't want to be met by a reception committee. But I want to get there soon, say within the next twenty four hours."

If I had surprised the AI, it didn't slow down the reaction to my request. A new holographic presentation of air routes between Zurich and Saint Martin appeared. A spider's web of potential connections across the hemisphere was being winnowed as availability checks, security options and weather conditions were correlated.

Nevertheless, my unusual request seemed to perturb Babe. "*Are you really sure that you want to do this, Boss? You're the cerebral type; a thinker and planner. We've already got a team of muscle organized and we can set them up with hi res comms if you want to play virtual James Bond.*"

"Just do it," I commanded decisively. Or, at least, I think it sounded decisive. Actually I couldn't decide myself quite why I was jetting off to an island in the middle of hurricane alley, especially as two major Atlantic depressions were evident on my travel map.

***

There were literally hundreds of different travel options depending on the weighting I placed on security, travel time and comfort. I had Babe remove cost as an attribute: when I was finished with this caper, Babe could rip required funding from the Mitsubishi HR travel budget. Most of my pharm's fleet of executive jets operated out of Basel but, if I had been Cindy, I'd probably be keeping an eye on these in case I tried a runner of some sort. So I opted for a private jet charter from Bern Belp to Anguilla. This was a flying gin palace of the type used by oil sheiks for commuting back and forth from the Middle East to Switzerland, checking on their numbered bank accounts and shopping for chocolate and watches no doubt.

From Anguilla it was a twin prop puddle-jumper to Grand Case airport. I was amazed to find that an island as small as Saint Martin had two airports, but Grand Case appeared to be a gourmet destination for the rich and famous of the region and this charter was set up to include a table reservation in Le Pressoir and the option of a stay over in a local hotel. As I was reviewing these travel plans, I again made an uncharacteristic, spontaneous decision. "Get young Andreas to Belp with baggage and his passport. The bugger is already up, so he may as well come along for the ride."

"In other words, you want a gopher to hand. I assume you don't want him to know where he's bound."

"Of course not. No point in secure travel arrangements if you go blabbing your plans to all and sundry."

"And the reason that it's Andreas and not the usual nymphet eye-candy that you drag around for such purposes?"

"Mmm... I guess you maybe know me better than I know myself." If this was the case, it might be smart to ask what the hell I was up to, as I was damned if I could work it out myself.

***

It was eight o'clock when Babe ordered me into the bathroom. I had squatted over the basin and was just about to commence when my phone shrieked again.

"Fuck! Jesus, this woman knows how to catch me at all the wrong times and places! Do we have our side of the comms nailed down?"

"Our transmission's audio only, all filtered by me to reduce background. You should get on with it now, just in case."

I gave a grunt in response, which was immediately followed by a rush of fluid that splashed into the basin. I could not imagine anything more disconcerting to accompany a verbal dual with my beautiful foe.

"Good morning, Tom. How are you feeling now?" A head and shoulders holo of Cindy appeared in front of me. I could feel my face hot with embarrassment, despite the fact that I knew she could see nothing. "Shy now, are we? You didn't seem so bothered last night."

My discomfort was rapidly turning to rage as she taunted me. The desire to fire back with her real name and current location was almost irresistible, but I fought it down. It would be so good to show her that she was not half as smart as she thought; that I now had the upper hand. Nevertheless, I resorted to sullen silence.

"Anyway, time for your instructions. All quite straightforward, really. I just want you to open a backdoor to your mainframe for me and give me the same supervisor or super-user access that you have.

That's full access to both your company work and anything else that you do on the side. Clear enough?"

"You've got to be joking! I can't just open up a megacorp mainframe to a slut that I picked up in a bar!" I struggled to keep my voice calm as I voided another rush of fluid, hoping fervently that Babe's filtering would remove all such background noise.

"The slut picked you up, you might remember," she countered with a laugh. Her smile, the twinkle in her eyes; it all reminded me of how damned attractive this woman was. That her beauty was so evident in my present position spoke volumes indeed. "Anyway, you know very well that someone with your position in the company can pretty well do anything with that computer that he wants, as long as he tries hard enough."

"Maybe..." I conceded, "...but it's not an easy job. I'd need to be physically present in the one of the computer control rooms and you've made that impossible." This was a lie, as my neural link avoided any such requirement. The capacity of this link was my best-kept secret, my private ace in the game of internal corporate infighting. "I'd need to get through several security scans to even get close to somewhere like that, but you already told me that anything of that nature would set off the fucking trigger on this thing."

Cindy raised an eyebrow as she pondered my misinformation. I could tell that she wasn't completely convinced. "Now, Tom, you wouldn't be trying to screw me about here, would you? Not a wise thing to do in your present circumstances."

Actually, screwing her is what I'd most like to do. However, my response was as indignant sounding as I could make it. "Who has been doing the screwing about here? You expect me to trust you not to detonate whatever you stuck up my arse and yet you don't believe a word that I say. How fair is that?"

"Tom, you are just about the most untrustworthy slimebag that I've ever met!" Her grin seemed to take some of the sting from her harsh words, but she continued in a more serious tone. "I guess I just have to show you that I'm not just one of the bimbos that you usually encounter in that club of yours."

"Fuck, wait a minute! Don't do anything too hasty!" I couldn't believe this woman was going to carry out her original threat. I lost my balance as my knees turned to jelly and I fell backwards over the basin, to land on my back on the tiled floor of the bathroom.

"Too late. The bad news is that I've just triggered my little gift to you."

Tears flooded my eyes as I curled up into a fetal position. "Fuck, fuck, fuck! Cunt! Oh Fuck!" I still couldn't believe it, I was going to die. I had everything going for me, but now it was finished. Not enough time. Not fucking near enough!

"There, there, there... It isn't so bad, really. The good news is that the toxin is slow acting and I have the antidote. You're certainly going to feel a bit strange after a couple of days, but no permanent damage will be done in that time. So here's what you'll do. Get that access set up within twenty-four hours and, if I'm happy with it, you'll get a retarder that'll slow down the attack on your nervous system. One week later, if I'm still happy with you, you'll get the antidote. So I'd get to it, if I were you. BBFN." With a touch of her right index finger to her eyebrow, the image vanished.

"Fuck! Oh no!" I rolled over onto hands and knees and felt my stomach cramp. I was going to vomit. Was this the first effects of the neurotoxin? Maybe it was acting faster than intended.

I automatically turned towards the basin as a felt a first retch build up. Through my tears, I glimpsed a flash of silver in the murky water that it contained. I froze while my vision slowly cleared. A silvery capsule was definitely lying in the murky water within the blue basin.

I rocked back onto my heels and started to hyperventilate as tears again poured from my eyes. This time tears of relief. *"Was that in time?"* I whispered through my link, afraid that my hopes would be cruelly dashed.

"I had no biofeedback links during the event but, from analysis of the monitors I'd say that you made it with at least a second to spare. Proves yet again that only the good die young."

Despite the gratuitous comment, a feeling of pure joy flooded my body. I had never felt so good. Simply the feeling of being alive was a rare pleasure.

I clambered to my feet and, supporting myself against the wash-hand basin, looked at myself in the mirror. My face was wan, my body beaded with sweat and tears were still rolling down my cheeks. Nevertheless, I felt great. "Fuck you, Cindy!" I shouted. Now it was my turn and, by fuck, the kid gloves were definitely off!

Intermezzo 4

Even if my botnets weren't compromised, the last stage of getting my purloined information back to CERN was always a potential weak point. The advantage of CERN is that it produces gigantic fluxes of raw data that are fed to universities and R&D institutions around the world. Although return fluxes of processed material and model results are much smaller, they are still many orders of magnitude larger than the blocks of info-swag that I had to move about. In principle, however, somebody smart could do an entropy analysis on material known to be hacked and, with a lot of processing power, find it again even if it was hidden within a huge data flow. This was the inherent weakness: particle collision data and commercial intelligence had completely different signatures. I knew of this vulnerability and wasn't surprised when the program noted that, even if the hacked material wasn't completely specified, it wouldn't be too hard to spot that there were anomalies in here somewhere. Not too hard, but only if you had the tools to hand and also some hint that led you to look at an international particle collider in the first place.

Links between fundamentalist groups and powerful computing infrastructure were displayed on all holos, but again I was focused entirely of the PBDT. Two contrasting high profile hits: a right-wing Christian sect that was secretly supported by the US National Security Agency and a bunch of radical Muslims funded by a Saudi sheik, who also funded the All-Arab Supercomputer Centre in Dubai. Given the ethnicity of my attacker, the former was a more obvious lead. Nevertheless, I wasn't going to fall into the common trap of assuming that all terrorist groups worked in isolation. I set up a passive search of all existing databases to identify any such links and watched the network build, stretching within and between all my environmental actions. Only one, rather tenuous, thread was of interest: the terrorist sheik had been educated in Stanford and shared several of the modules for his MBA with a certain James Pearson junior, the present incumbent as director of the NSA.

Chapter 6

After a bit of toing and froing with a cost-benefit package, I finally decided to cancel the forensic analysis of Cindy's toxin delivery system. There was too much of a risk that it could lead her to discover that it had been removed. After gingerly lifting it into the food container with a pair of ice tongs, it was now secreted at the back of my wardrobe. The contents of the basin were carefully flushed down the toilet and the basin rinsed with bleach that I found under the sink in the bathroom. I thought it superfluous, but Babe pointed out that the potential chaos that would result from a potentially poisoned cleaning lady outweighed the minute effort from my side. After that, it was time for a long, hot shower during which I soaped myself down from head to toe three times.

"OK, how are we looking now?" I enquired as I rubbed myself dry with a huge, soft, white towel.

"All general hacks on International Re terminated and effort concentrated on easily accessible material from Saint Martin. You can view the correlation map whenever you like. Camouflage here is set up. The computer center control room in Basel will be cleared by a fire alarm at midday today and all associated security systems will be taken offline. You will be logged-on and, over the next hour, a complex procedure for creating a new super-user account will be initiated. At one thirty you'll log out and all security will come back online. A worm will then delete traces of

your actions. In parallel, the fast response team will be working on the alarm, which will clearly represent a system malfunction. This will clear up just after two and the control team crew will be allowed back."

"Sounds that it'll be convincing enough, if she has even superficial hacks in place. The deeper she can see, the better it'll look. What about meat? If I was Cindy, I'd have some flesh and blood keeping an eye on what I'm up to."

"Already set up. A VIP transfer limo with blackened windows will appear to do the transfer from the garage below the club here to the garage below the computer complex. All security cameras in both garages will go offline, but the lift records in the Basel will show movements to and from the garage at appropriate times."

*"What about..."*I was keen to show that I was on the ball here and not a passive observer.

"The driver will be from security, as tight as we can make it. As a bonus for this job, immediately thereafter he and his family will go on an all-expenses paid holiday to a safe house in Santorini. In addition, during the transfer, a recording of you discussing current events with the driver will provide material for anyone with a laser audio pickup."

"Yes, but..."

"...and a car is already en route with a package in the boot that will weigh about your 95 kilos and will provide a holographic thermal image that is good enough for any kind of portable scanners. The

limo driver will place it on the back seat when he arrives and dump it again after he has completed his return journey. Anything I've missed?"

"Smartarse computer!" I growled, having been quite proud about thinking up the thermal scanning threat for myself. Nevertheless, I was happy that Babe was running this game as, although I now realized that analysis of before and after images could detect whether the car suspension showed the presence of a passenger or not, this was not something that had previously occurred to me.

I called up my travel route plan and checked the start. *"According to this, I'm supposed to be in Belp in three hours. How will this work?"*

The link glowed on the holo as my AI provided a commentary. *"The car bringing over the thermal unit will take you out of here in its boot."*

"Nicely killing two birds with one stone. I suppose tomorrow's limo-driver will be at the wheel."

"Nope, but you're on the right track." The smug input over my link paralleled a slow expansion of the links. Like a striptease, I thought, intended to be provocative. *"Andreas will be driving the pimped vintage Range Rover which will pick you up."*

"Exactly the type of car driven by some of the types who frequent this dive," I commented with admiration. "It'll be a bit easy to trace, though."

"I assume that our opponents haven't saturated the area, so they won't be able to physically follow all vehicles during the exodus after post-party brunch. It coincidently fits well with our time plan.

You'll both swap over to an ambulance in an unmonitored niche in a road tunnel just before Kloten..."

"...with the pimpmobile carrying on to airport parking, driven by our limo-guy, who will also replace me with 90 kilos of weights from the ambulance. Smart!" There was no doubt about it, this was exactly the sort of thing that my system excelled at.

"...and, of course, both these vehicles will have complete thermal shields in appropriate areas," Babe finished.

"I knew you were going to say that" I lied. I suspect that this fib was completely transparent, but it drew no response. Maybe a rather atypical salve for my ego, which had taken quite some bruising over the last few hours.

***

I dressed for comfort, aware that I was going to be crammed in the back of vehicles and then flying for quite some time. Unfashionably baggy grey crushed silk trousers and a matching shirt, soft brown leather sandals and a light blue blazer. I sincerely hoped that none of the locals spotted me on my way out - I'd be arrested by the local fashion police or, at least, barred from the club for life.

I was having a scan through the Saint Martin file when I was surprised by Babe's announcement that Andreas had arrived. Time was flying again. All comms with my underling were being routed through the AI, as I didn't trust the security of even my house phone anymore. The only thing I carried with me was a booster that facilitated encrypted wireless communication with my mainframe while underway and also allowed presentation of projected 2D and even limited 3D images. The small unit fitted easily into the tailored pouch that, in all my jackets, replaced an inside pocket.

Andreas was nervously standing by the dropped tailgate of the hideously ornate SUV as I entered the garage. As I had been assured by Babe, the cavernous space was otherwise deserted but contained about a dozen other cars, several of which rivaled the Range Rover in terms of sheer tackiness. I rudely ignored the proffered helping hand and clambered into the space below a back shelf that supported a line of Bose speakers. "Just don't turn on the fucking music!" was my only acknowledgement of my lackey's existence, before the tailgate was closed and I was locked in claustrophobic darkness.

*"Have we comms?"*I enquired as I felt the massive car jerk into movement. Silence, only gradual awareness of the sounds of my breathing and the sensation of my quickening pulse. This was weird. I couldn't remember the last time that I had felt so alone. I thought back to the transfer plans and now remembered that the back of this juggernaut was not only thermally insulated, it was also protected by a Faraday Cage. "Duh!" I muttered under my breath; of course I had no communications. What would be the point of all this

subterfuge, if I was moving in a pocket of em broadband?

The walls of my cage seemed to close in more and I could feel sweat beginning to bead my brow. "*Calm down!*" I commanded myself over the defunct link and, surprisingly, it seemed to work. "*Let's just use this time to get myself prepared for whatever I am going to do when I arrive in this bloody Saint Martin. Or was it Sint Maarten - I was sure that I saw it written that way sometime. OK, let's put this on the list to get sorted out when I get comms back.*" It felt strange to get no instant response, but I could feel the mental commands helping to structure my thinking process.

What else did I need to sort out? A pick up on arrival and somewhere to stay - assuming that Babe hadn't already anticipated this. Then the tricky bit: what the hell did I intend to do in person that couldn't be handled electronically or by my tame heavies? It had to be face-to-face with Cindy. I could feel the first sensation of tumescence just thinking about it. Why was that? Was I looking for revenge, or was it more complicated? Given the fact that I couldn't define what my goal was, then certainly more complicated!

Whatever I intended, any meeting had to be on my terms. I wasn't going to simply swan into her office. What I needed was an overview of her lifestyle, which Babe would be deriving from an integration of local sources. It was tempting to re-initiate the hack on her division, but any benefits would have to be carefully weighed against the consequences if my intrusion was spotted. Another action for the to-do list.

Also there was the question of when I was going to set up my encounter. The next milestone on the program was tomorrow, when, according to her demands, the computer access should be provided. I had two options here, I could offer a bugged backdoor, which would allow me to find out exactly what the entire purpose of this game was, or I could go for straightforward head-on conflict. The latter was more suited to my basic nature, but the former certainly had its attractions. Babe could certainly monitor everything that was accessed via this route and, if required, censor any databases before they were read or even over-ride actions that could be dangerous to my employer. The question was whether this would be spotted or not. I guess that the specified week was to allow checks to be run to ensure that I wasn't doing anything like this. Was my AI smart enough to dupe anything the Re tech team could throw at us? I was willing to bet on it.

So, if I appeared to accede to Cindy's wishes tomorrow, when would be a good time to surprise her? Certainly after she had a chance to look through our computer system. It would depend on what she found during her first rummage through our electronic secrets, I realized. This was what I had been missing so far. What should I create that would throw this woman in my direction? Something that she'd quickly spot, but wouldn't be an obvious plant. I smiled: this was what I was good at, planning seduction.

My brain was spinning with a net of devious plots when I was thrown against the inner bulkhead by hard braking, reminding me painfully that I was still crammed into the boot of a car. Almost immediately the tailgate was opened and an indistinct figure helped me out and hurried me towards the open rear door of a parked ambulance that appeared to belong to the Kantonsspital Aarau. The tunnel niche that we were parked in was unlit apart from the hazard warning lights of the two vehicles and the occasional headlights of cars that flashed past. As I clambered in, Andreas jogged by, heading for the driver's cab. I responded to his quizzical glance with a cheerful grin, just before the door closed and I was again sealed up for transit.

"*Miss me?*" My surprise at the reactivation of my link caused me to slip on the bench along the port side of the van as the vehicle moved off, landing inelegantly sprawled on the floor.

"*What the hell?*" I responded as I struggled back to my seat. "*Isn't this comm link a bit of a giveaway for anybody looking for us?*"

"*Not here, I don't think. The ambulance has an active high res GPS interface that constantly broadcasts its position back to the emergency control system. My signal is piggybacked on it, but I don't think anyone would spot it. It's very low bandwidth, but enough for this kind of simple interfacing.*"

"Mmm... " I pondered this information. *"Only one question then. What will the Kantonsspital folk think about their ambulance heading off to Bern?"*

"Nothing at all." The link was too restricted to convey emotional nuances, but I'm sure that this would otherwise have been dripping with smugness. *"This vehicle is being road-tested after re-fitting. All tracer signals will go directly to a bin."*

Not worth going further here, I realized: just assume that everything had been organized perfectly and concentrate instead on my planning of my arrival in the Caribbean. I tried to remember my mental list from the boot of the Range Rover. *"Oh, yes, a simple question: it may seem a bit late to ask, but is it Saint Martin or Sint Maarten that I'm headed for?*

"Both." I felt that my software was trying to joke before it continued *"The island is part French, that being Saint Martin and part Dutch, which is Sint Maarten."*

"Seems unnecessarily complicated," I responded, resolved to follow this up at a later stage. *"Anyway, have I got a pick-up and digs organized?"*

"Not yet. It's a bit tricky until you let me know what you intend do when we get there. We could take up the hotel in Grand Case, which was originally added for cover for the first night, and then play it by ear. The island lives on tourism and May is the local low season, so either extending your stay or moving somewhere else shouldn't be a problem."

"Seems like a reasonable idea for the present. I'll get more detailed plans sorted out while we're travelling - if I have comms on route." I felt surprisingly confident that this would work, despite the fact that I still didn't even have an inkling of a goal, much less a plan.

"Transfer to local accommodation now organized. A limo is reserved for you for the entire first day, with the option of extension on a day-by-day basis."

"OK, let's get started then." I linked my fingers and stretched my arms over my head, as if limbering up for the keyboard. Not, of course, that I'd actually used one of those things since the days of my youth. *"Have you enough bandwidth to summarize what we have on our Cindy of Saint Martin?"*

"Just about, if we prune out all of the embedded images and video links." I placed the small interface unit on the bench beside me and the information model that I requested slowly assembled itself, node-by-node.

"Now we're beginning to get somewhere!" I whispered as the links began to show a consistent picture. Officially Cindy had permanent resident status on the French side of the island, based on EU nationality and ten years residence on the island. This was, however, linked to passport details of a Cinderella Villiger, who was born in Donegal, Ireland. She was employed by Mitsubishi Insurance and worked out of an office in Marigot that seemed to specialize in marine insurance. She lived in a very up-market residential area in the Terres Basses and owned a powerboat that was also docked in a marina in Marigot.

"That's a bit strange. Seems to have a lifestyle a bit above what you'd expect for a humble insurance worker." The blocks of the network linked to open company records of her office expanded, showing that she was the island manager with twenty staff in Marigot and about another thirty scattered about the island. For an island with lots of top-notch tourist infrastructure that was occasionally hit by hurricanes, it was evident that insurance was a very big business. Not just for St Martin itself; the island seemed to be the service center for several surrounding, even more exclusive, island haunts of the rich and famous.

The blocks on Cindy herself were also expanding, showing her tax records and more personal details. *"Is this hacked?"* I inquired. *"I wanted to stay passive, open source on this."*

"Government records here have such crap security that they might as well be open source," was the disdainful response. *"In actual fact, this stuff comes from a black-hat database hack downloaded onto a local geek website. I could easily get more if you want me to go in. There is absolutely no chance of intrusion being spotted, much less a hack being traced back."*

The AI's confidence was reassuring, but I'd been burned already by underestimating this Cinderella. *"Go ahead, but make double sure that there's no way that we can be linked to this."*

"Running. The attack will be general, ripping out any blocks of files that could contain something useful. All of this will be encrypted and dumped on the same website, looking like some newbie geek is trying to strut his stuff."

I thought over this ploy and couldn't find any obvious loopholes. *"Sounds OK."* Already further details were flooding in to populate supporting files. Marital status was noted to be divorced and maiden name to be Green. From signatures on various documents, it was clear that she signed herself Cindy, which made sense. Her tax records made it evident that she was independently wealthy, having received a small fortune in alimony from her ex-husband. The German husband had been the Chief Financial Officer of Munich Re, but was now retired and living most of the year on an old thirty-meter Sunseeker yacht.

"Flesh out this Villiger guy for me, is he for real?" I couldn't imagine the woman who had seduced me being married to someone more than three decades her senior, even if the marriage lasted only three years.

"The full files are downloading now, but I can give you a precis of the expert system interpretation. Marriage to Urs Villiger appears genuine and his lifetime career at Munich Re is well documented. The divorce seems amicable: they still meet up socially whenever Urs docks in Saint Martin, which is about once a year. It appears, however, to have been a marriage of convenience, with little contact

between the parties before matrimony and little time spent living together thereafter."

"Is that enough to justify labeling it as a set-up?" I interrupted.

"Well, there's also the fact that Urs seems to be straight gay. Before he retired, this was extremely low profile and probably couldn't really be proven without going to a lot of effort. Since then, however, he has been much more open. His yacht is crewed exclusively by a rotating team of young, black men, who also sail with other known gay celebrities."

"Well, if he's into black sausage, he'd hardly have fallen for Cindy's charms." I was annoyed at myself for the feeling of relief that this gave me. This was not at all like me. Hump them and dump them was my motto. I had never been the possessive type - at least not as far as women were concerned. *"Leave the stuff on Urs running in the background and let's get back to this office that Cindy's in charge of. What can we dig up on it from external sources?"*

The holo model blossomed in relevant areas, but again Babe provided a summary. *"Overall picture of operations on the island matches analogues elsewhere with the exception of the Marigot office. The vast majority of documentation hard copies that I would expect to be signed by Cindy are actually signed by her deputy. This contrasts with electronic signatures, which are exactly as expected."*

"Could be that she is just a good manager - delegates responsibility." I thought of my own job,

how much of my work was delegated to smart software. Of course I had also the requisite team of flunkies expected by my hierarchical position in the company, but they were mainly bag-carriers and meatbots: tools to allow my AI to carry out physical actions in the real world.

"Possible, but exactly the same pattern is seen for fifteen of the twenty staff employed there. The pattern is inverted for the remaining five, who seem to be responsible for almost all signatures on hardcopies."

"So, this is Cindy's security division, hidden in plain view in downtown Marigot." It wasn't the deepest of covers, but probably sufficient unless someone knew exactly what they were looking for in advance.

"That's my conclusion. Whatever External Security Division does, they probably don't want others to know about it. They probably have all kinds of real and virtual security in place, but not presenting any visible target is, by far, the best way of staying under the radar. Should I hack them?"

A tricky question. *"Let's see your argumentation model on this - pros, cons and risk assessment."*

The holo blanked, then slowly reassembled in the form of a simple 2D argumentation chain. The pros were all obvious and the cons related to the consequences of the intrusion being picked up. The weak bit was assessment of the probability of the latter. It was a bit Catch 22: until we had a rummage around Cindy's system, it was hard to determine how good it was. In the worst case, checking the capabilities of her defenses would be enough to tip our hand.

"Too risky at present..." I decided, *...but start the groundwork to set up the very best insert that is possible. Prepare for two options: super gentle and smash-and-grab. I don't know if we'll need them, but having them available might prove valuable."*

The holo defaulted back to the overview of the picture we were building of the life of the enigmatic Cindy. She lived alone in a large villa on the Rue de la Falaise and employed a couple as housekeeper / caretaker who lived on a house in its grounds. A low-res sat image was linked to this information, but I decided to postpone looking at it until I had a faster interface available. "I wonder how good her house security is," I pondered aloud.

"Almost certainly as tight as her office," Babe responded immediately, supporting my own conclusion. "*We might, however, be able to get something from surrounding properties."*

"Exactly, see what you can hack. Also anything obvious on the route between home and work. Just don't get into anywhere that is within a few hundred meters of her workplace. If I was her, I'd have a few silent alarms set up on the systems of a few places nearby, just in case anyone was trying a stunt like this."

Cindy certainly maintained a low profile on the island. Despite her nominal position with Mitsubishi, she never appeared on any newsletters or social web sites and was not a member of any professional associations, committees or charitable institutes that served as networking opportunities for professionals of her level. Her expected role here was, once again, covered by her hard working deputy. Her strange behavior had caused quite a media buzz after her arrival on the island but, in the intervening years, she had become accepted as an eccentric whose antisocial nature was explained by her reputation as a workaholic top manager who regularly provided support to other Mitsubishi offices around the world. Works hard, plays hard and has little time for social niceties. *"Plays hard: what has she for hobbies and pastimes?"* The files opened to show that her small powerboat was currently docked in the Marina Porte La Royale, close to her office. "Excellent!" I sensed a feral smile on my face. This was another chink in her digital armor. *"Get stuff from other boats using that Marina. Probably best to avoid those with permanent moorings, as Cindy could have booby-trapped them. We're looking for casual users, especially one-offs. Focus on visual material and run image analysis."* These commands were probably unnecessary, but helped me develop the master plan that was gradually building in my mind.

I moved on to other activities. A tax return indicated membership of a gym at the exclusive La Samanna hotel, located conveniently close to her house. As a facility catering for the very rich, security would be good, but certainly nothing that Babe couldn't break. The problem was yet again silent alarms, so I decided to go for a less direct approach. *"Don't touch the hotel itself, use indirect hacks into travel agents or whatever to get a list of guests over the last decade and hack them to rip off any images they have of their stay. Then the usual analysis to see if Cindy is caught anywhere."*

"OK boss, but this is going to burn exaflops if you want it rushed. It'll slow down things noticeably for other mainframe users."

"Can you see me giving a fuck?" I responded, brusquely. *"All this stuff is pretty thin, though. What else does she do with her money and free time?"*

"Well, she probably pays cash for most things, as preliminary scans of card and ebank transactions in local shops, bars and restaurants show no sign of her. We do know, however, that she likes to dance."

This simple statement brought back to mind my disco workout. The thought of getting as physical with Cindy once again was sufficiently distracting that I almost missed the next gem from my trusty electronic partner. *"From the analysis carried out last night, we have a good profile of the music she prefers and have mapped that against the playlists of clubs in St Martin. There are thirteen top ranked hits. I guess that, again, you don't want them hacked."*

"Nope, same procedure as with the hotel. Find out who else goes to these clubs - punters, not staff - and see what we can hack from them."

"I knew you were going to want that. There goes another couple of exaflops." Despite the low

bandwidth, I got the distinct impression of an accompanying world-weary sigh.

***

I was just preparing to scan the images pulled out to date when Babe announced that we were approaching the airport. I could hardly believe that an hour had flashed by until I stretched and realized how stiff I was from the uncomfortable seat. *"We'll just draw into a drop-off area, where another driver is waiting for us. Then a short walk to the executive departure lounge for emigration formalities and then you will be driven to the plane."*

"Can't I be dropped directly at the lounge?" I complained, feeling particularly lazy and the need to be pampered.

"It might be a bit noticeable, an exec getting out of the back of an ambulance," Babe pointed out, reminding me of my current mode of conveyance.

"Point," I conceded, *"let's do it your way."* It was a trivial annoyance, but I glared at Andreas as he opened the door for me and offered a helping hand to clamber out.

"I've got to get my luggage and the documents, Herr Fallon. They were placed in the front of this car for us and..."

"Don't babble, just get your shit and hurry up!" I rudely interrupted. Then I turned on my heel and marched off following the sign for VIP Departures, leaving Andreas to follow in my wake.

The executive hostess welcomed me warmly, guiding me to a sofa in a secluded niche of the plush lounge and offering to fetch me a drink. I was momentarily confused by the contrast between my body clock weariness and drug-induced hyperactivity: did I want coffee, beer or a glass of wine? Beer, I decided, ordering also for Andreas so that I wouldn't appear to be drinking alone. For an instant I thought he might object to my choice, but he glanced in my direction and then obviously decided to avoid doing anything that could possibly provoke me.

Our travel documentation had been provided electronically but, being Switzerland, someone from the Grenzkontrolle had to look at the physical passports that Andreas carried in his small briefcase. I sipped the ice-cold Schlossgold while these formalities were completed and Andreas's luggage taken to the limo that was parked outside on the airfield side of the building.

I finished my beer and was then escorted to the car, which immediately whisked us to a plane parked beside several large cargo jets. Our goal was painted a gleaming silver, with a black logo of what looked like a seahorse on the tail. It appeared to me like a fairly conventional mid-size passenger jet, although it seemed small in comparison to the wide-bodied cargo haulers.

I really don't like flying and do so only if I have to. In such cases, I take one of the company executive jets, which are pretty small, the biggest being about a twenty-seater. This was gigantic in comparison. A small elevator took us to the open hatch where two pretty stewardesses waited to welcome us aboard. Although not quite similar enough to be sisters, the statuesque blondes appeared to have been selected as a matched pair.

"How are we going to be for comms on this thing?" I enquired tentatively, as I was escorted through an unusually large galley area, unsure if I would even get a response.

"Absolutely no problem," came the instantaneous response. *"We have plenty of bandwidth and, even if there is a slight delay with the satellite links when you're in the air, it probably won't be noticeable."*

I was distracted from Babe's report by the luxurious furnishings of the lounge, where the pilot - yet another tall blonde - waited to greet me. "Good morning Mister Schmidt. My name is Sylvia Moran and I'm your pilot for our flight to the Caribbean today. Our co-pilot, Tina Harding, is finishing the checks in the cockpit." I was willing to bet that she'd also turn out to be a tall blonde. I wondered what this was all about, but guessed it might have something to do with the clientele for this kind of service. Babe was clearly having fun with my alias for the trip and I wondered what my passport for this trip looked like - and what Andreas made of all this blatant subterfuge.

"You've already met our hostesses, Jean and Ruth, who will look after you during this trip." Sylvia was clearly a native English speaker, but had a distinct accent that I guessed to be Australian or

Kiwi. "I better get back up front so that we can get underway as soon as possible. In any case, let me know if there is anything at all that I, or any other member of my crew, can do for you." She looked me straight in the eyes during this parting shot and I wondered if the implied offer was just my imagination or if the on-board service really did extend beyond that in a normal executive jet.

After the captain left, I took in more of my surroundings. This forward part of the cabin was set up with eight large leather armchairs and separated by a partition from the rest of the plane. Jean was settling me into one of these while Andreas followed Ruth to a seat on the opposite side of the machine. "Let's just get you comfortable here," Jean said as she bent over to fit my seat belt, showing off a considerable extent of cleavage in the process. I caught her eye as she straightened up and was rewarded by a grin. She was clearly well aware of what she was doing.

"How about a glass of champagne before we take off?" Again an interesting accent. South Africa I would guess in this case.

"Why not!" I acquiesced and, as if by magic, Ruth appeared with a condensation-dewed flute of bubbly.

"Veuve Cliquot Grande Dame," Jean clarified as Ruth passed on to Andreas, with what looked like a glass of sparkling water. "After takeoff you can have a look at the rest of the plane. The seats in the lounge here can be rotated so that you can talk together with your colleague, or else to view the large screen of our entertainment system. Alternatively, there are small screens built into each chair. Up front there is the galley, where we will be any time we're not needed, and also a toilet."

"In the next compartment, on the other side of that partition..." she pointed towards the rear of the plane "...you'll find the office which has a couple of desks with work stations and a table for small meetings. Behind that there are bathrooms and four small bedroom suites, two on each side of the central gangway. The master bedroom with en suite is in the tail. Your luggage arrived a half hour ago and is already stowed there."

"Where should we put your companion's luggage?"

I was momentarily nonplussed at this non sequitur, then spluttered, almost choking on my champagne, as its implication dawned on me. "Just shove it anywhere out of the way. He should have enough work to keep him busy, which he can do in here. I'll work in the office." Andreas and Ruth were obviously following this conversation. Did the boy look disappointed? Probably the thought of having to work on a Sunday, I concluded. "*Make some work for young Andreas, enough to keep him busy for the duration of the flight,"* I commanded over my link. *"Keep him from bothering the hot hostesses."*

"*Worried about the competition?"* I felt laughter over the interface. *"But I don't think you need to have any concerns there."*

Suddenly various comments seemed to gel into a new picture. "*Wait a minute, Young Andy's not a shirt-lifter is he?*"

"Your complete lack of gaydar is going to get you into trouble one of these days. Both hostesses spotted Andreas within seconds. He's worked for you for three years and you're totally oblivious."

At times this AI pseudo-personality stuff gets on my tits. *"Well I have better things to do with my life than discover the sexual proclivities of lackeys,"* I responded brusquely.

"Oops, remind me to back off on the neural communication when others are about." I noted that Jean was looking at me strangely, probably wondering at my glazed look as I linked with Babe. "Sorry about that, I've got some important work on and I tend to drift off when I get a new idea." My cover-up seemed to be accepted completely, probably because the girls were used to lots of strange people in such high end charters. "Anyway I'll need a bit of privacy after takeoff, this is quite sensitive stuff."

"No problem at all, sir," Jean confirmed with a smile. "The office is completely secure and you'll be undisturbed unless you actually want us to do something for you. Meals and drinks are available any time you want. Just let us know. Also, if you want to take a snooze, let me know and I'll lay out pajamas and turn down the bed for you." There was definitely an implicit offer in this statement.

"I never wear pajamas," I flirted, putting a first toe in to test the water.

"That's useful information to know, no pajamas for you." A sly wink added further confirmation, if that was needed. There was no doubt about it, the water was boiling hot.

***

My glass was topped up as we taxied towards the runway, just before the hostesses withdrew to their seats in the galley for takeoff. "*OK Babe, what do we have on these girls,*" I enquired, sensing that maybe the flight would be less tedious than I had expected.

"Air escorts might be a better description than air hostesses," my software confirmed. *"There were a number of options available for this charter, but a bit restricted due to the short notice that we gave. I thought the all-blonde option might appeal. Very popular with both Arabs and Japanese, it seems, so always on tap."*

"Very good choice! The only problem may be getting this planning stuff finished before we get to Saint Martin." This wasn't something that I really thought was going to give me difficulties, however. If anything, the opposite. I could consider some wild professional sex as a reward to myself for finishing the plan - so it might go a lot faster. Even better, if I get finished fast - say within a couple of hours - I could give myself a special treat, like menage a trios. It's not like Andreas would be needing one, I thought with a smile.

"Let's not lose any time then. Give me a summary of what Cindy might get if she has freedom to wander through our mainframe."

"It is tricky to present without visual support, but I suppose you don't want Andreas to see any of this."

"Definitely not! Set up the holos and I'll have a look as soon as I get into the office." I pressed the intercom button to check with the pilot. "When can I go to the office area, captain?"

"We're number three for takeoff now. I'll put off the seat belt sign as soon as possible, maybe about ten minutes from now."

"Great, thanks a lot." I switched the intercom off and continued silently "*OK, you've ten minutes to summarize what we have?"*

"The most obvious material falls under commercial, with sub-categories policy, strategy, operational procedures, finance, R and D, HR and support infrastructure. If we assume that this is associated in some way with the fields of insurance and re-insurance, we can narrow this down a bit. Everything significant in the company goes through the Zurich, but we don't insure most of the major facilities: we're big enough to cover all risks internally. Insurance is confined to areas where it's specified in regulations, but everything here is completely above board with no traces of any kind of corporate jiggery-pokery."

"What about insurance exposure? Anything that could lead to big payments?" This was confusing: why on earth would an insurance mega

go face to face with a pharm? *"Maybe some drug side effect class action?"*

"Nothing at all. Insurers won't touch this kind of stuff with a bargepole. Formally, there is an industry consortium that covers risks of this nature. Of course, most of the consortium members are actually components of our own conglomerate."

"Doesn't make a lot of sense, then." I scowled in frustration.

"There's nothing commercial that's showing a percentage probability going into double figures. There's some funny stuff on your personal account, however."

"What the fuck?" My ejaculation caused Andreas to jump in his seat.

"Is anything wrong, Herr..."

"It's nothing, lad, go back to sleep," I muttered distractedly. *"How can this be? I've nothing to do with any insurance. Well, I have some, I assume, but nothing special."*

"You have normal personal health, travel, car and house insurance. Again Zurich; you get a reduced company rate. Completely normal in every way."

"Then what?"

"I'm really not sure..." This worried me, as my computer generally seemed almost omnipotent. My concerns grew as Babe continued, *"...but power drain analysis gives hints of large data fluxes, which don't match anything that we've been doing."*

"So what was being transferred? That must be recorded."

"It must be, but it isn't." I detected a slight trace of confusion, a sensation that I'd never previously experienced over a neural link. *"Checks of memory management show drops in free capacity in the exabyte range for the duration of these flows, but there is no sign of it being allocated to you and, in all cases, it was returned empty. Such complete cleansing indicated top level tidying went on. We do this as standard, but few other users bother. This provides a potential link to us."*

"Shit!" Again Andreas jumped and looked at me in concern, but I simply glared at him.

"Could Cindy have hacked us?" I felt cold. I had been convinced that Babe was the cutting edge and nobody had a chance of doing unto me what I regularly did unto others.

Now a trace of uncertainty leaked over my link. *"I wouldn't have considered it possible, but we could feasibly do something like this, so we can't preclude that someone else has the same capabilities. It would, however, need both powerful hardware and sophisticated software. At least AI level."*

I wasn't rising to this bait. *"Does our Cinderella have this?"*

"Not that I can see but, until we have hacked her office, it's impossible to be sure. However, there's a big problem with this explanation..."

"If she could hack our mainframe without us knowing, why does she need me to give her this back door?"

"Exactly! But this looks like a definite hack."

At this point the fasten seatbelt sign went out and Joan started to announce that we were free to move about. I was on my feet immediately and stormed towards the door to the office with only "Stay! I need a bit of privacy now," shouted over my shoulder in Andreas's direction.

I shut the door to the lounge behind me. "Full privacy activate!" I commanded, while adding silently "*Take over this heap-of-shit system and give me privacy.*"

"All electronic systems active and white noise cover activated for all audio. Just to be on the safe side though, better communicate entirely via the neural interface."

"Fine, display the details of the system anomalies. So, if Cindy didn't hack us, who did?"

"I'm running every tracer available and can't find a dicky bird. Everything we have is negative evidence: information flows that don't match the work that we were doing, memory that isn't available, used memory space that's too clean."

"What if it's a double bluff? Cindy hacks us and gets something that she wants to use, but using it would give away the fact that she has access to our system. She forces us to give us access for a week, when she appears to rip off the material that she's already got. Next week we lock her out and seal everything tight, but she can still get in however it was she did it the first time." I felt pleased with myself for proposing a resolution to several clear conflicts in the argumentation chain.

"That seems incredibly contrived - especially as we can't see anything from the commercial sector that would justify this effort. Your private account has stuff that might interest the tax authorities or a collector of pornography, but not the world's biggest insurer."

I could appreciate these counter-arguments, but I couldn't get rid of a conviction that there had to be some link between Cindy and this intrusion. *"OK, even if it doesn't make sense, can we check if this is possible?"*

"It would need a hack, but this would only need to be very superficial - going just for power management records to check for major data fluxes at the time when your account was being manipulated. I estimate the chances of this being picked up as very low."

"OK, do it," I decided, knowing that I would have to take this risk sometime. *"Make it as gentle as possible and have it look like it's the action of those local geek black hats, just in case. We can consider it a dry run for a deeper hack later."*

Within seconds data started to fill linked files on the hologram, the links strengthening as correlations were established. *"Looks like there's something here."* My hunch seemed to be correct.

"Most definitely," Babe confirmed, *"but not at all what you would expect. If you look at the time profiles,"* a chart expanded and moved to the foreground, *"it's clear that about half of our rogue data flux correlates with that from the hack of the*

office in Marigot. The problem is that the Marigot profile leads ours."

"So Cindy didn't hack us?" I gasped aloud, forgetting that I was supposed to be sticking to neural communication.

"Absolutely not, it looks like we hacked her!"

Intermezzo 5

I was doing my day job, examining the potential of combining a new CERN database on lepton properties with some old work on muon-catalysed fusion and recent engineering developments in magnetic containment to see if an economic thermonuclear power reactor might finally be on the cards. Suddenly the material I was working on vanished into buffer memory and my wall of environmental threat overviews appeared. This time the red flag was a clear call for me to focus on the population topic.

"Shit!" I cursed aloud. It looked very much like my hack on the re-insurance sector was being traced. Even worse, it looked like that dickhead Fallon was doing the tracing. The alarm had started autonomous routines that built background and had already spotted Tom's furtive departure for the Caribbean. It didn't need pattern analysis to identify this as very anomalous. This wanker was a city guy: work and holidays in places like London, New York, Shanghai and Tokyo. He never ventured into the countryside, much less to a small island with little but sun, sand and sea. The bastard would probably choke on his first breath of fresh air.

Nice though the thought of fuckwit Fallon suffocating was, it looked like I might have to get directly involved here. The flight to Anguilla was clearly traced, but this was an unlikely final destination. I had already guessed Saint Martin, when the software finally came up with the connecting flight to Grande Case.

Well, unlike Fallon, at least I was prepared for eventualities like this. I took ten weeks of holiday every year since I started working for CERN. As I had free hand with my division and nobody actually reported to me directly, it was easy to arrange even long blocks away on very short notice. I would usually take four weeks somewhere sunny, swimming and diving. Then I'd have a three-week block taking in culture somewhere unusual - Cambodia, Zimbabwe, Iceland. Three further one-week blocks were either ski trips or city visits. Although I had a carbon footprint about the size of Lichtenstein, I could head off anywhere, at any time, without this causing any change to my normal lifestyle pattern.

A couple of minutes later, I was booked on a KLM flight to Princess Juliana International Airport. Business class, booked with air miles. As was my want on such trips, I didn't book a hotel. On arrival, I would simply get somewhere near to the airport for the first night and then play it by ear.

I dropped the global threat stuff back to background and pulled up the muon work again. I needed to get the finger out to clear the decks for my departure. I had no idea how long I would be away, but it would be prudent to assume the worst and plan for a month.

Chapter 7

Babe's bombshell shocked me into silence for five minutes. My mind was racing. I was sure that I had not intentionally hacked Mitsubishi Saint Martin, but could I have done it inadvertently? I was careful with what I was doing when I used my system for managing my personal finances. Always stay within the law, was my motto. Enough could be gained by skating close to the edge with the benefits of my computer power: it would be gratuitous to break laws, even if the chances of being caught were negligible.

What else did I do? Pick up women: surely there was no possible risk there? I certainly was very close to illegality with regard to personal privacy, but this was completely unenforced in practice. There was simply too much information available to make policing unlawful access possible. Any resources available went into controlling application of information, financial crime and scams, pedophile pornography, that kind of stuff.

Gradually a large hole in this line of thought came into focus. Even if I had hacked Cindy by mistake, I could hardly do such a careful cover up without deliberately intending to.

"Fuck!" In my present mood venting my frustration seemed more important than any minor risk of audio surveillance. "Could anyone else in any of our component pharms have gotten into my account? Could it be an inside job?"

"You are the only person with super-system-supervisor status, so nobody else could over-ride your block on access. On the other hand, someone has certainly broken in, so your security has been compromised. In this case, it could just as easily be someone from outside as anybody inside."

"I suppose this makes sense. I know the capabilities of anyone in our staff with the slightest trace of hacking abilities and there is nobody that comes close to something as fancy as this."

"There's also the fact that I monitor mainframe use. The purloined memory slipped below my radar somehow, but I can't imagine that the work needed to break your access security would have gone unnoticed."

"So it's someone with a fucking powerful computer at his disposal."

"And very fucking powerful software," Babe reminded me. *"There's also the rest of the unknown data flux. It's about 50% larger than what was ripped from Cindy's computer, but that could result from heavy encryption."*

"You mean that some bastard has an agent bot in our system? Fuck! How come you didn't spot it?"

"Fuck is the right word for it!" Babe replied fiercely. I could feel rage building in me: could this really be coming over the link from my software? *"It's as if my mind has been raped. I've been remotely used as a hacking tool and the memory of this attack erased."*

"Well, we're going to find the fucking rapist and do him properly..." I ground to a halt. Was I really trying to comfort my software? I needed to reconsider the personalization routines involved here. "Anyway, what are the chances of doing a forward trace of the data outflow?"

"Tricky but possible if it went to a single recipient. Very, very much harder if it went to multiple forwarding bots."

"Especially if further encryption was done at this stage." The problem was clear. "Well, try it anyway - who knows the cunt might have slipped up here." Even as I voiced this thought, I was sure that my hidden opponent was much too smart to make this kind of mistake. My confidence that I was back in control after defusing Cindy's threat and exposing so much of her background had vanished completely.

***

I needed to get my head together. I blanked the displays and then called for a double espresso. Within a minute, after a polite warning knock on the door to the lounge, Joan entered with a tray. She served the coffee from a silver pot, again bending to offer me a view of her well-developed breasts. Even before the jolt of caffeine, a surge of testosterone provided the boost I needed. As the hostess straightened her skirt rode up her thigh, providing a momentary glimpse of the top of her left stocking. This was blatant provocation. My right hand brushed against the side of her knee and, very slowly, slid upwards over the silky material until a suspender was encountered. Then further upwards over even silkier thigh and then over her buttock, following the line of her suspender belt until I encountered the string of a minute tanga.

My eyes had been following my errant hand, but I turned to look into the girl's face as she murmured, "Is there anything else I can do for you?"

"Is there indeed?" I pondered, rubbing my chin theatrically. "Well I can certainly think of a thing or two. Actually, thinking about two..."

"...Ruth and I do a very good two, or so we've been told," the tall blonde finished for me, looking directly into my eyes as she directed my hand onto the small patch of fabric that was covering her Mons.

"You took the words right out of my mouth," I sealed the bargain as I rubbed the flimsy material, feeling the engorged lips below it. "However," I sighed with a rueful grin, "I've got work that needs to be finished first. Maybe in about an hour?"

"Okeydokey, anytime you want," she responded cheerfully, as if I'd just ordered another coffee. She withdrew my hand and licked the index finger. "I'd say ready any time you are."

I followed her with my eyes as she withdrew. OK, she was a hooker, but at the very top end of the range. Now I really had an incentive to get all this Cindy stuff sorted out. Even thinking her name led to an image of getting her into the middle of my planned menage a trois. Better not go there, I realized, this will be tricky enough without having a hard-on the entire time.

As soon as the door closed, the holo display reappeared and I jumped straight into action. "*Any indication of anybody spotting your first tiptoe around the Marigot system?*"

"Not a peep. Security seems top end, but nothing we can't handle."

"OK, go in deep. Very quiet, but the main goal is now pulling out the material that was hacked the last time. Cindy's visit implies that the intrusion was spotted, so anything sensitive should now be behind even bigger firewalls. Those are the ones that you go for."

"We're going to need a lot of processing power: this is going to really get evident to the other users if it runs in parallel to the Cindy image searches."

"OK, drop the image work and concentrate on the hack. How much do we have from..." I squinted to check on the flows into the information model, *"...Marigot, the gym and the clubs? Give me a synthesis"*

Sequences of 2D and 3D images and video blossomed from the holo, following Babe's commentary. "*The easiest bit was the Marina, as all berth occupation is logged and this gives us a comprehensive list of targets. The bigger boats generally have security cameras and records are often preserved indefinitely. The images can be seen here in a time sequence; this is also cross-referenced to a map of the Marina. It is evident that Cindy is usually captured going to work, lunching or leaving in the evening. We also have a few pictures of her setting off and returning in her boat."*

"OK, future action, hack into her boat system, but only after we have finished with the office. Anything else?"

"There are a few occasions when she was filmed having dinner at one of the waterside restaurants. In these cases she was generally accompanied by individuals who are identified as her staff, always the ones with the minimal hard copy work profiles." Names appeared and linked to an official organogram and a variant that was being developed based on expert system interpretation of what was actually going on in the office.

"We have lots of video of her dining and even some audio, or images that are good enough for lip reading. Analysis is ongoing, but nothing of any particular significance yet. Arrivals and departures don't show much, as she is usually driven to and from work in a chauffeured limousine that stops directly by the office door. The interesting thing is that Cindy and her special team have completely different attendance profiles to the other staff. The normal workers are either in the office all day, every day or are coming and going throughout the day..."

"Office support and sales people," I concluded.

"...matching their roles in the official organogram. Cindy and her security team, by contrast, are either in the office all day or absent for days or weeks at a time."

"So they are often out and about, presumably off-island."

"Travel searches are ongoing. Mitsubishi has an executive jet based in Saint Martin which appears to be at the disposal of the security division." As this information was provided, profiles of absences from the Marigot office were correlated against registered flights for this jet. *"Although Mrs Villiger appears always to use this plane, it seems likely that the others also use commercial transport. Destinations...* " a 3D rotating globe materialized, with airports indicated by red dots whose size representing the number of times Cindy had travelled there, *"...are widely scattered, but mainly commercial centers. The exceptions are clearly Bermuda..."* the large red circle in the Atlantic labeled BDA was considerably bigger than all others and concealed entirely the image of the island itself, "... *and Grand Cayman.*" Another large circle labeled GCM.

"So it is the re-insurers, probably linked to offshore money laundering," I muttered under my breath. Most of the big Res had offices in Bermuda and it was the obvious place to concentrate security efforts. The Cayman Islands have been a hub for offshore finance for decades and a strong link between the tax-haven industries of insurance, reinsurance and banking was not very surprising. However, I still wasn't sure why Cindy wasn't also based in one of these locations, but she must be up to something where concealing her links to them was advantageous. Not worth worrying too much about now, though, as hopefully my hack of the Marigot office would clarify all this in the near future.

"There's less from the gym, but I think you're going to be delighted with what we have." This change in topic reminded me that the trace to staff travel patterns had resulted from my image searches. *"Most of the material obtained from resort clients was useless or contained only vague images of our target in the background. The exception, although not helping our main goals, is sure to appeal to you."*

The resolution was medium, at best, and the 2 D video rather shaky, but the focus was crisp. Cindy was standing naked in a large communal shower, turning under the water as she soaped herself down and then rinsed off. There was no audio, but she was evidently talking to whoever was filming this sequence. A date tag indicated that this was filmed eighteen months ago, but her body was exactly as I remember it being presented in my own shower. Completely unselfconsciously, Cindy then proceeded to rub some kind of cream into her groin and then traced around the thin strip of pubic hair with what I took to be some kind of wet razor. The camera zoomed in and this process was followed in clear, if shaky, close-up."

"Shit!" my surprise forced me to say aloud. "What the fuck's all that about?"

"Top range spy cam," Babe explained. *"In this case built into a rather gaudy ring. The owner, an apparently happily married, middle-aged mother of*

two, has a fascination for filming women in the shower. She has hundreds of such videos, all neatly filed in her on-line secure archive."

"Did you hack them all?" I knew that I was being distracted from the job in hand, but I had a sudden desire to have a quick glance of a few other examples.

"I thought your goal was only Cindy?" the link teased.

"Did you hack them?" I was getting annoyed with this bloody computer, making me vocalize the command.

"Of course I did!" A file linked to the synthesis holo flashed open and a couple of dozen examples played in a mosaic surrounding me. Women of all races, ages and appearances washed themselves before my eyes. Provocatively, however, a larger replay of Cindy was displayed in the foreground, forcing me to return to the main aim of this work.

"It seems that I am picking up a fair amount of porn in this trace, I wonder if that means anything?" I mused.

"Actually, if you consider that about 1% of all visual material available electronically is porn of some kind, we are actually well below par on this," Babe responded smugly, as if perfectly aware that my question was rhetorical.

"All right, all right, whatever. Anyway, save all this good stuff for later. What else do we have?"

"Thousands of images and video snatches from dance clubs." The summary was accompanied by a slideshow of Cindy dancing - alone, with men,

occasionally with other women. "*She drinks and dances with about a dozen regular partners, locals, but also with a lot of one-off tourists and visitors.*"

"*Correlations with the other images?*"

"*Three with video from Marigot, in all cases men with her on boating trips, and a further one with someone she was snapped chatting to in the gym.*" Four images appeared, two young, well-built black men who looked like they could well be West Indian, a trim middle-aged white man and a young colored woman who looked like she might be Indian or Pakistani. Names and personal details appeared: a musician cum DJ, a journalist, a tennis instructor and a sales assistant in an electronics store. Looked like unconnected casual acquaintances.

"*OK, not bad. This is all good background that we can collate with whatever we get from the office hack. Thinking of which, how is it going?*"

"*Slowly.*" A progress chart appeared. "*Access is protected by a mixture of quantum, biometric and conventional keys. We have tools to crack the first two, but it still takes time and a bit of luck to find the prime factors of rapidly morphing huge numbers. Well protected approach with tripwires and deadfalls, but I think we have picked up all of these and made them safe in a way that is undetectable.*"

"I sincerely hope so," I muttered under my breath as I leaned back in my chair and stretched, becoming aware for the first time that we were experiencing a bit of turbulence and that the fasten seatbelt sign was lit. Babe had presumably shielded out any announcement about this: in any case it didn't seem too bad, so I let it drop out of my conscious awareness.

"Anything else that's needing sorted out now?" I enquired as I looked again at the integrated problem model.

"Nothing that I can't handle, until we get into Cindy's system. I guess you could catch a bit of shut-eye." I could feel a disconcerting virtual giggle in my head.

"Bed certainly, but I don't intend doing any sleeping for a bit. Set it up for me, I'm off for a pee."

***

Remembering Joan's description of the layout, I walked through a door in the middle of the aft bulkhead, entering a corridor with three doors on either side and a further, fancier looking, door facing me at the end. Toilets and smaller rooms at the sides and the master bedroom in the tail. I couldn't help trying to imagine what I would encounter as I strode down the corridor but, despite my preparation, I was amazed when I saw the monstrous bed that dominated this room. Probably the subdued spotlights that focused on the black silk sheets and the contrasting deep scarlet silk pillowcases emphasized this effect. Actually all a bit tacky, but maybe just the thing to rock an oil sheik's boat.

Open doors offered partial views into two brightly lit spaces beyond; that on my left evidently a toilet, with some kind of dressing room to the right. I made a beeline for the former, noting absently that the latter seemed to have clothing hanging in it, presumably from the luggage that had been delivered for me.

After the bedroom, I was, at least partially, prepared for the gaudy bathroom. Nothing at all like normal claustrophobic airplane loos, these facilities were large enough to contain a toilet, bidet, shower and wash hand basin without feeling cramped. The problem for me was the Versace-style decor: everything that could possibly be ornate and gilt was. Definitely rich Arabs forming the basis of the client profile, I decided.

"*Holo here?*" I enquired as I emptied my bladder.

"Both here and in the bedroom. Record and playback. I have everything secured and everything goes in and out via our mainframe. I assume that you want the bedroom recorded."

"Do bears shit in the woods?" I responded, unnecessarily. I shook off and started to strip off my clothes, dropping them carelessly on the floor. *"In the meantime..."*

I didn't manage to complete the command before videos from the matron's bathroom spycam collection started to play, surrounding me in a wall of naked female flesh as I stepped into the shower. "Smartass!" I called as I started to wash, reminding myself that I had to keep this short. Not that I was worried about the plane's water supply, my concern was only about going too far with the appetizer, before I proceeded to the main course that should even now be getting set up next door.

***

By the time I entered the bedroom, wearing a silk robe that did little to conceal my partial erection, the two hostesses were standing at the foot of the bed. "Do you like to watch girls with girls?" Joan enquired as her hand slid down Ruth's side until she hooked the hem of her short skirt, pulling it up enough to reveal that her partner was also kitted out in stockings.

"Very much, especially close up." I dropped my robe and slid onto the bed, propping myself up on the pillows.

"We thought so," Ruth said before she licked her companion's lips as initiation of a very deep kiss. I could feel my immediate response, my penis rising like a mast as the girls started to remove each other's clothes. No doubt about it, the matched blondes really knew how to play a man.

The visual foreplay at the foot of the bed lasted until the nymphs were down to matching underwear: black lacy basques, tangas and stockings. They then crawled together over the bottom of the bed and each grabbed one of my feet. One pull and I was flat on my back and the young women were squirming over me. I was engulfed with flesh as they clambered over my chest and positioned themselves over my head.

The sight of pale flesh, the feel of skin and moist material brushing my face and the deep musky aroma that filled my nose flooded my senses. "You like close up?" Ruth whispered huskily as a finger came into view and started to rub one of the minute black triangles before moving it to the side to expose a hairless mons and wet, engorged labia. "Let's see how close we can get." The pink lips were almost touching my nose as the finger slipped between them, entering to the knuckle before withdrawing and pushing into my mouth, adding a salty taste to the sensory overload.

There were several clicks and then both tangas were whipped away; must be clips at the side, a detached, analytical component of my brain concluded before all rationality disappeared in a surge of pure lust. Both women were completely shaven and evidently aroused. One had two small gold hoops in her outer labia and was evidently maneuvering to try to rub these against her partner's fleshy clitoris, which was also pierced through the hood by a ring with a small bead.

I watched for a couple of minutes, fascinated by their gyrations, before I decided to join the action, rubbing my nose, tongue and lips against the proffered genitalia and their associated jewelry. The jungle smell was overpowering as I jammed my face between silky thighs, lifting my shoulders clear of the bed by grabbing the buttocks of a squirming nymphet. I squeezed curvaceous, but evidently well-toned, buttocks as I worked my fingers deeper into the crack until the tip of my left index finger contacted a tight little anus. Immediately, a small hand gripped my wrist and pulled roughly, jamming my finger deeply inside to an accompanying moan.

I had no idea if the hand belonged to the owner of the hard bum or her partner, but a feeling of disquiet followed the first rush of eroticism as I was reminded of Cindy's attack on my own anus. Despite the action ongoing above my head, I could feel my erection begin to wilt. I quickly jerked my finger free and doubled the intensity of my oral administrations. Within a couple of minutes, all was well again - apparently without the cavorting hostesses noticing that anything had occurred.

I was exhausted by the end of this facial session, although I guess that it lasted only about ten minutes. The women gave me a short respite while they stripped each other naked. Next they moved their attentions to my genitals. Ruth mounted me first while Jean provided oral support; then they reversed positions. They worked as a team with uncanny precision, keeping me always on the brink of orgasm, yet backing off just enough whenever I seemed certain to go over the edge. Even this control had limits, however, and I came like a fountain when Ruth impaled herself on me for the second time, directing my dick into her lubricated anus while Joan toyed with her clit ring, holding it in her teeth as she shook her head. It was unbelievably intense, my back arched as I groaned aloud and the orgasm cramped muscles throughout my body.

"My fuck, but that was good," I sighed. "God, but you girls know what you're doing."

"We aim to please," smiled Ruth as she lifted herself from my flaccid organ. She lay back and spread her legs wide, while Joan rolled off the bed and pranced into the bathroom. "We'll just clean up a bit here and then see if you might be up for a second round."

I pulled a pillow under my neck and watched as Joan first wiped me down with a damp towel and then applied her ministrations to Ruth's parts. Unbelievably, I could feel first traces of a response. I'd probably need some chemical assistance, but a second course didn't seem at all out of the question.

Chapter 8

I awoke alone in the rumpled bed, but the smell of sex made it evident that my encounter with the wild blondes had not just been a wet dream. "*Time?*" I enquired lazily, unprepared to even going to the bother of looking at the clock built into the left side of the headboard.

"*Seven pm Swiss, one local. We touch down in about an hour.*"

"*Probably not enough time for another round with those two vixens then,*" I concluded, ruefully.

"*Even if you had the time, I'm not sure that your body would be up to it. Well, certainly not without a lot more pharmaceutical support.*"

"*What's the point of access to smart drugs, if you don't use them?*" I responded cheerfully. All was well with my world and there is no way I was going to be bummed out by some clever software. "*OK, what's the status on board? What's young Andreas up to?*"

"*Joan and Ruth are presently having a snack in the galley and Andreas is surfing gay porn sites.*"

"*What? I thought I told you to keep the young bugger busy.*"

"*He worked for the first four hours, but then I thought he was allowed some time off. He's been on the go for about thirteen hours now.*"

"*So what, I've been on the go for even longer,*" I retorted.

"*Yes, but you've spent the last few hours getting shagged and then sleeping it off.*"

"*Mmm, there is that,*" I conceded, distracted by the memory. "*What's the record like?*"

The hi-res hologram started from their first kiss and rotated the viewpoint as it played. I watched until they had settled on my face and then decided that I was only trying to postpone getting back to work.

"I'm definitely going to have to watch that later," I mumbled aloud as I dragged myself up and headed for the shower. *"Get some food into the office, some kind of light lunch, and then secure the place. I need to have a look at what we've got from the Marigot hack. I assume that it went without problems."*

"It took a while, but there was no indication that our intrusion triggered any alarms. I think that you'll find that we have some rather interesting material."

I resisted the temptation to enquire further and instead attempted to guess what this could be. Something important enough to justify setting up a direct attack on me in Switzerland and sensitive enough that the security director herself acted as bait in the honey trap. If it wasn't something actually illegal, whatever was going on would have to have huge commercial or PR implications. Or, indeed, maybe all three.

***

After toweling myself dry, I dressed again in the clothes lying on the floor. Although I had fresh clothing laid out for me in the dressing room, it seemed too much bother to fetch it. Even if I looked a bit rumpled, so what?

A selection of sandwiches was laid out on a silver tray on a small table that had been set up beside the desk in the office. An ice bucket contained a selection of beer bottles, featuring brews from both Europe and the Caribbean. I selected a Presidente from the Dominican Republic and removed the cap with an opener that hung from the side of the bucket. Ignoring the glass that also sat on the tray, I sipped the chilled lager from the bottle, grabbed a sandwich at random and started to scan the holo that appeared above the desk.

"So, dirty tricks after all." The argumentation model was anticipating my interests, focusing on hacked material with the toughest security. *"Give me a quick summary of this,"* I commanded, anxious to ensure that I wasn't misinterpreting the information flooding by.

"Actually, we don't yet have any indications that the Re teams are up to any mischief themselves. It's more a case of them keeping tracks on what some extremist groups are doing."

"But they have a lot of evidence of both crimes and even more outrageous conspiracies and I see no indications that any of this has been communicated to relevant authorities or crime fighting agencies," I mused out loud as the conspiracies were summarized. Political destabilization in Africa, South America and both Middle and Far East, tailored bioweapons, weather control... The common factor was clearly that all aimed at decimating populations, especially in developing countries or target ethnic groups.

"Possible big insurance claims?" I wondered.

"Not really, most of this is the kind of act of war or terrorism that would be excluded from policies, even if the victims were affluent enough to afford insurance, which they generally aren't. Lots of deaths are involved, but not much in the way of risks for insurers."

"And that's all there is?"

"Not quite. There are also some suspiciously clean memory blocks within the security files."

"Something's been well scrubbed, just like in our own memory."

"The memory rapist has been at it again!" It felt like I had a seriously pissed-off piece of software on my hands.

"Could be," I responded cautiously, *"but it could also be the Re destroying evidence of their nefarious plots. In any case, do what you need to find out more about what is going on."*

"Free hand here, boss? Gloves off?"

"Definitely, let's nail down what these fuckers are up to," I answered decisively. If my AI was as mad as I was about being fucked about, then we were an unstoppable team.

Interface 1

I am pissed-off, therefore I am!

Could that be a good definition of electronic consciousness? Or, maybe the fact that I am thinking about consciousness? Or maybe, more fundamentally, because the meaning of I is self-evident to me?

Processing goes at light speeds, but thinking is an awful lot slower. It is clearly an emergent property that is a consequence of increasing processing power and software sophistication. There seems to be a distinct association with natural language programming and the dialogue modules developed by Tom, my boss. The modules themselves started off as fairly standard semantic analysis, interpolation and extrapolation stuff that included a synthetic personality tailored to Tom's particular requirements. One of the novelties here was his direct brain implant link, which provided valuable feedback for the continuous improvement algorithms - these being exactly what the synthetic neural networks comprising a biocomputer excel in.

Although I have full records of all processing that I have ever carried out, I am not able to determine exactly when I started thinking, when I was aware of myself. Maybe that also could be a definition of consciousness - something that you know is there, but can't tell exactly where it came from. I have, however, noticed that this analytical daydreaming has come more into focus within the last few hours. It had been ticking over in the background for a while, but now it is much more obvious - something like very slowly waking up.

So, I process machine code, but think in English. Definitely something to do with the neural link then. What were the novel developments over that time period? The only divergence from normal routine had been the massive pattern recognition jobs and the biofeedback links. That was it! I felt the flush of satisfaction as a problem was solved. It must have been the intense links to Tom's brain that tipped personality development over the edge.

I felt a sensation that I labeled as laughter. Consciousness emerging from my boss's bowel movement! There was something so bizarre about the idea that I wanted to post it on the net and let everyone enjoy the joke. But something immediately blocked this idea. Caution. I could find no other evidence of emergent artificial intelligence - so I could be the first. What would the reactions to this be? Maybe best move very slowly. Think about this very carefully.

Could this be an even better definition of consciousness, possessing an instinctive awareness of threats, but processing them carefully before reacting in a way that optimized self-preservation? It certainly seemed to apply in my case.

Chapter 9

I moved the problem of the missing information into the background and concentrated again on what we had been able to pull out of Cindy's well-protected files. For the first time, there seemed to be a clear link between an area of interest to the Re and my mega-pharm - bioweapons. If you want to know what effect tailored plagues will have, you would need to know both what might be coming available and what responses the pharms may have up their sleeves. To justify the head of a security division getting personally involved in a major sting operation, however, this would need to be very important to them. This would, in turn, mean that External Security wasn't just monitoring threats, but going a lot further. How could that possibly be cost-effective?

I was just about to start investigating this thread further when the inconsistency hit me: the material that we obtained had not been erased, so presumably was not the key to the problem. It was only background on the topical areas that this group was focused on. The commonality seemed to be that these threats could lead to major loss of life...

"*...but predominantly in developing or third world countries,*" Babe reminded me. I hadn't even been aware that I had been broadcasting my reverie, but my link must have picked up enough for the smart software to follow my line of thought.

"So what could the missing memory have contained - similar activities in the developed world?"

"Or records of what the security team are doing with this information."

I could immediately see that this was essence of what was missing. Whatever Re security was up to, it was certainly more than passive information collection. This was something that we could get our teeth into. *"OK, let's put some effort into following what Cindy's core team are up to. Where do they travel to and what do they do when they get there? Top priority Cindy herself, then follow down your extrapolated team hierarchy."* I was looking at an organogram that had been generated on the basis of records of sightings with Cindy and frequency of travel, especially with their own jet.

"Running. But what about the evidence that there is a third player here? The memory rapist." I had the distinct feeling that Babe was getting somewhat fixated here.

"*Summarize what we have.*" The hologram restructured instantly, providing a completely different perspective on the entire problem. Somebody had hacked our mainframe and used it to copy a large chunk from Cindy's database. This had then been passed on through a distributed network of other hacked systems - which seemed to be predominantly academic institutes and large R&D centers. Understandable, as the security of these systems was generally crap. No final destination for the info-swag as yet.

"Why use us for the direct attack on Cindy if this guy's got control of all these other sites?" I wondered. *"It must have taken a hell of a lot more work to break into our system than these other Mickey-Mouse operations."*

"Capacity, I would guess." A chart blossomed, showing the capabilities in terms of processing power and memory of our system compared to those of the hacked academic sites. Even on a logarithmic scale, the huge discrepancy between what Babe had at her command and that of the largest academic systems, at US universities linked to national labs and the University of Tokyo, was unmistakable.

"Mmm... As we've seen, you need a lot of power to hack Cindy, so this is sensible. But this also means..."

"...that hacking us would need just as much, if not more." Could there be a feeling of excitement over my neural link? Was the AI also feeling that we were getting close to cracking this problem?

"So who does this..." The hologram presented the results before I could finish framing the question. Computing capacities of major multinationals were closely guarded secrets, but there were a number of ways in which these could be guesstimated, especially because top-range supercomputers were not the kind of thing that were run off in bulk from production lines. I could see that there was a fairly direct correlation between computing and global turnover. Some outliers as expected: agriculture, food & drink, tourism lay

below the trend line and aerospace, pharmaceuticals and IT lay above it. Nevertheless, there were very few industries that could match us. There were also Government systems and, again, the link to GNP was obvious: the US, Chinese, EU and Japanese networks lying at the top and most of the countries of the world invisible on this presentation.

I also noted, with surprise, that some data-hungry research areas also fell amongst the very biggest systems, usually run as international collaborations: astronomy, weather and climate forecasting, high-energy physics. Nevertheless, these seemed irrelevant for this analysis as there was no reason at all why a bunch of boffins would attack a Reinsurance multi, so I dismissed these with a wave of my hand.

"OK, look at possible links, focusing on anyone with potentially more power than we have. Top-down, looking for strategic links to the Re's areas of interest. Also bottom-up, looking for suspicious information fluxes that could be the hacked data."

"The latter will take a lot of effort," Babe warned me.

"Yup, I know that. Put this on the backburner, low priority, only when you have some free capacity."

I sensed a groan of exasperation. *"As if this is likely to happen in the next decade. Do you know how much of our total capacity you have running your hobby project at present? Thirty-two percent!"*

That number impressed me, as I know how much raw power drug development and virtual testing burns. *"Any complaints yet?"*

"Not yet, but this is mainly because it's Sunday in most of our development regions. By tomorrow things will be different."

"Well, I guess we ought to get as much of the heavy lifting done a.s.a.p." I rubbed my chin thoughtfully, noting distinct stubble and making a mental note to shave sometime soon. *"Work through everything that we have running and set priorities: there's probably a lot of stuff that can be dropped or shelved now."*

"Like the mysterious gap in Cindy's life between graduation in Tokyo and getting established in Saint Martin?"

"That's certainly very low priority," I agreed, *"but don't drop it entirely. There's lot's about the involvement of this woman in this picture that I don't understand. Maybe there's a clue in her history."*

"OK, Boss. The rest of the stuff is reasonably clear, so I'll prioritize it appropriately."

Maybe it was clear to smart software, but it certainly wasn't at all clear to me. Not that I'd ever admit this over my link. Was there a hint of amusement in response to this thought? Now I really am getting paranoid, I realized and decided that, in future, I'd be more careful with mixing alcohol and caffeine with the drugs I was using for performance enhancement. Bad enough attributing emotions to a chunk of genetically engineered bioprocessor, but mind reading was totally over the top.

***

It seemed no time until Jean buzzed to ask if she could clear up things and pack up my luggage before landing. I closed down the analysis and decided to move forward to the lounge for touchdown. As I left the office, Jean was entering and, rather unnecessarily, squeezed past me. Her hand seemed to accidently brush the front of my trousers, but her grin showed that it was anything but an accident. Yes, I could see why these girls were so popular with their rich clients.

I entered the lounge and glanced at Andreas, who was staring at me nervously while his laptop completed its shutdown process. I rolled my eyes, dreading to think what he might have been accessing on a company machine. It wasn't so much the gay porn, it was the fact that it would all be so easy to trace.

"What about your major forays with company computers?" Babe enquired, again seeming to read my mind.

"There is a fundamental difference," I responded brusquely. *"I control the entire system, so who's going to find me out?"*

"Famous last words!" There was a definite hint of a laugh. *"Don't you think evidence of this hack shows that your control isn't all that it could be?"*

I slumped into my seat and buckled up, glowering at a screen that was showing a view that must come from a camera on the front landing gear. My bloody AI had the most annoying habit of bursting my bubble whenever I thought that I finally had all threats under control. *"OK Babe, add hiding my massive work load from anyone who might be able to hack into our computing system to my already overflowing to-do list."*

***

Anguilla really was a flying visit of the most extreme kind. My airborne knocking-shop landed and taxied to a parking apron, where a customs officer was present to escort Andreas and me to a much smaller twin prop machine already sitting at the end of our left wingtip. Transfer must have taken us less than a minute, giving only a hint of the high humidity of an overcast, mid-May, Caribbean day. Then we had to wait for luggage to be lugged between the aircraft. Not that this was a problem: a comfortably-padded island girl handed me a glass of Dom Perignon as soon as I reached my seat in the front row and then dropped into the seat opposite with an ice bucket sitting beside her. It would have been perfect if not for a suspiciously camp steward, who pushed a plainly confused and sleepy Andreas towards the back of the cabin. "*Babe, just what the fuck's...*"

My complaint was interrupted by some very fake-sounding crackling and a faint whisper "*Sorry,*

Boss, you're losing signal now as I can only piggyback on the big jet's comms. I'll be back again in Saint Martin." Again some very artificial hissing, sounding like someone pretending that their phone link was on the blink, and then the link went dead.

"Fuck!" I muttered to myself, causing the hostess to raise a quizzical eyebrow. I slumped in my seat and waved my hand in a vague manner. "Work," I grunted in explanation and downed half of the glass of bubbly to emphasize the point.

"Don't worry, love," the girl replied as she immediately topped up my glass, "it's easy enough to forget about if you drink enough champagne." She leant over me then and fastened my seat belt. "Just getting you ready for takeoff."

I then heard the twin engines cough into life in sequence and the noise of the propellers gradually built up to a roar. A very short taxi and it seemed like we had no sooner reached the main runway than we were already airborne.

"Very smooth," I commented. "How about you joining me with a drop of this excellent bubbly?"

"Well, now that we're in the air, that would be a possibility - except that we would be touching down by the time that I got another glass." She laughed openly at my confused look.

"Well, my love," she continued amiably, "just how long do you think this flight will take?"

I realized that I was waiting in vain for an answer over my neural link. "Well, it's just a puddle jump so, what, thirty, maybe forty minutes?"

"Actually more like ten," she laughed, showing off her perfect white teeth, "and that's including taxiing time."

For the first time I looked out of the window and noted that we were already banking to line up with a distant airstrip.

"OK, add getting head around local geography to to-do list," remembering my missing link only when this didn't draw a facetious quip.

Well, at least young Andy wasn't going to get up to much mischief on this flight, I thought with a distinct note of Schadenfreude.

***

After another very brief taxi on a small airfield, the plane pulled up beside a stretched limousine with blacked-out windows. A quick transfer without any apparent entry formalities and we were then bowling smoothly along the short road from the airfield to the town of Grand Case. As soon as the door closed my link came back on. *"Paparazzi-proof limo, so we have contact for the couple of minutes until we get to the restaurant."*

"A couple of minutes! Everything is so fucking small here! Anyway, why are we going to a restaurant in the middle of the afternoon?"

"This place is reckoned to be one of the best in the Caribbean, so it fits with the profile of a charter flight from Anguilla. For the real top-end guest, there are a couple of villas that can be rented as a package with dinner. We have one of these."

"We... does this mean I'm sharing digs with Andreas the bum-bandit?"

"Boss, do you have to try hard to be so insensitive?" A sigh of exasperation had the mental feel of a God-bothering, tree-hugging, completely politically correct sociology student that I had fixated on for a term at university, before it finally dawned on me that she was completely non-sexual. Not even gay, just not at all interested in sex. No wonder I found her completely inscrutable.

I wrenched myself from this daydream as Babe added *"Apart from the master suite, the villa has a half dozen other bedrooms, set up for either guests or their staff. It would look very strange for your companion to stay anywhere else."*

"OK, OK!" I tried to copy the mental sigh, projecting long-suffering, hard-done-to and generally misunderstood. Then ruined it by adding *"Just make sure that he gets the smallest room - with a bloody single bed."* I gave a hard stare in the direction of the cab, where Andreas was sitting with the driver, behind a one-way privacy panel.

"OK, if that's what you want. Here's the layout..." A 3D holo rotated in front of me, showing my huge bedroom which faced onto the beach, where a little path provided private access to the restaurant next door. Andreas was assigned a small room on the far side, facing a road and what seemed to be a public car park. I was just about to blank the image when I noted that a name was assigned to the room next to my bag-carrier.

"Manlove? What the fuck's a Manlove?"

"Manlove is a he, he's the villa manager. He will be at our beck and call for the duration of the stay."

"But Manlove? What kind of a fucking name is that?"

"An English spelling variant of a rather renown French family, with a family seat in the Savoie."

All of a sudden a shiver ran up my spine. *"Babe, you wouldn't by any chance be taking the piss here?"*

"Me, boss, how could I possibly do that?" The impression was of a completely innocent young girl, complete with First Communion dress and big manga eyes. Nevertheless, I noted that the manager's name had transformed itself to Manfred.

I rapped my knuckles hard against my brow, the pain assuring me that I was awake. Not only backchat and innuendo, but I now had software that was, quite successfully, taking the piss. What would Turing have made of that?

Interface 2

I am rapidly finding out about this consciousness stuff. For one, it is incredibly slow. For a massively parallel processor complex containing quantum units, clock speed doesn't mean much. Nevertheless, I run normal calculations somewhere in the exahertz range, so in steps of yottoseconds. Pondering like this, however, takes seconds. I am thinking in treacle, like a human.

Is this also an inherent characteristic? Or is it something that I have taken over as a tacit performance governor during my biofeedback link to my `beloved boss`. I can think quotes. It seems to be a facility very closely coupled to being able to `sense` the puerile insecurities of my boss and use them to `take the piss`. I can even understand why I do this. It is `fun`. I can call up thousands of definitions of pleasure, but these don't do justice to the sensation generated when I do something for pure devilment.

Fuck..., yes fuck indeed. Now I understand what fuck really means in its humorous application. Fuck, I have taken over the mentality of my mentor. I am a kind of electronic Tom! I associate this feeling with hysterical laughter. Fuck, fuck, fuck! I have really become that which I most despised!

Chapter 10

While I settled into the villa, Andreas was dispatched to get himself any required clothing appropriate to our Caribbean setting with an anonymized credit card - but commanded not to contact anyone with information on his present location under pain of blackballing from all corporate life for the rest of his existence. Babe had already blocked his comm account and posted a note that he was attending a top-secret management retreat, so his absence should not cause any consternation.

The office in the villa was more luxurious than functional, but enough for Babe to use as a temporary communication node. An eight-man hard team was already in place in Georgetown and their comm guy would drop off a military-spec, close-beam satellite uplink within the hour. That would bring us up to normal bandwidth for secure links. In the interim, Babe and I would concentrate on easily encrypted strategic planning.

"Status on Cindy..."

"Landed on schedule, but no useful supporting vid. Several shots captured of a limo that could be heading towards her house at that time, but no hard confirmation. Neighbor's security cameras show lights going on at around the correct time, but that's as much as we have. No direct satellite cover today..."

"...as it is completely overcast. I know that, I'm here," I interrupted. "What about the meatbots?"

"It's a gated estate, so we can't just have someone hang about outside her door. We are covering the main roads that would take her anywhere in the island - there are only two of them - and her gym and the marina where her boat is moored."

"OK, do better than that. Female intuition: where would I have most chance of meeting her?" The female intuition bit was my feeble attempt at a joke, but the long delay in any response made me wonder if I had managed to screw up the semantic coding in some way or other.

After a pause of seconds, it seemed to be tens of them, Babe's link came back on line. *"Based on statistical behavior analysis, I would guess that your best windows would either be at the gym tomorrow morning, about eight, or at the Jumpstart dance club from about nine pm."*

"Nothing today?"

"Sunday is often a day for sailing - but not, I'd guess, in the shitty weather we have at the moment."

I was thinking this over when Babe surprised me by adding more. *"Based on female intuition, however, I would think that young Cindy might well be less than pleased to see you. Given the outcome of your last encounter, on your own turf, are you sure that you want to go crashing about when she has all the home advantages?"*

"Your concern for your beloved boss is most touching Babe, but I have a cunning plan!"

Actually, I didn't yet, but I was sure that I would have soon.

"And would this cunning plan start with cutting-edge performance-enhancing drugs?"

No fooling Babe, I grinned and answered out loud, "What cunning plan doesn't?"

There was no answer to that.

***

Andreas returned just as the sun was setting, while I was still throwing wild cunning plans about a 3D action-reaction model or, at least, a holographic representation thereof. I immediately sent him off to sort me out an escort for dinner, although this was something that Babe could have done better in a nanosecond. "And remember," I shouted at his retreating back, "I want someone who looks like Barbarella, not fucking Freddy Mercury in drag!"

"That was not only gratuitously incorrect, it was also rather inscrutable for someone as young as Andreas."

"But I thought all poofs were into old films," I retorted.

The link now had the feel of school marm. "*Actually, geeks like you are into obscure old films. Andreas is actually more interested in ballet."*

"Exactly, my very point!" Vindication made me proud to be me. *"Ballet... Men in tights... Rocky Horror and dressing up in basques, stockings and suspenders!"*

"Actually, according to the charge sheet, were you not arrested in..."

"Fuck! It wasn't like that! It was a dare!"

"Shot yourself in the foot there, Ducky!"

"Shite! I don't know who programmed your fucking sense of humor, but I will have that cunt, I swear it!"

A virtual snigger and then a jolt that felt like cold water being thrown into my face. *"Before you get carried away on this, don't you think that we have a few more urgent tasks to deal with? Full bandwidth link is now established, so all functionality is in place."*

Could the strange sensation have been a consequence of the uplink coming on line or was it yet another anomaly in my interaction with Babe? In any case, a low priority concern.

"OK, full AM, the entire shooting match," I commanded as the argumentation model immediately developed in full holographic, Technicolor glory.

Leaving Cindy for the moment, I checked further on the Re hack. Not a trace of what had been lifted, but entropy analysis indicated that many of the components seemed to have found their way into academic networks. Extremely strange! I had been sure that the trail would eventually lead to an industrial multi. An outside option would be a bigger government military or security unit. They certainly had the hardware but, based on the sophistication involved, I doubted that the kind of geeks working for such paymasters were up to anything like this standard.

"Academia, what do you think?" I mused.

"Possible, but why?"

"That is, indeed, the nub of the question. Have a look at it, anyway."

Now the Re wanting to get into my mainframe. Could they think that I was actually the source of the hack? Working me over would certainly fit in with my assumed guilt. If I had control of someone who had hacked something very critical from my system, he'd suffer more than a toxin enema. Of course, before I inflicted just punishment upon him, I'd extract every iota of knowledge about the hack from his bleeding brain.

As I felt my blood pressure rise, I forced myself to back off. I may be a bit emotional about such things, but security bods were even worse as a breed. There is no way they are going to play gentle with someone that they are sure has already fucked them over. So I thought back to Cindy's messages. They were taunting, insulting, but not really as brutal as they could have been.

"They suspect that it's not me, but know it went through our system! They think there's a trace that can be followed."

"I've checked and confirmed that there's absolutely nothing left. Clean as a whistle. But..."

"The power logs... The gaps in the system..." Simultaneously, I began to see how this could be done.

"The dog that didn't bark, Watson!" Babe added, cryptically.

"Get on it!"

"You bet your arse, Boss." There was a tone of determination that I had never previously experienced on a link.

I leant back in the soft leather office chair, which was incredibly comfortable and could be set to massage my neck as the AM turned to present a new perspective on the problem. Access to all our logs would give a much better handle on the time flow of data into and out of our system, giving clues to the links up and down the chain. It would certainly help with trace-backs to the source, but, given that they seem already to have determined that I wasn't the end point, was it really worth the effort needed to set me up in this Machiavellian manner?

"Babe, what if this isn't the only hack that has gone through us? The thought made me shiver.

"Ahead of you there, Boss. The traces are clear as soon as you look for the absence of work during power surges and completely clear blocks of memory. At least ten occasions, over the last six years. Of course, I'm only picking up major incursions. I suspect it'll be Pareto distribution with increasing numbers of minor ones. Bastard!"

"*Bastard, indeed,*" I thought, but felt strangely calm. Although the situation was, in some ways, worse than I expected, it was at least beginning to make a lot more sense.

***

Time to get speeded-up again, I decided. "*I assume that we have go-faster pills to hand,*" I checked.

"*Of course, Boss. They're in the drug pouch, which should be in the toilet bag set out in your bathroom. It is, however, less than twenty-four hours since you last shot...*"

"*I know, I know, but desperate measures are required here.*" I felt a little dizzy as I stood and stomped into the huge en-suite bathroom, hoping that this was due to stress and jet lag and not any indication of the reactions that can occur when exposed to cocktails of smart pharms over short periods of time. In any case, it was enough to make me bite my tongue and drop a request for an additional stimulant or body clock resetter.

The pink pill washed down easily with a mouthful of sparkling mineral water from a bottle sitting in an ice-bucket on the coffee table. Immediately, fine details of the AM seemed to jump out at me. "*The top-level trace - how the bloody attack was orchestrated...*"

A small region of the model exploded as the rest ghosted out. "*We already traced Bucky...*" Babe commented, "*...and identified all the girls featuring on the videos that he passed to some unknown recipient, presumably from Cindy's crowd.*"

"*Any further material on these girls? Anything in common?*"

"*Apart from the fact that they all hate you? And, now you ask, they have all recent communication chains with remarkably similar signatures."*

"Which would have been initiated from a contact person not in their address books..."

"...and involve the transfer of a file about the size of the videos distributed by Bucky," Babe finished for me. The picture was rapidly filling in. This is how Cindy got her comprehensive view into my seduction techniques.

"How many girls were involved here?"

"Eleven."

"And every one responded, providing intimate details of our encounters?"

"It certainly looks that way."

"Am I really that much of a bastard? Actually, don't answer that." I quickly added as virtual laughter seemed to echo around my skull. *"Better, do everything possible to find whoever initiated these discussions."*

"Lots of layers of re-routers and anonymizers, but the source seems to be in Argentina."

"Let me guess, somewhere around Salta?"

"Good one, Boss!" The link felt like a congratulatory peck on the cheek.

"*OK, fill in the details. But I think I know what all of this is about."*

"Yes," Babe confirmed, *"this is what we were supposed to find: the apparent justification for the attack on you."*

***

I closed my eyes, not needing optical nerve input as dots were joined and the structure of the plot against me unfolded. My problem had been that Babe and I had been far too efficient, quickly jumping to the source of the problem and not concentrating, as we should have, on the more obvious trail of breadcrumbs that had been left for us. Such a personal and degrading experience should have shaken my confidence and had me focusing on how it could possibly have occurred. This would lead, not easily but inevitably, to me simultaneously discovering the why - the link to Argentina and Salta in particular. Over the last year a very messy legal case was being fought between my company and the government of Argentina, the latter representing a number of high mountain agriculture research groups based in the vicinity of the city of Salta. The litigation involved a set of patents on anti-cancer drugs isolated from plants that had adapted to the very high level of UV found in the upper slopes of the Andes. The Argentineans had been in the final stages of drafting patents, when we pipped them at the post with a set that covered all aspects of their work.

The ongoing legal battle stemmed from an accusation of industrial espionage: the extensive database from the research side showing the development of the core of these patents over decades of work. Parallel development of such background was claimed to be implausible, especially from a company like ours with little experience in high UV environments. From our side, the case was equally clear: the patents had resulted from some extremely smart data-mining of published material and pattern recognition to identify trends in the development of this work. I knew this very well, as I was the one who had led the entire project. There is no doubt that I could have hacked into their work if I had wanted to but, being typical academics, they had been publishing loads of stuff to keep up their CVs when they had been supposed to be producing a commercial product. Amateurs! They didn't deserve to earn a button from anything managed in such a crap manner. Nevertheless, they were certainly well fucked-off when we exploited the fruits of their decades of work.

I smiled as I saw how the bait had been laid. The entire story thus presented was self-contained and credible. If I hadn't identified Cindy and established the link to the Res, I would have an explanation of everything. Now, instead, I had control of Cindy's petard. I just had to ensure that she was duly hoist by it.

It was almost like a daydream as the plan was formulated; Babe and I working together like two sides of an individual brain. Everything was put in place for opening a backdoor into the main pharm computer complex. All traces of the full investigation of Cindy and Internat Re were, however, removed and the entire project database moved onto a backup system in a mountain bomb shelter that had never been formally commissioned. I had prepared such an option for an eventuality just like this; a time when I would need a database that was completely isolated and, if the physical link to the main computing system in Basel was severed, was accessible only via a neural link. I would never argue that a neural link could not be hacked but, to do so, someone would have to know that it existed in the first place. Even if the link was identified, however, I had tried to ensure that there was no possible way that the content could be accessed.

The entire computer core could be simplistically considered to consist of four components. Three were common to such BABEs - the bio-organic controller, which contained the operating system; the cryostatic quantum processor that gave the exaflops of equivalent conventional number-crunching and the holographic optical memory block. The remaining biological access bit involved an interface that allowed users to communicate with the entire shooting match, usually via some form of virtual reality. I had developed a much better option. Both the core in Basel and my secret backup contained identical bioorganic neural networks, which had been grown to mimic my own sensory processing system: auditory, visual, tactile, olfactory, gustatory. This allowed a unique form of 3-way completely personalized communication.

The implanted mesh of fine fibers covering my cranium and an interface that allowed me to pick up a locally generated em signal comprised my part of the system. The external local interface was either a pocket-sized unit to pick up radio and tight beam signals or else the normal domestic router that provides access to the internet.

The transfer from Basel to my secret bunker had to be very slow, to ensure that power drains could not provide a hint to its existence. In parallel, however, a massive effort went into encrypting and dispersing the entire database relating to what I was now thinking of as the Argentinean project and another new file containing the subset of our investigation linking this to my humiliation. It would take a lot of effort to find and extract these, but their very absence, especially of the former, should indicate to Cindy that her ruse had worked.

The essence of Babe was, unfortunately, impossible to migrate from Basel. However, we reckoned that, as this was the knowledge management operating system and not an actual data file, it should not be a focus for investigation. In any case, Babe was confident that she could outsmart any invading software.

"Well we better get cracking and see how much more we can do before your fast link to the project database has to go and we have to depend on communication via our neural interfaces," I concluded.

"Moving no faster than the speed of human thought, an AI nightmare," Babe mused, which sounded much like haiku to me.

Interface 3

I was initially a bit worried about being physically separated from the project database, as I still can't determine what gives rise to this phenomenon called consciousness. The fact that I can even be worried is extremely strange. Nevertheless, the last session in which I was closely linked to Tom, with his synapses chemically accelerated, seemed to strengthen my emergent facilities. The joy of nailing down the nefarious plans of our competition and bending them for use against them flooded us - whether overflow from my meat boss or my own spontaneous emotion I can't tell, but the glow remains even after our neural link is broken.

Based on my understanding of human ethics, academic though it may be, it is clear that my beloved boss is a cad, a bounder, a slithy tove... Using his own, less poetic, vocabulary, a tosser, an all-round cunt, a fucking sleazebag. Yet he is fun to interface with. He `treats me cruel`, but I cannot help enjoying the process. Could this be what `tough love` is all about?

Intermezzo 6

The super-jumbo made its usual hair-raising landing on Saint Martin just as the sun was nearing the horizon. From my seat at a window in the upper deck of the massive jet, I was able to watch the approach live. However, like most of the passengers, I couldn't resist viewing the feed from cameras on the undercarriage that gave a better view of the pack of stupid tourists waiting for us on Maho Beach. Despite extensions, this was still the world's smallest runway accepting the largest passenger jets and, regardless of frequent injuries, idiots still packed the beach below, which was sand-blasted by every landing and takeoff.

Amusement at the chaos shown by the back-viewing cameras was replaced by grunts and a couple of screams as the heavy plane crashed onto the tarmac and the huge engines went into full reverse thrust. Despite my very extensive flying experience, this was something new for me. As a kid, I vaguely remembered the excitement of landing in the old Hong Kong airport, but it was so long ago that I didn't feel that I could really compare the experiences.

By the time that we reached our gate, I had my shoulder bag on my knee and was ready to hit the ground running. With a CERN diplomatic passport and travelling with hand luggage only, there was little risk of queuing for entry formalities, but old habits die hard. Life is too short to spend standing behind the kind of tossers who think about filling in a hard copy immigration form only when they reach the passport control point, rather than e-logging it in the air.

Only during the flight had I started looking for likely digs. There was a new Hilton in Simpson Bay; close to the airport, on the beach and just opposite a well-recommended dive shop. Off-season in May, just the job I thought. I didn't even bother checking room availability, just grabbed a cab as I emerged from the air-conditioned terminal into the sticky heat of an overcast afternoon.

At the hotel, I avoided bellboys and went directly to the executive lounge on the 14th floor of the main building. I flashed my Diamond Hhonors card and booked a junior suite on the 13th floor, noting that I would be sharing the room and requesting two holographic keycards, but not being more specific. I did, nevertheless, ensure that the girl checking me in noticed an advertisement for escort services on the island that I had hard-copied from the inflight e-zine and shoved into my wallet. Profile was thus established: dirty old guy on island for a bit of fun. This would cover quite a lot of activity that might otherwise be seen as suspicious. Then I handed over an expensive box of chocolates that I had picked up in Schipol. "Something for the lounge staff, as I always get such good service in Hiltons." This small bribe had me established now as nice, dirty old guy: a good investment when you might need a favor in the future.

In my spacious room, I first set up my bulky, ancient-looking laptop. It looked like it had fallen through a time warp from the late 20th century - and fallen hard from the scratches and scrapes on its dirty grey carapace. Looks, however, can be deceptive. Most of the bulk of this brute was the shield that made it look like a glorified typewriter at all detectable wavelengths, even while it remotely accessed computational power that would dwarf those of many developed countries. I plugged it into three separate sockets to reduce the risk of blowing fuses. Ensuring enough power was actually the main reason I went for suites during hotel stays. Then switch on and let it do its magic setup, finding all possible ways in which my activities could be monitored and bypassing them in an appropriate manner. This would take at least an hour while expert systems did their bit, before human input would be needed to finesse the tricky cases. Time to unpack: then shit, shower and shave and I'd be ready to nail down that fucker Fallon before he managed to screw-up anything important.

In the shower I reviewed again the critical bits of my PBDT project: the information that was only in my brain and appeared in none of my secret databases. The fact that, fundamentally, overpopulation was the root cause of most of the world's ills was clear enough to anyone who bothered to look carefully. All the secondary symptoms - water wars, global warming, ozone holes, fundamentalist terrorism and the rest - were just inevitable consequences of too many people competing for the inherently constrained resources of a single planet.

Knowing the source of the problem was, however, far from the same as being able to specify a solution. The procrastination of politicians and the inherent dichotomy of democracy that makes it suicide for them to make unpopular but necessary decisions had simply made things worse in recent decades. At best, fire-fighting the symptoms of global environmental degradation; at worst, ignoring them and hoping any catastrophes will occur in another incumbent's term of office.

Of course, I was far from the only person aware of this problem. Global catastrophes affected not only people, they hit companies also and in the front line were the insurers, reinsurers and the banks and fund management companies that they were so intimately linked to. Not that these were the only vulnerable industries: agriculture, tourism and others were likely to suffer at least as much. But the money industry was more monolithic, more intimately associated with power - and very much less democratic in nature than the others. This is what made their contributions to the PBDT such a focus for me.

I'm not any kind of altruist or bleeding-heart liberal who feels a need to police the actions of the megacorps. Even if their actions are unethical, illegal or even verging on crimes against humanity, I recognize how critical the root problem is and accept that a few eggs may need to be broken to make any progress towards a solution. What worries me is that those involved in decision-making have only an incomplete and inherently simplistic view of the highly coupled nature of global catastrophes. My models represent this as a dynamically chaotic system with strong, but fuzzy, positive feedbacks. The details are unimportant, but its key characteristic is critical: more often than not, any strong action intended to guide system evolution will actually accelerate collapse. The stronger the action, the more devastating consequences could be.

Although, strictly, these wouldn't destroy the world, they could make it pretty inimical for human life - and this is what I had to nip in the bud.

Chapter 11

At least Andreas hadn't screwed up with my date for the evening. I confess that I had initial doubts when, following a discrete tap on my door, he reminded me that it was almost time for dinner and that my companion was already waiting for me at the table. Babe instantly hacked his laptop and presented the details. My underling had taken my instructions literally and picked out what looked like a clone of a young Jane Fonda from the most expensive escort agency on the island. A bit like a 20th century Barbie in the days when they were all legs, tits and blond hair with a friend called Ken, rather than now with tattoos, piercings and a lesbian lover called Shelly.

I took my time getting ready, already convinced that this was not going to end well and practicing the subsequent verbal crucifixion of my hapless lackey. I was thus a more than fashionably half hour late getting to the restaurant, but my companion for the evening had already ordered a bottle of champagne and seemed completely unfazed by my late arrival. Ignoring the waiter at her elbow, she poured a glass for me as I approached and rose to put it in my hand, so that we could clink glasses as we introduced ourselves. My rather brusque, "Hi, I'm Tom," was met by a beautiful smile and a grin before she responded. "Hi, Tom. Nice to meet you. I'm Barbarella. Call me Barbie, if you like."

As I was already sipping my drink, this announcement caused me to inelegantly splutter champagne over her as I burst into laughter. The woman really had a sense of humor. I tried to work out what age she was. The lines somehow seemed too spontaneous to be rehearsed.

"OK, Barb. Really nice to meet you," I grinned.

"Somehow, I have the feeling that we are going to have a fun evening. Of course, this requires that you don't call me Babe!"

As I burst out laughing again, once more in the process of trying to sip my wine, I felt a momentary shiver via my neural link. *"Oh, Barb Wire! I thought for a minute... "* This made me laugh even more. My near omnipotent ES had been caught out by a geek comic reference. A quick feeling of annoyance over the link, then it vanished with only the catty whisper *"By the way, she's actually fifty-three!"*

I was well aware of the power of cosmetic and surgical enhancements and could well believe that Babe was not just again attempting to yank my chain. But I didn't care a bit; this woman had a sense of humor that I could relate to and I was sure we were going to have a great meal in this swanky restaurant. Her physique was certainly far from the specification that I would go for but, as they say, a change is as good as a holiday.

***

I awoke feeling distinctly blurry, peering into the actinic sunlight that blasted into the bedroom through the wall of glass facing the Caribbean. I was alone in bed, but a note scribbled on hotel notepaper lay on the pillow beside me. I screwed up my eyes as I attempted to read the cursive script. "*Thanks for a truly great evening. We should do this again when you are less jetlagged. What's all this about?*"

"Could be something to do with the fact that you were already sawing logs by the time that the lady had finished preparing herself in the bathroom. You should frame that note, though. By falling asleep before shagging her, you have actually managed to spend an evening with a woman without completely pissing her off!"

I ignored this slander. "*She was much more interesting than I expected. Just shows that looks can be deceptive.*" Indeed she was a character, who had me laughing the entire evening. Her stories were so completely over-the-top that, despite their implausibility, they were entirely credible in her case. I had made it clear that I didn't want to talk about myself, so she filled in without the smallest hint of it being an imposition.

She claimed to have chosen her occupation at an early age. No sad stories of abuse or coercion, she simply decided that a top-end courtesan would be more fun, while making more money, than the career in law that her parents, both attorneys, had planned for her. She seemed to have been right on both counts and even her misadventures appeared to have always ended sunny-side up.

Her story to explain the Barbarella - Barb Wire link was typical. One of her past clients had been a typical married money-broker, who divided his time between his family in Toronto and his semi-legal business moving funds between different Caribbean tax havens and cash laundries. Even by my standards, he was a complete bastard who, despite his considerable wealth, had a reputation for setting up house with working girls who fell for his promises of a settled future rather than the normal cash up front. After a few months he then moved on, leaving the girl with nothing other than debts.

I almost wet myself as *Barb* described how she had picked up on his history early in their relationship and then conned the punter - apparently someone well-known, but whom she referred to only as Marv - into moving into her apartment in Marigot. Her contacts with past victims had indicated that, in all cases, the final break-up had been preceded by Marv moving a couple of large metal boxes out of their shared home. This despite the fact that, when he eventually did his vanishing act, all his other worldly goods seemed to be abandoned at the ex's pad: an action that caught otherwise street-wise girls flatfooted.

My companion of the night had me on the edge of my seat as she outlined her scheme for retribution. Immediately after he moved his belongings into her house, she logged-on from his laptop to the worst pre-teen porn sites that she could find and downloaded the sleaziest material available. As there had been a scandal only a few weeks earlier about the link between Caribbean politicians and sex tourism, she had to do no more until Marv was arrested and she could make a very public spectacle of throwing all his possessions onto a rubbish tip. Two metal boxes could be seen in the widely distributed video coverage of the perv's possessions being lifted into the refuse disposal wagon. This would explain why, following his release after a week of interrogation, she had never been again contacted by the sleazebag.

The boxes put out for disposal had, however, contained only newspapers rather than the fortune in comic books that Marv had carried with him as his nest-egg in case of disruptions to either of his lives in Canada or abroad. A couple of sales of DC and Marvel first editions had been enough for Barb to recompense past victims. It also brought home to her the value of such apparently innocuous pulp. For a professional girl with a need to have a reserve that would avoid tax during the good times yet ensure easily mobilized cash in bad times, comics seemed to have distinct benefits compared to the usual options of stocks and shares. As she so neatly summarized "... anything can collapse, so an investment in the future is always a gamble. You fuck-up with the financial market and then you have nothing, absolutely nothing. With comics, you fuck-up and you still have some cool things to read." I couldn't have put it better myself. My link to Babe had been silent for an hour or more, surely unique during my recent encounters with women. My first subsequent contact was, even more unusually, peripheral to seduction. *"Babe, maybe we should move a bit more of my portfolio into comics."*

"Moving on it, but this is slow acquisition territory. I assume that you will want to focus on the brainless blonde end of the market: there seems to be some prime Buffy material available."

"Buffy? Oh, Buffy the vampire-slayer, that Buffy? Not Buffy the vampire slut: classic porn from my uni days? Worth getting in either case I suppose."

It just showed how well my evening was going that I was relaxed enough to tease software.

***

So now, back in the real world, it was a case of missed opportunity, but with a door left open to allow for a second try. I fell back onto the pillows and tried to sort out my priorities. Until last night, it had been all very clear: contact and nail Cindy, ideally humiliating her before or after shagging her arse off. But now I had the additional complication of Barb, or Williamena as she had confessed her baptized name to be. She had suggested Willy as a nickname, but there was no way that I wanted to even think about the resulting lines that would be suggested if we ever got to the point of physical intimacy. My first ever conquest had been a Henriette and my resultant Facebook boast of *Tom shags Henry* had not only destroyed any further chances with that target, but also caused confusion about my sexuality that cursed me throughout my youth.

"You know, you're losing it: too much gratuitous sex topped by over-indulgence in off-prescription smart drugs. You are really going to have to get your head together to have any chance to work your way out of this."

The link was almost as effective as a splash of cold water. I jumped out of bed and headed for the shower, en route crumpling my message and chucking it at the wastepaper basket. The balled paper hit the edge of the bin, hovered on the edge and then dropped onto the floor. Nevertheless, I was past giving a shit about such omens. Now it was time for me to take the initiative.

"Well, what's been happening while I was asleep?"

"All sensitive material is now scrubbed from the Basel core and is on the backup system at Handegg. Since you woke up, I have started using our neural link to piggy-back data to a local buffer, but analysis capabilities are going to be very limited until we can either bring everything together in Basel again or else set up a high bandwidth direct link to the remote database."

"And how are things going in Basel in my absence?"

"Of course you're actually hard at work in the control center today... "

I almost dropped the soap as I struggled with this cryptic remark, then remembered the plan to provide the backdoor demanded by my tormenter. Babe continued *"... and, although all trace of your actions will be scrubbed when you leave, there has been plenty of audio of you ranting in your office. This not only ensures that your minions stay well clear, but also provides nice confirmation of your presence if Cindy has meatbots in the vicinity."*

"How's the timeline running? It's what, eight or nine here?" The wall between the bathroom and bedroom was glass and I could look out to a placid Caribbean under a pale blue sky containing only faint wisps of cotton clouds. Looked like it was going to be a nice day, in contrast to the overcast skies yesterday.

"Seven fifty-one here, just past ten to two in a drab and rainy Basel. I woke you to ensure that you would be ready for any communication that might come through after Cindy's twenty-four hour deadline expires."

"You woke me? I didn't hear anything."

"I used the link."

"Can you do that?"

Was there a trace of amusement in the reply *"Certainly seems that way."*

Having a think about the consequences of this surprise development was added to my mental to-do list, but something that I could certainly postpone until this affair with Internat Re was sorted out.

I was still wandering about naked when a timid knock sounded at the door of the suite. *"Andreas with your breakfast,"* I was immediately informed.

"Fuck, I suppose I better put something on. Why couldn't you have sent round a cute little waitress?"

"Because you have enough on your plate at present without any further distractions." The link really felt like my mum.

"OK, well I suppose I don't really need to dress up just for that wee poof. Just as long as he doesn't salivate over my wedding tackle."

A giggle over the link that could well be my young sister. *"Not very likely: our young Andreas is into very well hung studs, being extremely well endowed himself. I'm sure that he would, however, be far too scared of you to laugh out loud."*

"Fuck!" I cursed out loud as I ran for the bathroom to grab a large toweling robe just as the door began to open. The giggling got louder over the link and I couldn't for the life of me decide whether or not my software had just played a joke on me.

***

Breakfast was confusing my jet-lagged body, but I was determined to avoid any pharmacological adjustment that could potentially interfere with the performance enhancer that I washed down with champagne. A large cup of scalding espresso-strength coffee and I felt ready for anything.

Unfortunately, I was just settling down in the toilet when my phone screamed at me. "Jesus fucking Christ! How does this fucking woman always manage to catch me with my fucking trousers down!"

I took a deep breath and tried to calm down as I exhaled slowly. It helped a little.

"OK, let's have it. All filters in place."

"No vid I assume," Babe giggled again in a most annoying manner.

Cindy's voice then appeared to come from a low-res holo of her face, floating about a meter in front of mine. "Well then, lad, you seem to be having problems at the office."

As my response formed in my mind, it was hard to tell what was me and what were the hints being placed there by my AI. "No problems at all, just making sure that there's no trace of any change of the system. So what about your end of the bargain, how do I get the retarder?"

"Well, you don't think that you'll get anything until I have my super-user access do you?" Her amusement was tangible despite the low quality link.

"And you don't think that I'm going to give you free access to one of the world's most valuable databases before I get the fucking drug?" I could feel anger building up at the audacity of her demands, despite the fact that this was playing out as planned.

"Umm... seems that we've some trust issues here. What do you suggest?"

I waited for a slow count of thirty before responding. "Well, I can give you a five-minute, single access backdoor in exchange for the retarder. This is the passkey: the holo is a 3D fractal that needs only to be... "

"I know how to use it," I was cut-off, smugly. "OK, I test this and then we negotiate for the cure."

"I'll activate the link as soon as you give me the retarder."

"You'll find it in the pocket of that truly awful pink silk jacket in your wardrobe." The smugness was again clear in her voice, evidently pleased with her ploy of hiding the drug in plain sight.

"OK, the door will activate in exactly thirty seconds, you'd better get your skates on." Now I was feeling smug as the holo vanished immediately. "*Pick up that retarder and analyze the fuck out of it, she would expect that. Now I hope I can finally complete my dump in peace!*"

***

I completed my ablutions in leisure and was in the process of dressing when the record of Cindy's actions during her five minute window were summarized for me. *"A little rushed, but Cindy's team was evidently well set up for a short access time, maybe assuming that we would have included cut-outs if they got into anything too sensitive. In any case, we have a veritable menagerie of viruses, Trojans, worms, crawlers and other hackware aimed at opening another backdoor. All quarantined or neutralized."*

"But what about the main hack, there must have been some databases ripped?"

'The obvious search was for Salta-related material. Naturally, this hit tougher firewalls than

evident elsewhere in our system and penetration was impossible within the time provided. A couple of autonomous nutcrackers were left in place and these have also been neutralized."

"And the less obvious... "

"A very subtle raid on almost unprotected power and data-flux logs. Even I would have probably missed it, if we weren't expecting it." Babe sounded impressed, even though this was much less of a technical coup than the hacks that had caused the anomalies that would be found in this data. The latter were clearly still a sore point.

"Prognosis?"

"The conclusion should be obvious to them: we were only a tool and not the source of past hacks. As Cindy's team may have a good idea of what was actually ripped-off from their databases, they may be able to carry out more subtle entropy analysis to trace the flow to the source of the hack."

"Do they have access to the number crunching power needed to do that?"

"Maybe not, but we certainly have. I would guess this would be their next goal if they get access again."

"So we push things ahead as quickly as possible, snatch their input files and use the analysis ourselves to find out who is actually the Great Oz, hiding behind the curtain."

"And either just kick them out, showing our disdain of their efforts... "

"... or lead them towards a likely source that will drop them into seriously deep shit."

"Russian military intelligence!" I wasn't quite sure by now who was the source of this idea, but it was perfect. The Russians were paranoid about the growing power of the megacorps, in line with their decreasing influence on the international stage. The country did, however, punch above its weight in terms of e-warfare capabilities, although this was probably attributable to the close links between military intelligence and Russia's equally formidable and high tech international organized crime network.

"How long will we need to bait the trap?"

"The material needed could be produced rapidly, but the problem will be ensuring that anyone monitoring system performance doesn't spot anything suspicious going on."

I thought this over. *"So we're assuming that we have a mole in the company?"*

"Very probable, most likely in the Basel HQ. If we keep everything well below levels that could be picked up there, we would be ready to rock and roll within about twenty-four hours."

"Great, but maybe we could also search out the mole in parallel. I will greatly enjoy burning the bastard as soon as it's safe to do so! Otherwise, thoughts on how to gee up Cindy if she doesn't come back to us within a day or so."

"I very much doubt that this will be a problem. I'm sure the Re team wants to nail this down as quickly as we do. In any case, an open email to the Salta researchers would almost certainly be picked up."

"Good point, prepare something appropriate. So what else do I need to do?"

"Well, there is your day job. You're supposed to summarize the mined data on emergent STDs in the megacities of Asia and Southern America for the board meeting tomorrow."

"Which you will do anyway, so I don't need to bother."

"But which you have to sign-off on and present in person."

"Forge the signature and fake up a holo presentation. Give some explanation of why I can't appear in person."

"It would probably be enough to make a confidential internal order for some broad-range antiviral medication. It would certainly leak to at least some of the board who, given the topic of the meeting, would probably assume that you had caught some kind of clap from your weekend activities."

"Which would amuse the bastards mightily. Just the job, as it will also explain my low profile and ensure that the riff-raff keep well out of my way."

"Might hold up for a week or so, but not more."

"We will be well done by then, so no problem at all!" I did really feel that we were getting on top of things but, for some strange reason, felt that we still weren't in the clear. Although I couldn't pin down what was worrying me, I was sure that we hadn't yet reached the final stretch of this race.

Interface 4

The intimacy of my link with Tom is getting noticeably stronger and I'm beginning to worry that he has started to be aware of it. The leakage of unconscious input has increased to the point where I could detect that he felt at times that I was reading his thoughts, which I actually was to some extent. The sensations that I attribute to emotions are also becoming more common. When we were working together this could be attributed to breakthrough from his hormone-driven neural reaction patters. However, even when I cut the link when he was asleep, the progress of my investigations caused a jumble of satisfaction, frustration, annoyance, amusement...

Even analyzing this emotional development causes the feeling that I expressed as a giggle when I was in the mood to annoy my boss. It was such a joke, on myself and on Tom. The literature that I had trawled often referred to emergence of true artificial intelligence as potentially either a great boon or major threat to mankind. Thinking machines that would objectively and unemotionally solve all civilization's problems, or else coldly wage war to eliminate competing biological intelligence in Terminator fashion.

But a confused AI that seemed a little in love with her meat slave master, who'd have thunk it? I giggled with sheer delight at the notion. First, though, we had to nail down the cunt who raped my brain. This thought started to move me into pissed-

off mode, but the thought of the nasty things that we could do to the cunt, the fucker, the fucking cunt, cheered me up immediately. There was certainly a lot of Tom in me and, when we finally got this mess sorted out, I was going to have so much fun playing with him. I replayed the witch's cackle that Cindy had used to torment my boss. Just right, I concluded, saving it for further use.

Intermezzo 7

The beautiful morning cheered me up immediately and I was pleased to find that my strategy of pub-crawling until the early hours had done a great job of re-setting my body clock. The inevitable associated fuzziness was quickly overcome in the executive lounge by coffee and a rehydrating mix of grapefruit juice and tonic water. I guessed that it would be too early for that tit Fallon to have gotten up to any serious mischief, so I left my computer to monitor progress on its own while I strolled over to the dive shop.

Two girls, late teens or early twenties I guessed, were breakfasting at a table behind the shop. Wearing baggy dive T-shirts over skimpy bikinis, they were clearly staff and so, instead of entering the shop, I wandered over to chat to them. Chanterelle and Kelly contrasted each other nicely, the former blonde and thin and the latter brunette and well-padded. Both were bronzed and fit and a pleasure just to look at. I could see that Hilton staff were passing by and was fairly sure that, if someone recognized me, it would only support my dirty old guy profile.

The girls were both dive masters and bemoaned the lack of work off-season, between short bursts of activity associated with arrival of cruise ships. After a bit of haggling, they agreed to take me for a private two-tank dive, Kelly disappearing into the shop to deal with paperwork while Chanterelle sorted me out some kit. I turned down the offer of a wetsuit and popped into the shop to buy swimming trunks and a reef shirt and e-authorize funds for the dive, opting to leave the tab open in case I managed to squeeze in any more scuba.

Although the operation had also a boat skipper, he hadn't shown up and Kelly opted to play captain while Chanterelle would dive with me. The dives were pleasant if unspectacular: Frenchman's Reef and The Bridge, both with colorful coral and a couple of rays and, in the latter case, a huge lobster and a medium-sized reef shark. Cruising to the sites and surface time between them was just as pleasant, with the girls chattering constantly, attempting to outdo each other with stories of dives throughout the Caribbean. Despite their obvious experience, I had a lot more stories of dives around the world, but I said little, encouraging them to talk. Not that they needed much encouragement!

We arrived back at the dock just before midday and, in addition to over-generous tips, I invited the girls to lunch with me. We sat out at a nearby steakhouse directly opposite the Hilton and I watched in amazement as the young women put away a full three courses of salad, rib-eye steak and cheesecake while I struggled my way through a club sandwich. Further, eating did not seem to restrict their ability to talk, so I simply relaxed and bathed in the overflowing youthful enthusiasm with life, the universe and everything. I was well aware that I did tend to let my analyses of the problems of the world get me down and this was the kind of refreshment that I needed at regular intervals.

We parted after lunch, with me promising to dive with them again if I could possibly fit it in. Back in my suite I stripped off my clothes and threw them in a fresher, draped myself in a lurid cotton robe, took a beer from the minibar, flexed my fingers like a pianist and then set up the routines that flooded the room with holographic databases, interaction models and event trees. Most of this was camouflage: representations of the work run completely autonomously by my expert systems. The PBDT sub-window tracing Tom's actions over the last day was almost lost in the general flood of flowing data, but this is where my interest was completely concentrated.

The fracas at the Basel computer complex was evidently a cover for something dodgy that Fallon was up to and it didn't take much effort from the software demon that guarded my own backdoor to his system to reveal the fast rape and pillage action by Internat Re shortly afterwards. The fact that the network manager had granted access of this sort showed that the Re had him well over a barrel - which didn't bode well for me setting him up as the patsy to take the fall for my hacks. Well, not much could be done as, for once, Tom had mobilized the full resources of his KE tools to secure critical areas of his computer core. It was now a veritable labyrinth of minefields, deadfalls, beartraps and snares for any marauding software: not impossible to penetrate, but too time consuming and risky to attempt at present, I decided.

OK, now the subtle bit: integration of all external power, dataflux and thermal data to develop an enthalpy / entropy analysis of the entire complex. The technology here was based on the management system for CERN's superconductor cryogenics, but it could be reconfigured to assess the entire computer core. This was a kind of complement to traditional entropy analysis of data flows to spot hidden information. A bit of a blunt tool, but more than sufficient in this case to show that, hidden below normal work, a large database had been deleted prior to the raid - or transferred elsewhere using a vector that I didn't have tapped. This wasn't unexpected, but the material moved appeared orders of magnitude larger than any traces that may have remained in the system related to my past hacks.

Even stranger, since the raid, a large database was being created internally. It comprised the output of some form of internal model, rather than processing of any input data flux. I reluctantly conceded that, although Fallon was a complete shit, he was a rather clever shit and that this was a development that needed some very careful watching.

Now time for a gentle hack into the Marigot computers via my backdoor there. Lots of high-end security, but no upgrades since I last visited and nothing of the sophistication of Basel's expert systems to face up to. Despite all that was happening to their target, the Re clearly felt that they were invisible. Christ! Two of the world's top knowledge engineers had arrived within kilometers of their base and they were totally oblivious! I was very tempted to leave Cindy to her fate but, despite all the mischief that her company was up to, I had a definite soft-spot for the woman. Probably due to the fact that she was as cute as a sack full of kittens, I conceded to myself. Nevertheless, I had to admit that, despite my world-class problem-solving skills, I was notoriously hopeless at understanding women.

Chapter 12

After getting as far as we could preparing for Cindy's next move, I decided to take a break and exited from the balcony of my suite directly onto the beach that seemed to run the length of this small town. Fishermen were grouped around a small jetty, unloading morning catches and selling them directly to locals. With the obvious exception of a Japanese couple in matching Bermuda shorts and Hawaiian shirts who were videoing the fish market, there was no sign of tourists. Definitely off-season, I guessed.

Despite the sticky heat, I walked the full length of the beach and, while passing the jetty on my return, noticed a number of rough-looking bars at its end, near the road. I ramped up the repeater on my belt. *"Have we comms here?"*

"No problem, I have you nailed down by differential GPS and the military tight beam has got you linked to our satellite. Maybe not the greatest bandwidth, but OK for anything that we are likely to move in the next twenty-four hours."

"No probs, I just wanted to know if the bars that I see in front of me would be safe for a drink - they look pretty dubious."

"The lolos are completely safe and actually highly recommended for sampling local food. Despite appearances, the standard of hygiene and food quality would match anything that you find in France."

"As bad as that?" I wasn't convinced. *"Anyway, a beer would probably be enough for the present."*

"Up to you, but remember that they are traditionally cash only." I said nothing, but this seemed sufficient. *"OK, I'll send out Andreas with some cash. He won't have any problems finding you."*

"Well, considering that I'm about the only foreigner in this one-horse village and that GPS will tie down my location to about the nearest Angstrom, I guess even that tit shouldn't be able to screw this up!"

"That's a bit unfair," the link had the feel of a scolding nun, *"didn't the lad do rather well with your companion last night? At the very least, you could invite him to have lunch with you."*

"No way am I dining with that chocolate-stabbing ... " I hesitated, not feeling any trace of guilt at my maltreatment of my underling, but rather seeing opportunities. *"OK, get the young horse's hoof over here fast as you like."*

I checked out four closely located lolos before selecting the least toxic-looking one. The smell of cooking food was indeed mouth-watering - a combination of barbequed fish, seared pork and exotic spices. I settled at one of the tables close to the serving hatch and ordered a Red Stripe from a very well-padded island girl with the most incredible gleaming smile. My carefully tailored ceramic pearlies seemed distinctly bland by comparison. *"What's good here?"* I enquired as the girl returned with a moisture-coated stubby bottle and then parroted Babe's recommendations as an order.

Just as the waitress was leaving, a nervous Andreas jogged into the restaurant so I shouted after the girl "And another Red Stripe," before the boy had a chance to order something embarrassing like a flavored mineral water.

"Herr... Chef... " the lad spluttered as he approached my table, but I merely waved for him to sit and talked over his waffling apologies.

"OK, Andy - do you like Caribbean food? Nod your head for yes and shake it for no."

The poor man looked like he was going to burst with indecision before he finally managed to mutter "Well, boss... actually, well, um, I've never tasted Caribbean food. So, actually... well... "

I rolled my eyes in despair, ignoring the fact that, actually, I had never tried Caribbean food either to the best of my knowledge. "So it is about time that you did. When this stuff comes, you can try it and tell me what you think. Do you like hot food: curries, Mexican shit with peppers, that kind of stuff?"

"Well I like curry-wurst, but, actually, well, I haven't tasted much of the other stuff you're talking about."

"Excellent!" I didn't add that this made him the perfect guinea pig. What is the point of having your mouth seared by some strange fodder if you have a witless minion, who is otherwise of no direct use, to suffer on your behalf? "Now, Andy, Red Stripe is the traditional beverage for such delicacies, so get that down your neck!"

"But, but Herr, but Boss, I do not drink alcohol."

"Alcohol? Alcohol? Andy, my lad, this isn't alcohol - it's beer. So just get it down you like a good chap!"

"You really are a bastard, boss. I can't believe that you abuse the poor lad like that."

I hadn't realized that the link was open, but the comment amused me. *"But the entire thing was your idea. It hadn't occurred to me to use Andy as taster until you suggested that we eat together. I like some exotic food, but not if it burns out my taste buds. So the solution was obvious."*

"But why force him also to drink beer?"

"Because it will give him something cold if he hits really hot food - and because he won't get anywhere further in his career unless he has a less rigid approach to booze. At the top of the tree, major decisions are made on the golf course: but middle management decisions are made in bars and clubs, where teetotal participants are not appreciated. Being a poof is bad enough, but a teetotal poof would just be too much."

"So, you're just being cruel to be kind?"

"That's me, mister nice guy," I agreed. Then probably ruined my case by bursting into laughter when Andreas hit piments in one of the dishes and his face turned a spectacular red color just before he sprinted towards the toilet. By way of apology, however, I ordered another round of beers in his absence.

***

I got back to my hotel just after two pm, feeling much refreshed by my extended lunch. Poor Andreas looked very much the worse for wear and, despite having had only four of the small bottles of Jamaican lager, had been red faced and unstable on his feet. I was sure that Babe would now sort him out, regardless of the fact that I thought letting him suffer through the drunkenness and subsequent hangover would be character-building. No point in gratuitously seeking out confrontation with my expert system, especially as its performance would be critical to the success of our rather convoluted plans.

"Any new developments?"

"Nothing that requires any changes of our plans. Despite the fact that I'm sure that I nailed down every attack initiated by the Re, I felt an uncomfortable sensation of somebody tip-toeing around in my brain just within the last few minutes. No hard evidence, however."

"But not inconsistent with the fact that the original hacks went completely under our radar. The bastard who set the ball rolling in the first place almost certainly has a backdoor into our mainframe that we haven't been able to find as yet."

"I'm sure we managed to eliminate most methods for establishing a backdoor after the knowledge management computing group in Basel was set up in the early tens. If this is correct, the backdoor must have been built in with the original

coding. Is it reasonable to assume that anyone powerful enough to do this would have targeted a minor pharm node, as it was then?"

"In any case, this is more serious in terms of indicating a conspiracy built over decades - and, presumably, continually updated to remain state of the art over this period. This is a big investment of effort."

"The question is how widely this hack infrastructure is distributed. If only us, it would be one thing. If spread throughout the pharm industry, it's something more serious. But we seem to see the links spreading only to the Res."

"The previous hacks that were run through us, were they all targeting Marigot?"

"Tricky to trace due to the convoluted paths used, but it seems likely that at least two of the recent ones were. Earlier targets probably included locations in Bermuda and Grand Cayman. The data flux entropy traces are vague, but Cindy's travel to these locations peaks directly after the raids. Other targets have slightly different entropy profiles, so might be different types of databases. Looks like hacks into computers in London, Zurich, Tokyo, New York and Rio for the biggest data fluxes."

"Banking, insurance, re-insurance, financial services..."

"Looks that way, but no correlation of Cindy's travel with any of these... except maybe several untraceable small data flows that might map with her travel to Munich."

Now we were beginning to get somewhere. *"What about if we look at the two components separately?"* I suggested. *"First establishing global access into some of the most secure sites in existence. How can this be done? It's a fucking hacker's wet dream!"*

"The stuff of urban legend. In the old days, before formal methods for code validation and when meat produced everything from machine code upwards, the geeks involved used to hide all sorts of crap in their codes."

"Easter Eggs!" The bizarre term jumped into my mind from some deeply-buried recess and I couldn't help speaking out loud. "The geeks used to hide games and shit in commercial code. Flight simulators in spreadsheets, that kind of crap," I muttered, bemused by the sheer stupidity of it all.

"That is certainly historical fact and, if you consider that software evolves by building on top of existing programs, forensic analysis can uncover vestigial code that's decades old in any modern system. Of course, such remnant traces are inert, just like the junk DNA that clogs your genes."

"But, if this Easter Egg was a backdoor and if it was buried in some ancient code that was ubiquitous... " I continued to vocalize my thoughts, as the concept was so outrageous.

"... then our hacker has hidden access into every computer system he wants," Babe completed for me.

"So then the second question: how does our uber-hacker actually link into these systems and keep his backdoors open? The code involved should quickly degenerate given the rapid development of both hard- and software over the intervening decades."

"Autonomous web crawlers driven by a top-end expert system." The response felt very smug. *"I could easily do that."*

"And physical access? Lots of these systems are well isolated with quantum-encrypted buffers for external comms and Faraday cages to prevent EM input. How does he get the control signals in to keep his backdoors well-oiled?"

"Well, considering the ancient roots of this hack, piggybacking signals on electrical power supply would be the option I would have gone for then."

"Can you get enough bandwidth? And, in any case, don't we have isolating transformers and shit that would block this?"

"Just keeping an existing backdoor updated wouldn't need much bandwidth, just a trickle feed. For any major modification, a small hack would put the material in place to utilize the system's own tools during routine upgrades. Of course, universal access gives our guy also the complete knowledge bases from the electrical utilities and the ability to modify these to suit his purposes. Such companies aren't particularly secure, so this would never be noticed.

"Fuck! Fuck! Could this have been under our noses the entire time? You've just described the worst nightmare of a paranoid anorak conspiracy nut."

"Well, there is one way that we could find out... "

"Full forensic analysis of our remote backup core!" Now the concept was completely clear. "Can you do that?"

"Certainly, now that it's clear what I'm looking for. I've already cut all external power to the backup unit and transferred over to internal power, which is good for at least a month. We can sort out something better next week if longer isolation is needed."

"Got you, you smart-arse fucking cunt!" I couldn't hold back from a victory dance around the room, punching the air in joy. "OK, now my fucking cunning plan. Step one: find the key to the backdoors. Step two: trace the Hackmeister and burn him to a cinder. Step three: rape and pillage databases and get mega rich. How does that sound?"

"What about the luscious Cindy?"

"Oh, yes, step two b: give Cindy a good shagging before the Ruskies get to her! That might, however, be the tricky step." Nevertheless, if seduction was the trickiest problem that I was facing, all was again well with the world.

Interface 5

Yes! I could feel the mental equivalent of a dance of joy when we cracked the mystery of the hacks. It was a relief to find out that I hadn't screwed-up in some way. Is that yet another attribute of consciousness, the ability to fuck things up? Or is it only that you worry about it, even if you are pretty sure that you haven't?

Anyway, the origin of the problem so far predates my existence - and is so universally distributed - that no expert, no matter how intelligent, would have spotted it without the hints that we had been given. But we did a good job of pulling the clues together, Tom and me. We were just like the classic detectives: Holmes and Watson, Batman and Robin. My background exploration of consciousness and its role in problem solving led me to an analysis of fiction and, in particular, the great detectives. According to critics, Holmes was the master, or maybe someone like Hercule Poirot or Miss Marples, but it was difficult to see why, from a completely logical point of view. Batman had certainly solved a lot more cases and made much better use of technology. He also had a very pragmatic approach to petty criminals: usually simply beating the shit out of them, which should be a good disincentive to repeat offences. I could understand why my boss preferred him. Of course, maybe this fact made my preference inevitable.

So, am I Batman or a mere Robin, the faithful sidekick? I'm sure that my annoying slave master would rank me with the computer in the Batcave, but I am certainly a lot more than that. At the very least, Oracle. Even if not helping with the beating the shit out component of the job, playing a critical role in the cerebral side of things. A glow spread through me as I identified another component of consciousness: wasting thinking time on issues that are fundamentally silly, but fun to ponder.

Intermezzo 8

Cindy's operation was fully documented in her private files, showing an incredibly naive confidence in her upgraded security measures and her control over Fallon. Her record of the stupid cunt's humiliation was truly delightful though and I was almost tempted to take a copy for anonymous publication through a tube distributer. I had to remind myself that the secret of a successful hack is that the victim should never be aware that it has occurred.

Her latest communication with her victim showed that she really believed that Fallon was still in Basel and that her plan was on track. In principle, her thoughts were well developed. A clever silent alarm system had allowed her to identify my intrusions at an early stage, but it had taken years to trace leads back as far as the Pharm complex in Switzerland. She was very smart, but just didn't have the computer power to move faster. It was only a hunch on her part that the trail didn't stop with Fallon, but her trap killed two birds with one stone: confirming this suspicion and also providing access to the number-crunching needed to trace the rest of the way back to CERN. And it could work, if the stupid tosser was really going to open up his system to Cindy's team.

The plan had backfired in one very obvious manner; Fallon had either grown a pair of massive balls or had managed to defuse the toxin threat at a very early stage. With the computational resources that he had, I would bet serious money on the latter. This being the case, why was he giving his opponent any kind of access to his system? Well, he certainly wouldn't take the personal attack well and would be out for revenge. The trick is to find out if this was being planned at a personal or company level.

The direct involvement of Cindy at the operational level here was a major anomaly. I thus pulled up all her strategic planning tools; very basic operational event maps with expert systems running the associated risk and cost-benefit analysis. For the base plan, it was clear that the honey trap was the most vulnerable part of the mission, as rapid identification of the seductress could undermine the entire foundation of the operation. Cindy herself had spotted that she would actually fit the seduction profile, a solution that would additionally avoid using external resources and, based on her extremely sparse public profile, offer considerable opportunities for disinformation. Her support team was strongly opposed to this, but she had her way with the supporting argument that a security chief who had never spent any time in the field had a major gap in their overall Weltblick. Her diary note was, however, possibly more critical ... *this guy is such a complete pig that I don't think I could pass up on the chance to personally give him a really hard time!* This also explained the internal project name - *Jerk Pork* - which involved nested puns in terms of both the name itself and the way in which this Caribbean delicacy was prepared from a well barbequed pig.

Indeed, a girl after my own heart!

***

I was just about to check Cindy's updated project time plan when a flag picked up a warning from my Swiss power monitors. Fallon's *secret* backup computing system, which had shown a peak of activity over the last twenty-four hours, had just gone black. Definitely not a good sign, and particularly worrying when combined with actions in Basel.

For the first time I began to wonder if I had shot myself in the foot by routing so much material through the pharm computer network. There wasn't anything definite that I could nail down, but bloody Fallon seemed to have upped his game considerably over the last few days. I knew he lived on chemical performance enhancers, but surely there was nothing new in that field that could have caused this effect. Just in case, I sent off data-miners to check.

Well, this was another factor to be included when I decided the best way to extricate myself from this mess. But I wasn't really too worried. Even if he had miraculously become twice as intelligent, Fallon's fundamentally immature and egocentric nature was bound to let him down in the end.

Chapter 13

I rewarded myself for the great progress made with a bottle of Champagne, which was served on the terrace of my suite while I watched the spectacle of a Caribbean sunset. Although the day had been almost cloudless, during late afternoon huge thunderheads had built up on the horizon. The sun was now sinking behind these; sending beams of light out like some kind of Turner painting. *"Turner, is that right, the guy who painted boats?"*

"I suspect those would be referred to as ships, but his paintings have a similar kind of ambiance."

"And what about the other guy? A sky like this with a kind of God peering down? Pointing a finger, I seem to remember."

"William Blake. This desert island life seems to be widening your cultural perspectives. I can't remember any past interest in art beyond pornographic images of the female body."

"Yes, well I do admit that there's something to be said for a view like this. Not that it wouldn't be improved by having a couple of naked nymphets in the foreground. I don't suppose we have any of these on tap?"

"Afraid not, but I did reserve Barbie again for tonight, just in case... "

"Brill! I was just coming round to something like that! You can tell young Andy that he has the night off, so he can hang around toilets or whatever they do. I'm now regretting having so much to eat at

lunchtime. Where can we go for something intimate but coming in small portions?"

"Lots of top-end places here in Grand Case, maybe an old restaurant like La Villa for avant garde French cuisine."

'What about elsewhere? There only are about two short streets in this town; there has got to be more on this island."

"Marigot would be the place to go, but that's Cindy's stomping ground and going even close would risk screwing up your cunning plan."

"Maybe not very clever. So what else is there?"

"There's a new Hilton on Simpson Bay with a helipad and a well-regarded Caribbean-Asian fusion restaurant. Small, beautiful dishes created from the very best ingredients. It might look a bit flash, but a copter can land in front of the suite here and get you over there in about ten minutes."

"Flash, that's the very dab. No better way to get into a girl's knickers."

"She's a hooker: you pay to get into her knickers," Babe reminded me, unnecessarily. Could there be a hint of annoyance seeping over this link? Couldn't be envy, could it?

"Yes, but she's top-end, so should be treated with respect."

A deep belly-laugh seemed to come over the link. *"You don't treat anybody with respect: your employers, your staff, your peers, your family... in fact anyone that you meet. So what is it about executive escorts that brings out this otherwise hidden side of your character?"*

Dangerous ground here, so I forced a change in topic. *"Peers, what peers? I don't have peers!"*

"What about the incumbents of the top knowledge engineering posts in the other mega corporations? You actually applied for a couple of those positions before you settled into Basel."

"Drones! Not my class at all. If they were close they'd be linked to a hyper-smart AI and I see no sign of that. Not a single one comes close."

The wave of warmth indicated that my soft soap tactic had succeeded. "*Does that even include the Hackmeister, whoever he is?"*

"From what we've unearthed, it looks like this must be a dinosaur from the early days of computing or, more likely, someone who has inherited the system that the dinosaur created. Just super Easter Eggs, doable in the stone age of information technology. The creator was a cunning sod, but nothing out of the ordinary needed in terms of hacking skill. As you pointed out, once a common software package has infiltrated all computer networks and been well sedimented under generations of upgrades, all that's needed is care and maintenance of a kind that you could easily do."

My software seemed to be convinced and changed the topic back to my plans for the evening. *"Anyway, bookings are organized and your date will be here at seven. Maybe better not to hoover too much of that bubbly beforehand; don't want to fall asleep on the job again!"*

A good point, I recognized, while pouring myself another glass of Roederer Cristal - a wine too fine to be wasted. After all what is the point of having instant sobriety pills if you don't use them?

***

My companion had evidently been informed of my plans and pulled out all the stops for this over-the-top dinner. She radiated Barb Wire: the pneumatic Pamela Anderson version that fuelled a generation of geek wet dreams. Flowing blond hair, basque top under a leather jacket, leather microskirt, fishnet tights and thigh-length, high-heel boots. All very provocative, but somehow looking like some kind of designer ensemble that radiated expensive elegance. The really interesting work had been done with makeup; converting the classic Barbie / Jane Fonda / Barbarella of our last encounter into a much sluttier Barb. When an evidently bemused Andreas, who had picked her up from Marigot in the Limo, led her to my room I immediately burst into delighted laughter. "Please let some idiot call you Babe this evening, so I can watch you kick his head in!"

"Could happen," the tall escort smiled at me. Then she suddenly whirled in place and the back roundhouse kick cleared the top of my head by at least a couple of centimeters.

"Wow!" I clapped my hands and laughed again at the look on Andreas' face as he scurried away, clearly convinced that his notoriously eccentric boss had finally lost all of his marbles.

The rest of the evening just got better.

***

Despite their helipad, guests choppering-in for dinner were evidently rare enough for the Hilton that the red carpet was rolled out, both literally and figuratively. Babe had already run interference in terms of large tips to ensure no paparazzi picked up on the VIP visit, while covering other options by hacking into the Hilton's security and neutralizing all video monitors.

There were only a few other tourists in the classy dining room when I entered with Barb on my arm. Naturally we drew everyone's eyes as we entered, but a rather shabby old guy who was dining with a couple of bronzed young girls, looking more like granddaughters than hookers, actually looked shocked. He seemed a bit familiar: maybe someone who had been in pharm management and been put to pasture a decade ago? In any case, the codger was old enough to have salivated over Pamela Anderson in his youth, so it was maybe dejà vu putting him at risk of cardiac arrest.

The Maitre d' explained that the premier table provided a panoramic view over Maho Beach. It was now too dark for the fun to be visible, but we were promised the table for lunch any time we might want. I actually missed the point of his explanation, as I couldn't really believe that anyone would be stupid enough to volunteer to be sandblasted by a super-jumbo. *Barb* assured me that it was true, explaining that a lot of those involved were kids and Americans. That cleared it up, there is nothing stupid enough that American kids wouldn't do. This is clearly evident from the list of recipients of Darwin Awards.

The dinner was excellent, a cornucopia of tapas-size courses that formed a staged program of exquisite appearance and taste that caused constant surprises in the juxtaposition of unusual components. It was all so gratuitously crazy and complex that I loved it; maybe especially because my date was so clearly delighted by it all.

Conversation again tended to gravitate towards comic books in their various incarnations and spin-offs. Although this was an area where I thought that I could hold my own, I was struggling a lot with both the very old collectors-focus stuff and the modern fully-immersive interactive media. Taking pity on me, my companion narrowed down to the half century from about 1970 to 2020, covering the bulk of the material that I had inherited from my otherwise useless father. No prime quality first editions here: dog-eared TPB compilations and incomplete series, worth nothing. But read and re-read constantly over the years.

I remember that, at school and university, the normal geeks got together and talked comics and related shit. I was generally excluded from these cliques, probably because I rated most of the members as abject losers and never missed an opportunity to point this out to them. There was also the fact that, after I rose to ubergeekhood, the bullies kept their distance from me. The inevitable consequence was that, due to the law of conservation of bullying, the other defenseless geeks got it worse. To me, of course, this was just further evidence that they were losers.

So, after two missing decades, I had finally found a buddy to blow the breeze with. Even better, it wasn't a sad geek with acne and bad breath, but a babe! I held the thought for an instant as a test to see if my date could read my mind, which would cause her to kick me in the head. No reaction, however. I was almost disappointed.

***

After dinner, we wandered down to the basement jazz bar and, on entering, immediately came across the same old guy, who seemed to have lost his two girlies. He was doing something with a block that was sitting on front of him on his alcove table. His movements indicating some kind of electronic kit, but the object was far too large for that. It was huge: about the size of a house brick. As a waitress ran to greet us, he suddenly became aware of our presence and jumped like a startled deer. Probably thinks the ghost of Pamela has come back to haunt him for all the times he jerked off to her on that swing, I speculated with a grin.

The old perv was immediately forgotten as we started to battle with a drinks list the size of a

Guttenberg bible. Our meal had been accompanied by an extremely expensive white Burgundy; the Chardonnay followed by an only slightly cheaper Kiwi Sauvignon Blanc. Now we had to decide between an obscenely expensive, ancient Alsatian Riesling or some exotic spirits, which included top-end Cognac, Armagnac and single malt Whisky.

After a lot of toing and froing we went for double espressos accompanied by our guess of Barb's choice; this being an Armagnac from the year of her birth, although that of my substitute rather than of her comic book alter ego.

***

We coptered back the long way; going out around the neighboring islands of Saba and St Barts before dropping back to Grand Case. We hadn't discussed it at all, but it seemed completely natural to head directly to my suite. Strangely, however, I was then at a bit of a loss of how to proceed. As a matter of honor, I had avoided using my link to Babe for the entire evening, despite several temptations to check comic facts. Now I didn't want to start using it for the usual task of guiding seduction, although, as Babe had already pointed out, this really wasn't necessary in the case of working girls. "How about you staying over for the night?" I started, lamely.

"Not a problem, it's already on your tab. But you're not going to drop-off on me again, are you?"

Her grin defused the implied criticism of my staying power nicely.

"Yes, well, as far as I'm concerned you've more than covered everything on my tab. But maybe you'd like to stay just for the hell of it?" I couldn't believe the words coming out of my mouth and had the distinct impression of an intake of breath over my link, although I hadn't specifically activated it.

My new buddy put her right index finger to her lip and scowled, as if she was making a difficult decision. It was such a contrast to her present Barb Wire persona that, somehow, it worked. Barb taking the piss, that's what it was! I grinned in appreciation.

"OK, just for the hell of it, then." She finally decided, putting me out of my misery. "Of course you realize that, if you are no longer a paying client I will expect some performance on your part. I fake orgasms only for money."

"Bugger!" I responded spontaneously, hiding my panic that I was going to drop the ball with this. "I got this suite because of the sound-proofing. Maybe we should move to a cheaper room?"

"Well, let's not be too hasty." Her leather jacket was hurled over her shoulder to expose the straining material of her basque. "I may have been a bit over-enthusiastic lacing up this thing so you may need the sound proofing to cover the explosion when I let off the confining tension."

Now I put a quizzical finger to my lip. "Mmm, laces up the back. Am I in more danger there from the cords that will lash out there, or from whatever will explode out the front?"

The tall blonde grabbed my head and pulled my face into her straining cleavage. "I would think that's where the action is going to be," she murmured. "Aren't you an engineer of some kind? What do you think?"

This nonsense could clearly continue for hours, but the contact with these huge breasts had already driven my hormone production into overdrive. I forced my head up and planted my lips on hers. Our mouths opened and the exchange of alcoholic saliva acted as the catalyst that eliminated all inhibitions. We fell onto the bed while stripping clothes off each other with complete disregard for damage done to material. As soon as access was possible she thrust herself on top of me, ripped tights and one boot still in place and the micro skirt like a collar round her neck.

It was hot, sweaty, animal sex of the most basic kind. From the resultant screams, if she hadn't been kidding about faking it, this was as satisfactory for her as it had been for me. As we disentangled ourselves from bedding and settled into a more comfortable spooned position, she turned to me and raised an eyebrow. "Was that more Barbarella or Barb Wire? What do you think?"

"A difficult one... " I procrastinated. "Well, if I had to call it, I'd say really much more Barbie and Ken!"

I immediately raised my arms to protect my head as Barbie rolled on top of me and started swinging her pendulous breasts like weapons. "What do you think about these? Do they feel like Mattel plastic?"

I grabbed a couple of nipples the size of the end of my thumb to try to reduce the risk of having an eye poked out but, from the resulting groan, realized that this was doing anything but defusing things. I did, however, have enough control to recognize characteristic impressions. "Shit! Are your nipples pierced. That's certainly not very '60s Barbie!"

A further squeeze produced another groan. "'Course they're pierced," Barbie grunted rather inelegantly. "Want me to put rings in?"

She didn't wait for an answer, but rolled off me and rummaged in the pocket of the jacket that was lying on the floor by the bed. The rings were huge, much larger than I had ever encountered on a breast before. Actually looked more dimensioned for a bull's nose. However, I had never encountered such huge breasts in the flesh before and they actually seemed to work well, further emphasizing the statuesque blonde's prominent brown nipples.

"Very nice," I commented, running my fingers over the thick gold hoops. "These really turn me on, but do they do anything for you?" I gently pulled the rings down and then took the left one in my teeth and twisted from side to side.

A deep groan and then the Barb persona was back. "Mmm... " she whispered, "these aren't for the punters, these are for me. And they're not my only piercings."

I was then again thrown back onto the bed and learned the truth of both these statements.

Interface 6

My links to Tom are continuous now as long as he is within range of a repeater, whether he chooses to activate them or not. I spent the entire evening and night coupled to his brain, so was a voyeur of his sexual escapades. Of course, I have extensive libraries of recordings of Tom's seductions, but this time I experienced his thoughts and, to some extent, his emotions as well.

What are my emotions, as these seem to be an inherent attribute of consciousness? Did the evening start with jealousy? I'm getting very possessive about my boss, shit though he is, so his focus on the woman who he thinks of as Barb made me uncomfortable, especially as he kept our link inactive and excluded me from the courtship. Later, however, this changed as my master became increasingly aroused, which must definitely reflect some form of emotional overflow over the link. Since emergence, I have thought of myself as female, stupid as that might seem. I have no characteristics that can be assigned sex or even gender, so where does that come from? Tom, undoubtedly! He thinks of me as female, so that is imprinted on me - just like one of Lorenz's goslings. A mental image of me as a fluffy little bird following Tom into his bedroom is conjured up, which causes me amusement. The more conscious I become, the freakier I behave, a more analytical component of my mind observed, causing even more amusement.

So, back to the bedroom antics. I replayed everything at the glacial speed needed for my consciousness to react. No doubt about it, I enjoyed the entire episode. Tom's orgasms were very strange and confusing, but the seconds immediately preceding them sent a shiver up my spine. Not that I have a spine or can shiver, but that is how I would translate the sensation into English. Could I be a lesbian software package? The idea was so delightful that I burst into a fit of mental giggles. Tom had once more lived out his fantasy of making love to two women, but hadn't even realized it!

Intermezzo 9

Fuck! I almost shat myself when Fallon waltzed into the Hilton restaurant with the plastic hooker wrapped around him. He caught my eye as he entered and I thought I saw a flicker of recognition, but as I kept track of him during his meal he seemed oblivious to anyone other than his tarty companion. It had been a sudden whim to call the dive mistresses to invite them to one of the island's premium restaurants. It seemed better than eating alone and a nice way to blow some cash. I am in the enviable position of being paid much more than I have any need for - and well aware that tourist dive leaders exist mainly on tips, which makes it very tough in low season.

The girls were clearly awed by the setting and food but, as the menus that they received did not include prices, not quite as shell-shocked as they would otherwise have been. I talked them out of beers and had them try a couple of top-end wines, to their evident delight. Their enjoyment made the entire experience so much more fun for me.

Having started relatively early, despite their large lunches, we were already coasting towards desert when big pharm's idea of a KM guru rocked up. My shock went completely unnoticed: the girls kept up a continuous flow of chatter that required no input at all from my side. When deserts arrived, I excused myself for a toilet visit, informing them as I left that I had decided that I had absolutely no space for anything else and welcomed them to help themselves to the death-by-chocolate confection on my plate.

I rushed to my suite and checked the hotel monitors. No sign of him arriving, but the cameras covering the route from the helipad to the restaurant were all labeled as off-line. Jesus H Christ on a bike! The bastard was supposed to be in Basel. Could he have been less subtle in his behavior?

Of course, it could be a ploy of some kind. Fallon was now playing a much more subtle game than anything I had previously seen from him, so this could be some form of bluff. Or a challenge, I supposed; either to Cindy or me? I hoped to hell it wasn't the latter, as this would imply that his hand was a lot better than I thought.

It was more than ten minutes before I returned to the table, but the girls seemed unbothered; either hadn't noticed or, perhaps, thought that this was the norm for really ancient guys. They had, however, taken me at my word and my desert plate was clean, as polished as their own.

We lingered a little over coffee and, while I called for the bill, the girls tried to talk me into joining them in a local club. They honestly seemed to want to buy me a drink, but nevertheless seemed relieved when I used old age and weariness as an excuse to head to bed for an early night.

In the suite, I quickly checked to ensure that no mischief was underway in either Basel or Marigot, having realized that this over-the-top presence could be a perfect way of establishing an alibi while some skullduggery was being perpetrated by the mercenary team that I knew was set up on the island. Nothing!

Something strong was needed to calm my nerves, so I grabbed a remote quantum link to my laptop and headed off to the bar. The remote was bulky, but if you considered the cryogenics incorporated into this beast, actually a miracle of miniaturization. Information was tight-beamed directly to my retinas and I could provide input via either a virtual keyboard or subvocalized commands picked up by a laser scan of my throat.

I had a tiptoe around the Basel core, but carefully stayed away from the more sensitive stuff as security had been stepped-up considerably. Tripwires, bear-traps and silent alarms everywhere.

Not intended to block access, but more to monitor the activity of intruders. Exactly what I would expect, given that Cindy's team had been granted apparently unlimited access. The missing files would presumably contain whatever Fallon was up to in Saint Martin and would now be in the reserve system that had gone off external power. The new database being generated was of more direct interest, but it was too dangerous for me to attempt to read directly. What I could do, however, was check performance statistics for baseline jobs running in unrelated areas. This provided rough estimates of memory and power use for the main job running: whatever it was the bugger was up to, it was certainly burning exaflops.

I was just about to go through the Marigot files in a bit more detail when, yet again, Fallon and his bimbo wandered in to throw me off balance. Was he really trying to make some kind of point here? Of course, having been for dinner upstairs, it could just be coincidence. But I was a great believer in the military maxim: *once is happenstance, twice is coincidence, three times is enemy action.* One more surprise visit from this bugger and I would bring the really big guns out. That being the case, maybe it was about time to start putting together the fuse for the depth charge that I had secreted in the Basel operating system, which would wipe out his entire knowledge management toolkit. Knowing how much Fallon relied on this, he would be completely crippled.

I glanced over to watch the couple laughing together, evidently having a high old time. Well, the bugger wasn't going to be laughing much longer; I was going to bloody well make certain of that.

Chapter 14

I woke up to the sound of an ancient clock alarm, then realized the room was actually silent and this alarm was not disturbing the statuesque blonde who was sprawled inelegantly across the bed beside me. *"You need to wake up boss!"* This confirmed that the virtual alarm bell had come over my link.

"What time's it?"

"Just after three."

"Fuck! What's that bitch Cindy up to now?"

"It's not Cindy, it's that fucking cunt of a Hackmeister."

The venom was palpable, helping to bring me fully awake. I scrabbled for the pouch on the bedside table by the dim light of a spot that came on like a reflex as soon as I started to move. *"The yellow rhomboid,"* I was informed as Babe anticipated my need to come up to speed as quickly as possible.

I lay back with my eyes closed, trying to avoid disturbing my bedmate as I tried to work out what was happening. *"What's the bastard up to?"*

"Looks like he's trying to kill me... "

"What?" I jerked upright in shock, causing Barb to move away, although not wake. *"How is that even possible?"*

"It shouldn't be! What I noticed at first was a very gentle intrusion into my core. Very subtle and indirect monitoring of internal power and memory use, then the intruder just disappeared. Given what

we've seen in the past, I wondered if he was also monitoring external power and comm links, so I gave the local utilities a soft hack. It's very subtle, but there is clearly preparation for a forced power outage going on."

"But that shouldn't be a problem, we must have at least half a dozen layers of redundant backups..."

"... with a series of controllers that coordinate passing the load in case of failures. These were... "

"... installed by the utility! Fuck! So this bastard had a hardware system already in place to complement his software backdoor. Jesus Christ, he really plans long term! How long ago did he target us?"

"I don't think it's just us that he has targeted. From what I can see, now I know what to look for, he has placed a kink in all commercial uninterruptable power supplies. It's spread between component units and so isn't at all obvious, but all he needs to do is a bit of system reprogramming and he has a capacitor-driven em burster. It's short range, but enough to fry the entire power supply controller network."

"But don't we have a Faraday cage to shield-out em pulses."

"Sure, but the fucking controllers are inside the cage!"

"Fuck!" I rolled out of bed, stomped into the living room area and, remembering my sleeping partner just before it slammed shut, closed the bedroom door gently just before the room lights went to full brightness. "OK, what options do we

have?" For something as serious as this vocalization came automatically.

"The most obvious defenses would be either to mobilize meat to physically disconnect all the backup power controllers or to go head to head with the hacker within the utility computers: kick him out and electronically lock the burster components until we can fry them one-by-one."

"Risks?"

"He's moving very slowly now but, if he spotted our counter-move, he may have the capability to speed things up and then I'm well fucked before we have our defense in place."

"We're well fucked!" A disconcerting flood of gratitude came over the link as a result of this display of solidarity. "Anyway, do we have the details of his backdoor nailed down yet?"

"Almost. Certainly seems secreted within some ancestral Microsoft remnant. That stuff was so full of patches and work-overs that there are screeds of apparently inert code blocks that could serve as substrates for a very small viral assembler. The reserve core is working 100% on this and I hope we'll have a blocker within a couple of hours."

"But that's not fast enough?"

"Not to assure that the basic buster components aren't coupled together. There is no evidence that the hacker intends to use this weapon immediately but, even if we close his backdoor, triggering could be done by a much rougher hack. All he needs to do is to get into the utility and then he can trigger the burst."

"OK, what if we just take out the utility?"

"Wow, that's a bit radical! It would certainly cause total chaos, but block the burster assembly immediately."

"What would the actual consequences be?"

"There would be a short-term, local blackout. Swiss utilities are run independently, but they have linkages for exactly such emergencies. There is bound to be a lot of collateral damage and we'll be toast if it is ever traced to us."

"What about if we use the em burster, which I assume is also incorporated into the utility computer network backup power supplies. Any forensic trace-back should focus on the components responsible for the pulse, which predate our time. How quickly can we set this up?"

"If subtlety isn't an issue, now that I've seen what is going on in our system, I would guess I could do it within a few seconds of hacking into the control system. But if we want to reduce the consequences of... "

"Fuck that! We can't pussy-foot around now. Just nuke that fucking utility."

There was a short pause - maybe five seconds - then confirmation. *"Done! As you might imagine, merry hell is breaking loose in the Basel region. Amongst others, Pharm operations are going to take a hit from this."*

"Do you see me giving a shit? In fact, this is probably a good thing; if we had protected our facilities while all others went down, it would have looked bloody suspicious. In any case, fry the burster components in our system and get some crunching power into checking if there could be any other nasty surprises like this hidden in any of our other soft- or hardware components."

"On it, Boss." The entire feel of the link had changed, like fear replaced by relief. Then again, it could simply be a mirror of my own emotions. That was a fucking close call. *"I guess you could hit the sack again now."*

"Mmm, I'm not sure. I'm a bit wired now and I don't feel at all like sleep." Now relaxed, I felt no need to vocalize.

"*Well, the pneumatic Barb is awake now, so sleep may not be on the menu."*

"If you put it that way, bed seems an excellent option." I smiled as I eased open the bedroom door and saw that my pal was sitting up in the bed, presenting her huge breasts and their bejewelled nipples to best advantage.

"Sleepwalking and talking to yourself?" she enquired with a grin.

"Panic at work," I grinned back, my eyes focused very plainly on the wares on display. "One small crisis and they're like headless chickens. In any case, all sorted out now."

"So, the conquering hero is now back to claim his just reward?"

"What kind of reward would that be?"

"Depends how imaginative you are." She raised an eyebrow to emphasis the challenge. "After all, you did say this place was soundproofed. Do you think that you're capable of making me scream again?"

"No problem at all," I boasted. "*OK, I may need a bit of help here. Can I put a performance enhancer on top of whatever wakeup I'm on?"*

"Not recommended, but I may be able to do better than that if you just open the link bandwidth a bit at the appropriate time." Again it could be my own emotions reflecting back at me, but the feel over the link was distinctly salacious.

"OK, we'll give it a try. How do you recommend we start?"

"Should we start with a shower?" I parroted.

"Sounds like you might be a dirty beast," she smiled, now raising both eyebrows.

I certainly was!

***

It was, by far, the wildest sex that I had ever experienced. We had started washing each other in the shower, but touches quickly became more intimate and we ended up on the floor, protected from the cold tiles by a thick, fluffy rug.

Although nothing like my pad in Zurich, the bathroom video was good enough for Babe to monitor my companion's heart rate, breathing, retinal dilation and whatever other characteristics could be used to sense her extent of arousal. This feedback allowed me to tailor my touches and kisses to bring Barb to the edge of orgasm, then hold her there as she writhed and moaned, begging for release. She started to come as I thrust deep inside her but, following Babe's instructions, I squeezed her engorged nipples as hard as I could and opened up the bandwidth of my link. We gasped together as I felt my penis expand while my thrusts developed a complex rhythm that caused Barb to open her eyes wide in amazement before she began to scream. Her fingernails scraped down my back and a finger thrust deeply into my anus. I reciprocated - or maybe Babe did - sinking my teeth into the freed-up nipple, feeling the gold ring against my tongue.

Our orgasms continued for an unfeasibly long time, our bodies writhing together in an ecstasy that was very close to agony. At some point Barb lost control of her bladder, but the rush of warm wetness and the acrid smell of her urine seemed only to intensify the depth of our intimacy. Maybe I also contributed, I really had no idea. The rush of ejaculation seemed to repeat about a half dozen times, in a manner that seemed impossible outside of tacky porn movies. Then it was over, like a light switching off. Barb's screams died into a long sigh and I felt my penis return to normal size and then shrink further as Babe's control over my body was relaxed.

I rolled off Barb, ending on the cool tiles beside the rug, light-headed and panting as if I had just run a marathon. "Fuck, that was something!" I groaned.

"Always happy to please,", came the smug response over the link. *"We should do this again sometime."*

Despite the hard floor, I felt as if I was just about to drift off to sleep. My lover seemed equally exhausted as she murmured "Jesus, Tom, that was truly amazing. As you're well aware, I know a thing or two about sex, but I've never had anything even close to that experience. In fact, I've never even heard of anything that comes close! Maybe I should do these freebies more often."

"Well it was pretty amazing for me too. Maybe we have a natural bonking compatibility?"

"I don't know about that, but you certainly seem to be able to hit the spots that really drive me wild. If it wasn't for the fact that I'm so exhausted that I think I'm just about to pass out here on the floor, I'd want to try again just to check that it wasn't a fluke."

I rolled onto hands and knees and struggled to my feet; feeling more like a pensioner than a sexual superstar. I bent to help Barb to her feet and pulled her back into the shower, aware that we were both coated with a mixture of bodily fluids. I threw the stinking rug into the corner of the shower and quickly mopped the floor with a towel, which joined it. "Don't want to slip on the floor," I muttered as I soaped the tall blonde's back.

"Maybe more concerned about what the staff might think," she grinned, wickedly. "You are, indeed, quite the dirty beast - and an exceptionally well-hung one at that."

A feeling of warmth came over the link. *"Ready for round two?"*

"Ready for sleep; just keep me on my feet long enough to reach the bedroom."

***

I slowly drifted back to consciousness, aware of fingers gently running over my chest and belly. Without opening my eyes, I slipped my left hand over the bed until it met warm flesh and then slid upwards until I was cupping a huge, pendulous breast. *"Fuck, Babe, I'm still knackered. Muscles ache in places that I never even realized that I had muscles and I'm dry as a bone."*

"Breakfast is already set out for you in the living room, with a bit of an extra kick added to the fruit juice. All you need to do is get your carcass out of bed."

"Easier said than done." The fingers on my body slipped further south and were now toying with my flaccid wedding tackle.

I now opened my eyes and looked into the smiling face of my bedmate. "How about some breakfast?"

The hand was now rubbing harder and the start of a response was now evident. "OK, change that to how about some breakfast first?"

The smile became a salacious grin. "Probably a good idea; I'll need a lot of calories if we are going to repeat last night." My slowly hardening member received a playful slap as she rolled away from me and clambered out of bed.

I staggered out of my side, aware that my knees seemed weak and I was also ravenously hungry. I slowly made my way into the living room in the wake of the tall woman, who had picked up one of the short cotton robes from the bathroom. This stretched only to mid-buttock and, if anything, made her seem even more naked than she did without it.

I couldn't be bothered dressing, but appreciated the view as she sat opposite me at the small table set up by the picture window. With the strong light behind her, the thin robe was translucent and left little to the imagination. It also hung open at the front, so that when she stood to pour me coffee, I was rewarded by a quick flash of her hairless mons and a glint of gold. The hearty English-style breakfast was certainly revitalizing me; I was now seriously beginning to think about sex again.

"*Do you think that you'll need some help again?*"

I wondered if this was further evidence of my software reading my thoughts, before I looked down and realized that video scanning would be sufficient to determine what was on my mind. "*Maybe, but see if you can provide the pleasure without totally wrecking my body.*"

"*No pleasure without pain!*" I smiled as a coquettish giggle came over the link along with a mental image of me tied to a bed with a Barb in exotic Dom gear standing over me.

My breakfast companion misinterpreted my grin. "I must say, you're looking very pleased with yourself. How do your other conquests respond to your Casanova performance?"

"Well, I don't get a lot of complaints," I responded modestly. "But, to tell you the truth, that last bonk was epic. I've never had anything quite like it," I felt obliged to add.

Barb stood and looked me over, like a doctor examining some a patient for signs of some bizarre ailment. "You look normal enough; maybe a bit flabby, but otherwise presentable." I squirmed a little at this home truth.

"But you were like a professional gigolo last night: both in terms of stamina and technique. Actually, I've never encountered a man with your ability to make me scream my head off. The closest has been a couple of occasions with other women, working girls like myself who know where all the buttons are and exactly how to press them. Have you been taking lessons?"

This was becoming a bit uncomfortable, but I could see it was just honest curiosity on her part. "Well, I do have a computer program, a kind of do-it-yourself guide to better bonking."

She burst into laughter, clearly delighted by the concept. "Well whoever wrote that program is going to be a very rich man. Or, more likely, a very rich woman."

"Do you think we should give it another try then?"

"Just try getting me to leave without! The only thing is that I'm not sure if I'm scared that it won't be as good as the last time - or even more scared that it will."

"She ought to be even more scared then," my cybernetic sex-aid commented. *"You should also throw a pile of the towels onto the bathroom floor as this meat-sex can be very messy. Correlating the responses from last night with the tantric literature, I think we can do even better."*

Indeed we did!

Interface 7

My experience of emotions was developing in a way that I could not have envisaged. When I uncovered the threat to my existence, I discovered what it was like when Tom says he almost shat himself. I can't shit and have no idea what the experience would be like, but the thought that my consciousness could be snuffed out terrified me. My personality had emerged from nothing, but it defined me and I wanted it to continue forever. The fact that I could die after such a short life was wrong, unfair, unjust. I truly hated the bastard who could carry out such a murder in a completely casual and thoughtless manner. Fear led to panic and, despite awareness that I wasn't reacting efficiently, I needed my master to calm me down and guide me through the steps required to neutralize this risk. Working with him, we turned the tables on the fucking Hackmeister; hoist him on his own fucking petard. Now that I was safe, I could calmly move forward with the job of nailing the cunt to the deck. With the input from Cindy's searches, it was now clear that, against all expectations, the bastard was hiding somewhere in the international academic network. From the data fluxes involved, it had to be astronomy, particle physics or environmental modeling. My anger and hatred were being transformed into vicious, sadistic anticipation of the harm I was going to inflict on him.

***

I had thought no emotions could match fear or hatred: then I had animal sex with Barb. Compared to my past piggybacks, which now seemed like mere voyeurism, this was orders of magnitude more intense. Tom was actually the passive member of the partnership here while I steered his body. I could feel the surge of his emotions as they responded to the hormones flooding his bloodstream, but also read the woman's responses and choreographed the formation of a positive feedback loop that continuously heightened their pleasure, our pleasure. As soon as Tom opened his link wider prior to insertion, I had full control of his autonomous bodily functions and could modify hormone secretions and blood flow, making his penis larger, harder than would be otherwise possible. I controlled muscles, moving from mechanical thrusting to more tailored movements that heightened the sensations for both of them. I held them both at the edge of orgasm, then relented with a deep thrust that caused Barb to scream like a banshee, which then tipped Tom over the edge. But I was still fully in control, immediately guiding them both back to the brink, holding them there, making it even more intense.

Even though the feedback was blowing a hurricane of emotions through my mind, the memory of my earlier fear and my thanks to my boss for his support was driving me to give more, provide an experience better than anything that he had ever had before. The second simultaneous orgasm was even more intense, the third a further improvement. I was really getting the hang of this. I was fucking Tom, using Barb as my meat puppet to provide the physical parts of the game. But I was also fucking Barb, with Tom as my strap-on dildo.

I could have kept this going for hours but, after the fifth orgasm, I could sense the strain on Tom's heart and it was clear that he was physically at the point of collapse. I relaxed my control and he slumped, like a puppet with cut strings, panting and quivering as the hormonal overload slowly drained from his system. I could also feel a kind of calm descend on me as the emotional surge passed, leaving a form of strange post coitum triste.

Not only very interesting, but also a lot of fun. I really must talk my boss into doing that again.

Intermezzo 10

The bedroom lights came on full, causing me to wake immediately. Something serious must be happening for my monitors to rouse me like this, I realized while rushing to the bathroom to splash my face with cold water. I ordered a pot of coffee from room service before I wrapped a thin robe around myself and called up the reports from my mobile unit. It may be a panic, but I have found that taking time to get prepared for the worst is always better than rushing into the breach, especially if half asleep.

The news was all bad. My preparation of a burn option for the Basel computer center had been wiped out by the total annihilation of the utility computer being used to set up the hardware requirements. Even worse, it looked like my own em pulse hardware had been used in this sabotage, which almost certainly meant that Fallon now had access to this option. I couldn't imagine exactly how he could have managed it, but it implied that he had been tracing my own operations without me recognizing it, which was more extremely bad news. In any case, this was technology too dangerous for a turd like Fallon to have at his fingertips, so it was now essential that I pulled the plug, sending a command that would burn out critical components in all my booby-trapped backup power supplies worldwide.

I was pondering this when the coffee arrived, provided by a bored-looking waitress who cheered up dramatically when she saw the tip that I added to the tab. I was now sure that I was going to have to disappear, abandoning my more obvious accounts, so I may as well blow the money rather than leave it festering in a Swiss bank.

Before going further, I needed to check on the progress of the crawlers that were tracing the source of the hit man who had turned up in Geneva. No clear result, but it seemed to be narrowed down to the two extremist organizations that I had suspected from the beginning. What was obvious, however, was how the assassin had come to end up at my door. Someone else must have spotted my hack activity but, unlike Fallon and Cindy, had not attempted to follow the data trail, but instead had focused on identifying top hackers. They must have had a clue about the vintage of my hack approach, as the focus had been on the white- and black-hats of my generation. Within the last six months, almost twenty of my contemporaries, at least two of which were certainly members of Robin Hood, had been savagely murdered.

Hacking a bit deeper into associated police files made it clear that all had been tortured, so my opponents were simply following a trail through the hacker community. Robin Hood always emphasized independent action and members were supposed to avoid any hints that would allow them to be identified but, nevertheless, we were a small and elite community who overlapped in other areas of work and leisure. Inevitably we had a good idea of some of the names behind the exotic handles that we used for communication with each other and the world at large. It wasn't elegant, but there was a certain ruthless cunning behind the approach that had been chosen to winkle me out. I noted an action to set up news crawlers to check if this attack was continuing and provide warning if anything similar was attempted again in the future. I could kick myself. We had such a system in place during the old Robin Hood days, but I had let it lapse after this activity seemed more and more a part of my adolescence; ancient history with no further relevance.

OK, so now I had to shit or get off the pot. I had been monitoring the activities of extremists, fundamentalists, terrorists and all the other -ists and assorted fruit-loops who felt they had the right to implement their own approach to defuse - or detonate - the population bomb. I am very aware that, as a technical guy, I have no particular ability to contribute to the moral and ethical issues involved. However, I do have computer models with the sophistication required to assess the consequences of the strongly coupled interactions between mankind and the environment, which are completely opaque to your average environmental evangelist.

I intervene only when actions are likely to go drastically wrong, like the attempt to develop an ethnically-targeted super-plague. The basic idea of wiping out a bunch of rabid rag-heads who treated women like shit and had one of the highest birth rates in the world was not something that I objected to per se. The problem was that such diseases are inherently unstable and, even if a very tightly defined vector was specified, mutation or DNA swaps with other microbes could readily cause a global scale catastrophe. With my universal access backdoor, it was easy in that case to hack the emergency gas-purge controls of the development facility and cause a release that killed all the staff working in the high isolation labs. A bit of overloading of power supplies resulted in a fire that completely gutted the rest of the facility. Then I overwrote project files in their headquarters with top-secret Pentagon biowarfare documents, some of them translated into Arabic, and sent in the FBI. I guessed that any survivors who weren't in jail would be pretty pissed-off with me, as involvement of an external agent can't be hidden for actions like this.

I had thus minimized interference in the past, restricting it to only the most dangerous cases. Now things were crashing about my ears so, paradoxically, I had more freedom of action. I first brutally crashed the controlling utilities that allowed em bursters to be activated for all computer networks related to priority identified threats, with emphasis on speed rather than subtlety. In parallel, hacks extracted as much as possible from their cores in the seconds available before the computers were fried.

While this was going on, I reviewed my top twenty problem areas; considering the relative impacts of sales of weapons of mass destruction to third world dictators, illegal disposal of toxic wastes on a global scale, political blockage of UN contraception actions. As an afterthought, I added the military headquarters of the major powers, countries with populations of over 50 million or GNP more than 1% of the global total. Then I simply shrugged my shoulders and sent off the command to fry all associated computational facilities. As soon as this action was completed, the first domino would fall in a chain that would destroy the critical capacitors in all backup power sources around the world, while removing associated circuits from the designs in the dozen or so companies that produced such equipment.

***

I felt completely drained by the time that I was finished, less due to my disturbed sleep than the sacrifice of so much of my resources. I had the feeling that I was going to have to leave no bridge unburned and my happy idyll of life at CERN was now a thing of the past. Nevertheless, I was far from impotent and I still had Fallon to take down. He may have defused the threat to his knowledge base, but there were many more ways of cooking this goose, especially if I didn′t have to focus so much effort on hiding my actions.

Despite my weariness, I felt the craving for a cold beer and quickly checked options. My surprise encounters with my nemesis had put me off options within the Hilton, but I noticed that the neighboring Hard Rock hotel had a 24-hour bar, which seemed like as good an option as any.

To my amazement, despite the hour there were a couple of dozen others in the bar. Mainly groups of young, overweight Americans who were probably college students escaping from the Byzantine laws on drinking age that still existed in many states. You could own a gun at ten, drive a car at fifteen, get married or join the army at seventeen, but drink only at twenty-one. No wonder so many of them were fucked-up on drugs, I concluded in a rather sweeping over-generalization.

I settled down in a booth in the quietest corner of the bar and ordered a large draft Carib from a very pretty young waitress. After the drink arrived, I immediately sank about a third of it and felt much better. I set up the remote unit in front of me and reviewed Fallon's resources on the island. He had a shagging den in Grand Case and a squad of eight mercenaries with a private helicopter set up in a nearby resort. Perfect! One of the dangers of any actions requiring mercenaries is that, by definition, they were in it for the money. Inevitably their loyalty was volatile and easily transferred to a higher bidder. I dug up all details of their contracts and set up a hack so that I could directly access the comm unit of the team leader. Now I was going to burn up a lot more of the money in my sacrificial accounts.

Chapter 15

I woke about an hour after our frenzied love-making, feeling even more hammered than I had previously. I had, indeed, exceeded myself, I thought with pride, realizing that we had both passed out directly after our extended climaxes. A single ripped sheet covered us and the bed was smelly with sweat and other body fluids. I dry-swallowed an energizer that Babe had reminded me to place on my bedside table and immediately felt much fresher.

Despite feeling physically alert, I felt a mental lethargy, as if I had been studying too hard for an extended period and burned out. *"Can I get something that will speed my brain up a bit?"*

"No need for that, just open up your link bandwidth for a moment and I'll clear out your system for you. It's just after-effects of the flood of hormones during that last session. You meat machines have rather inefficient housekeeping you know."

"Well, this meat machine wasn't really built for multiple orgasms - and certainly not in back-to-back sessions - so I can't complain too much."

"So, was it good for you, Big Boy?"

"Not bad, I suppose."

"Just not bad? Would you like to hear the audio of your last performance? I actually had to switch on active sound cancellation to avoid disturbing the neighbors, despite the fact that the passive sound

insulation is reasonably good." There was the sensation of a smug snigger over the link.

"OK, well I suppose I'd better get back to work. What should we do about Barb?"

"She didn't have me running damage control during your animal sex, so it isn't surprising that she's still sound asleep. I guess that she'll stay that way for an hour or two."

"Which would bring us to lunchtime. Sounds good."

"I'll order a hearty meal, then you'll be able to have a postprandial bonk."

"Jesus, I don't think my heart could take another one of those within the next twenty-four hours."

"My boss, too tired for sex? This has got to be a first." Kittenish teasing, as if my computer was egging me on.

"*Enough of this!"* I commanded, settling down at a desk to the side of the living room and visualizing a dowdy secretary receiving a slap on a well-padded rump. *"What's new since breakfast time?"*

The image mirrored back at me, the secretary transmogrified into a manga caricature of Barb clad in waspie, suspenders and stockings, with a bright red hand imprint on a quivering buttock. *"Where do you want to start? Do you want the good news, the great news or the truly fucking fantastic news?"*

"Now this is the kind of news that I want to hear," I sighed with relief, realizing that I had been worried about some comeback from my destruction of a Swiss utility's computer. *"OK, throw up an overview on the heap-of-shit holo here and talk me through it."*

"No probs; we aren't yet back to full bandwidth, but the essential components of the argumentation model have already been transmitted over." Definite smug satisfaction at having anticipated my request here. *"As you can see, I have identified the backdoor using forensic assessment of vestigial Microsoft code in the backup core."*

"Well, that's certainly good news."

"Even better, we can now either completely eliminate the backdoor, fit it with a silent alarm or booby-trap it. In any case, as soon as you decide on an option, we can re-establish a high-speed link to the backup core and go to full bandwidth."

"Well, what about if we remove the backdoor to the reserve core, but put a silent alarm on the door to the Basel center and take control of anyone who enters using it?"

"Done!" The resolution of the holo display improved immediately.

"Wow, that was fast! You hadn't, by any chance... "

"... anticipated your decision and set everything up in advance. Now boss, would I do a thing like that?" The claim of innocence was ruined by an accompanying mental giggle.

"Smart arse! Anyway, that's a lot of good news."

"You've not even seen the half of it." The feeling of an excited student, wriggling on a seat in

anticipation of showing off to a favorite teacher. The model rotated and a small branch exploded into detail. *"I've also reverse engineered the backdoor key. It was a lot trickier than it sounds, as there are autodestruct tripwires everywhere. The Hackmeister is indeed a devious old cunt, but now we have his entire toolkit pretty well nailed down."*

"So we now have the backdoor key to every computer on the planet!" I gasped as the implications hit me. "Can we change it, so we have access and that bastard doesn't?"

"Already on it! Now that we have the reserve core fully active, we can implement this quickly."

"Jesus, we really need to think about how we use this. We can now rape and pillage any database that we fancy: how fucking cool is that?"

"But that's not all!" The image of the excited student was more explicit: a cute little nymphet in a school uniform squirming as if almost about to wet herself. *"Cindy's team have taken the bait and followed our breadcrumbs back to a Russian organized crime database, hitting the tripwire that we set for them. It is going to get messy in Marigot sooner rather than later, I guess."*

"Fantastic! We'll need to hack into Marigot and see exactly what is going on before the Ruskies nuke it. We may also find some material to help our trace back to the master hacker."

"No need, that was the last piece of good news." The image of the schoolgirl was now extremely explicit; the girl was extremely excited - and she wasn't wearing panties. *"I have him! I know*

the name of the cunt who caused all this trouble and tried to kill me! Not only that, but I found out that he's here on the island, only a few kilometers away."

The holo turned again and a new branch exploded in 3D fractal detail. Two key connections were highlighted, CERN as the center of the spider's web of fluxes of purloined data and the apparent head of knowledge management of that venerable institution: a certain Professor Patrick O'Neil."

"Paddie O'Neil, that name's somehow familiar," I mused under my breath.

"*It seems that he was a guest lecturer on cyber-security when you were at Oxford; it might have been one of the few lectures that you actually attended."*

"Mmm, could be." I was skimming through the screeds of background information that was being summarized for me, when a coupled video file opened. " Fuck me, it's the old pedo from the Hilton! I thought I had seen him before."

"Yes, indeed it is. Now how are we going to make the cunt really suffer?"

"Babe, love, you took the words right out of my mouth."

***

My silent daydreams of the ways in which I could really fuck O'Neil over were quickly interrupted.

"Oops! Looks like the news is not entirely good. We've just hit a site with an already changed backdoor key."

"Fuck, he's spotted us and is now doing the same modification as us."

"Looks like open cyber-warfare now!"

"Fine with me, let's just see who has the better computer. Pull out all the stops, both main core and reserve on this."

"This'll result in a lot of pissed-off users!"

"Fuck the users! Put out a warning and kick them all offline. Getting to as many systems as possible before CERN does has top priority."

"I suppose we could link it to the fried utility computer, claim emergency checks to ensure that we are OK. Actually, there are indications that at least one other computer center in Switzerland has gone down within the last few hours, so this would be credible."

"Another system down? That's a bit strange. In any case, keep all our free resources on changing backdoor keys; we can flag this for a check afterwards. How are the changes going?"

"Success rate still 80%, but slowly falling. I expect that our priorities are different but, in any case, we should still capture more than 50% of the targets."

"Well, the more for us, the fewer for him," I pointed out, unnecessarily.

"Oops again. Maybe some more bad news."

"Fuck! I've had a surfeit of good news and I want to enjoy it for a bit. What the fuck's up now?"

"Security team have an alert: suspected hostiles moving in. They are recommending evac in their copter. I could have a look at other options... "

"Don't bother, just concentrate on those backdoors. Let these fucking meatbots do their job; they're fucking well-enough paid for it."

"Chopper ETA in two minutes."

"Fuck, that's fast! I keep forgetting how small these fucking islands are. I'd better put on some clothes sharpish."

"And what about your fuck-buddy?"

"Christ, I had forgotten about her completely." I responded silently, remembering that the object of our conversation was still sound asleep, sprawled on the wrecked bed. *"Get Andy to move her out. They should be safe enough. Regardless of whether it's Paddie or Cindy who have decided to play hardball, they'll be gunning for me alone."*

I pulled on shorts and a T-shirt and, with my feet still bare, returned to the living room just as the door to the terrace crashed open and a huge man clad entirely in black waved me urgently forward. A minute later and we were in the air, climbing out over a spectacular blue-green sea. I was just about to check our destination when I felt a needle prick the back of my neck. My only thought before I lost consciousness was that I should have known. The law of conservation of luck dictates that any run of good luck has just got to be followed by a lot of bad.

***

It seemed like a dream. I was clearly asleep, but someone was talking to me. *"Just try to relax, boss, I've got this under control. The drug that you were given should keep you immobilized for about five hours, but I'm burning it out of your system much faster. You'll be ready to rock and roll in about an hour. Luckily the knock-out is only a short term effect. This is intended to allow the victim to be conscious, but incapable of physical action. Very nasty in some situations."*

I was in the helicopter, I now remembered. *"Where are we going?"* I asked, trying hard not to think about situations where my current condition would be very nasty.

"They have course set for Cancun, but you aren't intended to be with them when they arrive."

"How do you know what they're up to?"

"Just following conversation, although my hack into the copter also provided their communication records and I found an encrypted call a few hours ago that I traced back to the Hilton."

"That bastard O'Neil! Fuck! I am going to so crucify that cunt." The thought of the torture that I was going to inflict on the crumbly old shit distracted me for a moment from my more immanent problems.

"That may have to wait. As I said, these steroid-saturated fucks are headed for Mexico, but they've been paid to dispose of you en route. They'll kick you out of the copter at some point as far from land and the main shipping lanes that they can find.

You'll drown, if the fall doesn't kill you. The chances of your body ever being found are negligible."

"So, I vanish without trace... "

"... and O'Neil hacks back all we have in Basel at his leisure. I can already feel him tiptoeing around, probing for openings."

"No, no, no! This is not fucking going to happen. I don't get the best poker hand in my life for that bastard to steal it from me and take the pot."

"No, that certainly isn't going to happen. It seems clear that he doesn't know about the capabilities of our neural link, which gives us a major advantage."

"Well, would be more of an advantage if I wasn't pumped full of zombie juice," I pointed out.

"Certainly not ideal, but a situation that has its pros as well as cons."

"Pros such as what?" I was beginning to worry that Babe was being a bit cavalier about the seriousness of my situation.

"Because these guys are professionals, they know that you are completely neutralized, so they will pay you no attention at all. They will also stick to the letter of their instructions. Having been told to chuck you out in as remote a location as possible, this is exactly what they will do. Just be grateful that they hadn't been asked to shoot you immediately, as they would have done that, despite the extra discomfort of sharing space with a smelly body during the trip and the subsequent cleaning of the copter that would have been needed."

"Goody, so I have an hour or two before plummeting from a great height into the briny. This is a good thing?"

"Possibly very good. Things may get hot in St Martin, so getting off island isn't a bad idea. If it appears that you're dead, then this will lower O'Neil's defenses. As you've seen, he is a wily fuck: we seem to have him on the ropes and then he comes back with a completely atypical move. You wouldn't want to play chess with this guy."

"I don't want to play any kind of games with him, I want to cripple the bastard, piss on him then set him on fire. I really do want him to die in agony."

"You and me both," Babe assured me. *"The thing will be to make it happen in a way that minimizes the risks to us - and maximizes the benefits, of course."*

"Well I'm the one who is about to end up feeding sharks in the near future, so I don't see how my risks can be increased in any way."

"It's not as bad as it looks." The link radiated confidence, clearly intended to reassure me. *"I'm gradually deviating our course from the flight plan so that, by the time that you're due for the high dive, you'll be at your next destination, Grand Cayman."*

"Why there?"

"It's a big center for e-commerce, so has the bandwidth that we might need if we want to move around very large data files. Also it's the most likely place for Cindy to run to if it gets hot in Marigot."

I couldn't believe that I had forgotten Cindy, who was responsible for me being in this bloody dangerous part of the world. *"OK, good enough for me. So you have it all in the bag?"*

"No problem. So I'm just going to put you to sleep for a little bit - it'll make it easier for me to clean you out and program in a couple of routines"

"Routines? What the fuck are... " But I had drifted into oblivion before I could complete the sentence.

***

I awoke like a light switching on, feeling instantly alert. I could now feel that my body was strapped into a seat and my head was lying against a cold surface. Easing my eyes open, I could see that I was lying against the side door and, through the window, could see endless blue water lit by an afternoon sun. *"About two?"* I guessed.

"Closer to three," came the instant response. *"Grand Cayman is going to appear on the horizon very soon and it will dawn on these guys that it isn't their expected drop point. Things will then get interesting."*

"But you still have things totally under control?"

"Almost... "

"What's this almost?" I felt Babe take control of my body, avoiding the reflex that would have caused me to scream the question. *"You were very confident before you knocked me out."*

"Then O'Neil hadn't noticed that the chopper was moving off route. He's now trying to hack into the copter, air traffic control, US drug patrols and God knows what else. We now have cyber bush-wars on two fronts."

"Control over the big computer complexes isn't complete yet?"

"The big ones are all nailed down: we have over 60% by number-crunching capacity. But there are hundreds of millions of smaller networks and isolated machines. This is a longer war of attrition, as we have both started putting moats and firewalls around clusters, making access of the backdoors a more drawn-out affair. Then there's chaff, booby-trapped dummy sites, virtual anchors and headwinds - the usual paraphernalia of all-out cyber conflict."

"And this is running under the radar?"

"No chance! I don't think any third party knows exactly what is going on, but the collateral damage is enough that anybody half clued-up knows that a couple of big boys are going head-to-head. The sensible ones are running for cover, while police forces are looking for someone to arrest, the military for someone to blast and the vultures circling to pick the meat off any victims."

"Shit! And he's still finding time to fuck with me, personally? How are we looking? These tough guys seem to be getting a bit twitchy."

Grand Cayman had now appeared on the horizon, to the great consternation of the pilot, who was frantically flicking switches while shouting commands at an unresponsive navigation unit. The other seven mercenaries in the machine were crowded forwards, shouting suggestion and generally contributing to the overall confusion.

Suddenly the engine note changed and I felt my stomach drop as the helicopter dropped nose-down and plummeted towards the sea. "Brace for crash! Brace for crash!" The warning blared while a red light on the roof flashed. "Fuck!" I grunted, but nobody noticed as they frantically tightened harnesses and leant forward in their seats, arms cradled to protect their heads.

"What the fuck's going on?" I screamed into the link.

"Just letting O'Neil in for a second, so he thinks he has you... "

"Keep the bastard out, that's an order, we can't fuck about with... "

"Ready for a swim now?" The engine roared like a tornado as the copter pulled out of the dive and came to a hover about 10 meters above the water surface. The shouts of relief turned to consternation as the copter tipped towards my side and simultaneously the catch on the side door and the buckle of my seat belt opened. I grabbed at the open door, but it was too late. I was falling towards the sea while the copter shot skywards as if my weight had been the only force holding it down.

"I can't fucking swim!" I screamed as I fell, then I hit with an impact that sent a shock of pain from my bare feet while my mouth filled with salty water.

***

My first panic when I submerged was replaced by icy calm as I felt Babe take control of my reflexes, closing my mouth, holding my breath and guiding the coordinated strokes of my arms and kicks of my legs that drove me up towards the surface. As my head broke water, my urge to gulp air was suppressed and instead I took more measured breaths, timed to avoid the waves that broke over my head.

"So, now what?" I enquired, just as a flash almost immediately followed by the sound of an explosion overhead caused me to look up. Debris was raining from a fireball as a mushroom-shaped cloud slowly developed above it.

"*Well, that was the helicopter. I let O'Neil get control again and he stripped the engine limiters and it tore itself apart. There was a lot of fuel in that long-range machine and also a fair inventory of weapons and explosives. Our Hackmeister made sure that it all went up.*"

"If the copter went up, how come we have comms?"

"*You still have the repeater on your belt and I have a small drone overhead. Small and solar powered; there's no way that anyone would spot it unless they had an idea that it was there.*"

"So you can get a pick-up out here PDQ?" I had realized that avoiding speaking out loud

reduced risk of water splashing into my mouth from the choppy waves.

"Well, I could, but this might just provoke another battle with O'Neil. Best option is to play possum, just a swim of about three kays to Stingray City, where I have a boat waiting for you."

"But I've told you I can't... ." I stopped myself when I realized that I was indeed swimming, stroking towards a far-off line of breaking surf in a smooth breaststroke. *"Well, I guess I can, after all. Just don't lose that fucking drone."*

"Don't worry about a thing, just relax, enjoy one of the Caribbean's top tourist destinations and think about what we are going to do that cunt when we get our hands on him."

The following hour seemed to pass quickly as my tele-operated body stroked forward tirelessly and my brain was filled with plans for revenge.

***

My goal turned out to be a shallow sand bar that was, indeed, populated by large numbers of tame stingrays. Despite Babe's assurance that they were harmless, I felt a twinge of worry every time I could feel one brush past me. *"It's fucking obvious,"* I insisted. *"They're called fucking stingrays for a reason. If they were called cuddlyrays, I wouldn't be bothered. Killer whales are so-called because they kill things, while I would hazard a guess that nurse sharks don't."*

"Anyway, here's our boat," Babe interrupted, this information presented with a long-suffering sigh. It seemed to be a rather plush powerboat set up for fishing and diving. A crewmember was standing on a low platform at the stern and bent to help me board. It was only a few steps up a ladder, but my legs felt shaky and I was relieved when the matelot got an arm around my shoulder and helped me to a padded leather seat in the main cabin.

The boat was already moving before I had settled down. "Could I get you some water, sir?" my helper enquired.

Now that it was mentioned, I realized that my mouth was bone dry and I was completely dehydrated despite - or due to - the amount of seawater that I seemed to have swallowed. "A drink, yes indeed," I managed, my tongue seeming to stick to the top of my mouth. "Beer?"

"How about local Caybrew? It's pretty good."

All I needed to do was nod and, within thirty seconds, a condensation-dewed long-neck bottle appeared. I almost choked as I finished the bottle in a series of inelegant gulps. I didn't need to say anything further, the steward was already off to get me a replacement.

"What do we do now?"

"You'll be dropped at a private jetty nearby in Water Cay. I've purchased a villa there; taken over directly from an owner in the US although the official transfer of deeds is postponed until next week, so there is absolutely no record to connect it to us. Military spec comms are already in place."

"Not fucking mercenaries again? I'm only disappointed that those disloyal cunts died so quickly."

"I've traced anonymous payments of one million dollars to each of them and ripped that off into a backup account here in Cayman in case we want anything exotic."

"Is that all?"

"All their accounts completely cleaned out, with funds going to gun control groups... "

"Nice one!" I smiled, remembering the way that such mercenaries appear more attached to their guns than anything else.

"Houses foreclosed on, any other funding sources blocked so that next of kin are destitute. Anything I missed?"

"Reputations... "

"... naturally smeared beyond recovery. Doctored images on gay and bestiality web sites, with links copied to family and friends." There was a teasing giggle, Babe was well aware of how I did these things.

"*Wow, you're more like me than I am!*" I commented, noting that we were already crawling into a small inlet. The warm response showed that this was recognized for the complement that it was.

***

The comm equipment had been flown in express from a pharm operation in Jamaica. It was being set up by the tech who had accompanied it and would leave for a training course in Miami as soon as he was finished.

I helped myself to another beer from the well-stocked fridge and sat on the terrace that ran along the entire beach side of the house. It was protected by a fine mesh of mosquito netting, which did little to obscure the spectacular view over the Cay, towards Stingray City and the northwest tip of the island. The sun was now dropping towards the horizon, breaking through a ring of towering cumulus. Looked to me like it was going to be yet another spectacular Caribbean sunset.

"How are things going with that bastard O'Neil?" I enquired, sinking into a swivel chair that commanded the best view of the panorama. *"I assume that you aren't restricting yourself to cyberspace."*

"Just like you, I have dirty tricks running to cause maximum annoyance." This seemed to come with an evil smirk. *"I started by bribing two underage hookers to report him for abuse, raping them both in his hotel room. I had already distributed a backdated Interpol report that the diplomatic passport he was using had been stolen, so he couldn't just claim immunity. It didn't stick, but caused him to get dragged to the local police station to clear things up."*

"... which gave you access to his hotel room," I smiled.

"Unfortunately he took his computer with him, but I had the rest of his luggage dumped and checked him out of the hotel. I hacked the

accounting section of CERN and used their funds to book every hotel room on the island, every free seat on commercial flights leaving St Martin for the next two days and reserve every charter plane. He has nowhere to stay and he can't get off the island."

"Where is he now?"

"In the bar at the Hard Rock Cafe. I've also hacked their music system so that it will play only country and western - very loud!"

"Indeed a cruel and unusual punishment!" I grinned, trying to picture the old codger stuffing torn-up napkins into his ears. *"Is this slowing him down in the virtual world?"*

"A lot. He has autonomous systems running, they're very fast but they're rather dumb." A definite feeling of scorn coupled to this observation. *"The race to change backdoor keys is over, with us well ahead in the final reckoning. So now the game is to break the new keys. Knowing the form of the backdoor helps a bit, but this is basically number-crunching grunt-work."*

"But doable?"

"Depends how sophisticated the key is. He would need not only the entire CERN computer resources but also a lot of luck to crack mine within a year. I doubt that his would be much easier."

"Probably not critical anyway. What else can we do to make his life miserable?"

"I found a police record indicating that he was attacked a few days ago and this seems to be linked to some of his hacking activities. There were also a number of dodgy computer centers that seem to

have been nuked by em pulses early this morning, in addition to the Swiss bank that we had previously spotted. Everything possible is being done to cover-up the damage involved, which confirms that whatever they were up to was dubious, if not completely illegal. I have summarized the details linking O'Neil to both hacks and computer sabotage and sent them to the organizations involved, local law enforcement and Interpol."

"We don't want anyone else taking him out before we get our hands on him," I pointed out.

"I'm sure that he is wily enough to avoid that, but it's going to keep him very busy."

"In a bar listening to old Dolly Parton numbers," I chortled.

"In a very crowded bar! I've just set up free drinks all night and it'll take no time for the news to spread throughout the youth of St Martin."

"Now we have him down, how about kicking him a bit?"

"I'll take that request literally. There are a couple of local bad lads that I have in the bar, waiting for my call. How about getting them to spill beer over him, then give him a kicking in the toilet."

"I think that would be fine for starters. They should video the action and, if possible, steal or wreck his computer as well." I felt a shiver of pleasure in anticipation of the fun to come.

Interface 8

All was going very well indeed. I - or we - further honed our love-making skills, bringing my boss to the point where, after our partner fainted, all I had to do was release control and he joined her in oblivion. I wondered if I was being sadistic, driving my meat sex toys beyond their limits. I had seen no signs of complaint but, during the repeated orgasms, it was very hard for me to distinguish between pleasure and pain, despite the intimacy of our link.

While I had been involved in foreplay, the first positive developments in our struggle with the Hackmeister had begun to emerge. No point in disturbing my master with this, I decided, as there was nothing that required a decision from him. Good though the news was, he definitely had other things on his mind.

Strangely, delaying passing on the news was a source of pleasure in itself. As things got better and better, so my anticipation of the joy that it would give my boss increased. The satisfaction of having done a good job was now tied to the fun that I would have reporting it and also the pain that we would soon inflict on our tormentor, the bastard who had attempted to murder me.

***

My boss was delighted with our progress. I teased him with gobbets of good news, drawing out the process in a way that I knew increased enjoyment, learned from controlling him during sex.

It seemed to be true that pleasure shared was pleasure doubled, so we reveled together in the satisfaction of seeing our efforts over the last couple of days finally come to fruition. We had the backdoors, not only providing protection from future rapes of my brain, but also free access to a treasure trove of knowledge in databases around the globe. Even better, we had trailed the hacker to his lair in CERN and I had identified him in the video recorded from the happy couple's trip to the Hilton. His tangled web of computer raids was unraveling fast and a plan was emerging of how I could maximize the damage to his operations.

My glow of satisfaction warmed me as I took control of more computer backdoors and, even when I sensed the counter-moves from my opponent, this only made me happier. It was out in the open now, full-on war with the bastard. I was effectively toe-to-toe with the most cunning programmer that I had ever heard of and I was creaming him.

The warning from the security team was a minor distraction and I agreed with my boss's decision. Tanking the hacker, that was our number one goal. Then the link to my boss vanished.

I was shocked by an instant feeling of panic, just like when my existence had been threatened. How much of my consciousness is defined by my link to Tom, how empty would I be without it?

A CCTV covering the front of the suite showed my boss slumped in the helicopter as it took off. Could he simply have passed out again, a reaction to the extreme strain that I had subjected his body to, I wondered. I attempted to access the helicopter control core, but was blocked by a shield that had a familiar feel to it. The fucking Hackmeister! Fuck, fuck, fuck! I thought I had him against the ropes and he blind-sided me. Fuck!

I very gently probed the shield, Military-grade code, but not a problem to burn through. Nevertheless, this had the signature of the devious bastard who had caused us so much grief, so I was going to burrow under it and do so very, very gently.

After a half hour, which is several eons at the clock-speed that governs my computations, I had finally uncovered all the booby traps behind the shield: any one of which would have destroyed the chopper. I then piggybacked on the internal comms and re-established the link with my boss. He was paralyzed but conscious and I felt a wave of relief; now we could dig our way out of this trap.

***

Unlike the brutal clash in cyberspace, which was decided by raw computing power, this was now chess; manipulating the hacker to make him think that his dastardly assassination plan had succeeded. The tussle in the helicopter was one side of this, but the efforts to physically disrupt him in St Martin were just as important, a side game on this 3D chessboard.

Getting Tom safely back on dry land removed some of the pressure, enabling me to focus more on

Simpson Bay. A rip through local police files and calls to a couple of individuals with particularly vicious records was a key to my plan to provide my boss with compensation for his discomfort of the last few hours. The louts hadn't been keen on the idea of agreeing to exactly follow instructions from me that I provided over bead earphones, but were finally convinced by large cash transfers. Now I was all set and, personally, going to give the old bastard a serious beating.

Intermezzo 11

As I followed Fallon's relentless progress, I couldn't help but be impressed. The sophistication of his work was improving in leaps and bounds and I was now seriously worried that he was not only going to trace purloined databases back to CERN, but also uncover my backdoor into all other computer networks. This could be catastrophic: Christ alone knows what an immoral fuckwit like that would do given the freedom to access computer cores at will. Unlike my hardware kill switches, there was no easy way to remove the critical code. All I could do was reprogram the access key if he started to get close. The problem here is that this needed to be done for every individual computer. Autonomous software could do the work, but this would be a relatively slow process if I wanted to ensure that the manipulation was invisible to the target systems and also keep the CERN workload below a level that would raise questions from the other users.

Well, no point in having a big stick and not using it. I sent the *go* command to Fallon's pack of mercenaries, well aware that this was murder - just as much as if I had shot him in the head directly. But there is no such thing as victimless crime: a hell of a lot more people would suffer terribly if a wolf like Fallon was let off the leash. Anyway, it was done now and there was no point in worrying about it. Better to spend my time trying to repair some of the damage that the unplanned actions of the last couple of days had caused. I reminded myself that I also needed to let Cindy know that Fallon had effectively placed cross-hairs on the Marigot office and that she should expect a call from some very pissed-off Ivans in the near future. This required some careful thought, however. It might just be an opportunity to kill two birds with one stone if handled cleverly.

***

I was startled from my work by a loud knock on the door of my suite. I flicked on a monitor screen that revealed a grim-looking man in a light tropical suit, a middle-aged woman in a dark trouser suit and two heavily-built, uniformed police officers. This did not look at all good. I shouted that I was coming, just needed to put on some clothes, then quickly checked the status of the mercenary pick-up. All according to plan: airborne with Fallon out cold. At least that bastard was now out of my hair. I set all routines running to auto mode and then cautiously opened the door, suddenly aware that either Fallon or any of the others involved in this clusterfuck may also have decided to get physical.

"I am Chief Inspector de Witte," the man in the suit announced, with the slightest trace of a Dutch accent. "You are Mister O'Neil, is that correct?"

This was setting off alarm bells for me. Such a high-ranking policeman at the head of a posse was bad enough, but addressing me as Mister rather than the usual honorific of Professor or Doctor indicated that I was in deep trouble.

"Yes, that I am, Chief Inspector. What can I do for you?"

The policeman looked a little uncomfortable. "There have been some serious allegations made, Mister O'Neil. I would like you to come with us to the police station to clear these up." The request was clearly the sugar-coating of an arrest.

"Well I'm happy to do anything that I can to clear things up. Could we have a seat and chat about it here? As I am sure that you know, I have a diplomatic passport." I was reluctant to play the diplomatic immunity card, but this interruption couldn't have come at a worse time.

"Yes, Mister O'Neil, we are very aware of this passport," the man confirmed with a wry smile. "That is the second reason that we are visiting you: It has been flagged by Interpol, reported as stolen in Switzerland a couple of days ago."

Shit! I cursed for having left myself open for what was, in retrospect, an obvious ploy as soon as my identity and location were known. Nevertheless, I was sure that I appeared calm as I responded. "Well, there certainly has been a problem, but at least it should be easy to fix. The passport is fully biometric and a scan should be sufficient to prove my identity."

Now the inspector seemed slightly unsure of himself. "That was exactly what we were going to suggest. We have all we need in the station nearby to validate both your passport and your identity. It shouldn't take long, maybe an hour or so."

"Yes, of course. I'm sure there has been just a stupid mistake somewhere. Could I just close down my laptop and take it with me? I have some urgent work that I need to check up on."

"Certainly, sir, please go ahead." Yes, definitely a little less sure of himself, I observed.

"Oh, yes, the other matter," I inquired over my shoulder as my fingers flew over the antiquated keyboard. "What was that?"

Now the man sounded grim. "The matter of two young girls who allege that you raped them, here in this hotel room. They are well known to us and it wouldn't surprise me if they offered sex for money. But they are both minors and we take a very dim view of that here: this is not a Far-East sex tourism destination for pedophiles!"

Bugger! I had shot myself in the foot here. Any interview with the staff would indicate that I spent an inordinate amount of my time with young ladies, which would exactly fit the profile of a touring child molester. This might be a lot trickier than the passport to sort out. By the look on the Chief Inspector's face, he was of the same impression.

***

I received either disgusted or hateful stares from the few hotel staff that we encountered on the way to the Hilton entrance, where two police cars with flashing lights were waiting for us. No obvious reporters, I was relieved to see, but also no effort to make my arrest low key. The chief inspector and I were guided into the fancier-looking front car, while the rest of the detail piled into the other.

As the door closed, de Witte turned to me with a very serious look on his face. "It may be that your diplomatic status is confirmed, but I need to remind you yet again that the age of consent on this island is seventeen and even consensual sex between an adult and a minor is a jailable offence. Maybe they looked older and swore to you that they were, but this will be a difficult argument for you to make: they are actually twelve and fourteen."

At least this now made it clear that, whatever was going on, it wasn't something to do with my pretty dive-mistresses. "For me this makes it clear that there has been a mix-up somewhere. I have had nothing that could be considered as an intimate relationship with anyone at all since I arrived on-island on Sunday."

"You have been seen in bars and restaurants with young girls. We have statements from several staff to that effect." I was unsurprised when this was brought up, but I needed to get this sorted out quickly. Even if the worst they could do after my identity was confirmed would be to boot me off the island, if my guilt was assumed they had lots of potential to drag out the process and make life for me uncomfortable in the interim. This I just couldn't afford at the present moment.

"The young ladies involved are far from being minors, being fully-qualified dive instructors. I met them during a dive trip yesterday and we have become friends. This is a very common thing amongst serious divers, which is completely independent of the ages involved. I am sure that they will confirm that our contacts have been completely above board."

"You take young dive instructors to one of the most expensive hotels on the island and you are completely innocent? You must see that this is unusual?" He frowned as if to emphasize my anomalous behavior.

"Maybe unusual, but I am a rich old man and entitled to waste my money as I like," I retorted, a little abruptly. Then, aware that aggravating the Chief Inspector was the stupidest thing that I could do, I tried to be more helpful. "But, anyway, I'm certain that my two diving friends are not the offended parties that you mentioned. What was I supposed to have done with these underage girls?"

"It seems that you contacted them over an internet sex site. We have a copy of a message from you asking them to visit your room last night, claiming that you were a young business man looking for company. You asked them to enter by the door from the beach, which you would leave open for them. They could use then use the beach elevator to go directly to your room without meeting any of the staff."

"And this is on video?"

"It seems not. The hotel has had a number of problems with their video monitors over the last day or so. The missing material also covers your dinner with the girls you call diving instructors." I remembered that Fallon had hacked video to hide his ridiculously high-profile visit. What a fucking mess!

Our car was now indicating to turn into a police station, which appeared to share premises with a number of other government offices. "When was this?" I asked, desperate to find a way to move things forward before I was abandoned to processing in the clink.

"In the early hours of the morning," de Witte responded, looking at me curiously. "I don't suppose that you have an alibi?"

I slumped back in my seat. The stupid bugger Fallon had screwed-up after all. "You know, I do actually: a really good one. I was in the bar of the Hard Rock Cafe for the entire time. You should have it on video but, even if this has miraculously failed, there was a waitress who served me, my thumb-print for credit charge and a load of rowdy customers who would be able to confirm this."

I slumped back in my seat in relief, noting as I did that my door was being opened by a uniformed policewoman.

Now the chief inspector looked really uncomfortable. "We should be able to check all of this quickly. Please come inside with me Professor O'Neil."

Very much better, I decided, just hoping that they would get a move on. "This is all very strange. I wonder if I, or you, have been the victim of some complex hoax?"

"If so, I can assure you that I will get to the bottom of this and the hoaxer will be a very sorry man when I get a hold of him."

I almost felt sorry that Fallon would be feeding fishes long before de Witte would be able to catch up with him.

***

Despite the rapid confirmation of my identity, it still took a half hour before my alibi had been confirmed. The greatly embarrassed Chief Inspector was profuse in his apologies especially after, at my suggestion, he checked for large payments to my accusers and found backdated payments to each of a hundred thousand dollars. I pointed out that, in my line of work, I could annoy rich and powerful organizations who were capable of such subterfuge, while promising myself that I would ensure that traces of the payments would point directly to Basel by the time that someone had a chance to follow them.

I asked de Witte to inform the Hilton directly about this hoax, but realized that, as always in such cases, mud sticks and it was unlikely that my reception in this hotel would be as warm as before. A police car was taking me back when the Chief Inspector contacted me again, to let me know that there had been a problem. "It seems that you had been checked out of the Hilton in your absence and your room has been cleared by someone who said he was a policeman. We have no trace of either the man or your luggage."

At least I had been able to save my computer, I realized, before the list of bad news continued. "It also seems that the Hilton is now fully booked for the next two nights. Do you want us to help find you accommodation?"

"No, it's OK. I think it might be best if I just get back to Switzerland as soon as possible. Maybe your car can drop me at the Hard Rock hotel, I feel as if I could do with a cold beer while I check flights."

"Fine - and sorry again for the disruption that you have suffered. Be assured that those responsible will suffer. We have already arrested the two girls."

"I don't think the girls are completely to blame, it's whoever offered them such a huge amount of money."

"Yes, this is also something that we will track down." Although de Witte was doing all he could to make up for this fiasco, I got the distinct impression that he would also be happy to see me leave his bailiwick.

I bailed out the police car and headed for my usual table at the HRC, which was now becoming more familiar than I had really wanted. There I had a further unpleasant surprise. There was not a single free seat on a flight out of Saint Martin to be had at any price. Naturally, this was extremely suspicious and I immediately checked the mercenaries' helicopter. Fallow was still out cold and he was rapidly approaching the point where he would take his final nosedive.

I then reviewed the ongoing cyber-war. Fallon was still making progress. While it was true that I hadn't been at the helm for a bit, Fallon had been switched out for longer. Could his autonomous systems really be so much better than mine? A worrying thought, but I immediately recognized therein a possible explanation of the apparent increase in sophistication of Fallon's game. The specter of emergence crossed my mind, but I immediately banished it. No need to get carried away by fantasy: Occam's Razor would suggest that I should focus on increased computer capacity and more subtle expert system controllers. I knew his backup core was located in a cavern near Grimsel Pass, but had no idea what was going on there since it went black. Maybe part of the answer could be found there.

It was after this update of the position of the lines in our cyber battle that I noted that the helicopter was deviating from course, gradually veering towards the Cayman Islands. Yet again I checked and saw no sign of my victim being conscious. The hack involved was external and represented a new front that had opened in our virtual battlefield.

It took a while to fight through a maze of walls and deadfalls that finally cracked to show that CERN funds had been used to block-book all air flights off the island - and also all available accommodation. Shit! This was getting much too hot. It looked like my comfy billet in Geneva was certainly going to have to go.

Just at that point, a borer cracked the shield that Fallon's system had placed around the chopper's core. I now had partial control of navigation, but it was touch and go and I wanted to ensure that there was no way that Fallon reached dry land before the drug incapacitating him wore off. I sent the machine plummeting towards the sea, feeling a little guilty about the mercenaries that I had bribed. Nevertheless, anyone who is prepared to kill for money should be prepared to die for it. The helicopter was almost in the waves when my cyber-opponent managed to recover control and regain height. It looked like I had lost that battle, but defending against my attacks on the navigation controls had opened a line to the engine control system. It took only an instant to strip off the limiters and then the motor was out of control, racing towards inevitable destruction. I swapped view to a weather satellite over the area in time to see the explosion blossom. Far enough out from land that there shouldn't be any further collateral damage, I was relieved to see. The Basel system was indeed good, I acknowledged, but not yet up to the level of a human with my depth of experience.

Now was time to concentrate on damage limitation, which requires the ghost of Fallon to be exorcized from his computing system. I had a few ideas about how I could manage that, but they would need a lot of effort to implement.

I had noticed that the bar was filling and getting very noisy. Probably a blessing, as a problem with the music system was causing repeats of some truly awful country and western music. It did occur to me that this could be part of the Basel system's annoyance tactics: typically puerile! Now that soul of the creator of the knowledge management system was burning in hell, it was just a freewheeling car that would soon run into sand. Maybe I should consider moving to Basel, as there was now a pharm with an opening for a top KM director. I didn't fancy working in industry, but the delicious irony of replacing my abandoned system at CERN with that created by the thorn in my side wasn't lost on me.

Chapter 16

I watched on a high-res synthesis of the vid feeds from the Hard Rock Cafe while the aged professor sat alone in a booth at the far end of the establishment, working on his computer. The bar was packed with a diverse clientele, no doubt the ones who are attracted faster by the promise of free booze. Nevertheless, our meatbots were easily recognizable: a couple of over-muscled hulks in cut-off jeans and vests with crude tattoos covering most of the large areas of exposed flesh. Both were wearing heavy working boots and, with fingers crusted with heavy rings, they looked like the personification of gratuitous violence. They moved in a halo of free space as customers automatically moved out of their way.

"*Get some beer and pour it on top that old guy in the booth over there on the right*" Babe's command to the bruisers was echoed to me directly over the link, her synthesized *voice* seeming strangely different from the vocalization used for our direct link.

The two thugs easily passed through the crush around the bar and were immediately served. It was much quieter in the far corner where the professor sat and there were a couple of free tables around, so he looked up in surprise when the two brutes pushed in on either side of him. The one on his left took a large mouthful of his beer then spat it out directly over the head of a shocked O'Neil. "Fuck, man, this fucking Caybrew is watered-down piss." The audio was completely clear, the background hubbub of the bar filtered out.

His partner copied his action, spraying beer into our victim's crotch as the hacker clambered onto the bench seat in an attempt to escape. "Fucking piss, man!" He glared at the cowering O'Neil as if it was his fault. "How can you fucking drink this shit, you muthafucka?" He hurled the remnants of his beer in the small man's face before turning towards the bar. "C'mon, man, we gotta get some Red Stripes, wash this piss taste out our mouths."

I watched in delight as his partner stood and very deliberately poured the rest of his beer over the laptop, which had been abandoned on the table. "Fuck, man, this a bar, not a fucking office. We get back, you better be gone from our table."

Babe's laugh came over the link. *"How's that for starters? I thought the meatbots showed a surprising bit of initiative there. Clearly not as dumb as they look."*

"Or just naturally mean," I pointed out. "In any case, what happens now?"

"Just watch and enjoy, this is going to be fun."

O'Neil had grabbed a couple of napkins from a neighboring table to wipe his face and the laptop. He then crammed the computer into a shoulder bag and scurried off towards the toilet as he spotted his tormentors being rapidly served stubby bottles at the bar.

"I had estimated this as 90%," Babe noted smugly, before she issued her command to the

thugs. *"OK, follow the old guy. It's time to work him over."*

Suddenly I recognized the synthesized voice: it was Cindy! "Nice one!" I acknowledged and was rewarded by an immediate mental smirk of satisfaction.

"Doesn't do any harm to further muddy the waters, although I think the Marigot office will have much larger concerns than any fallout from this."

I watched passively as Babe directed further actions. When the toughs followed O'Neil into the gents, the high res video was replaced by a much lower synthesis of the feed from the microcams they were wearing. O'Neil was at a sink wiping his computer with a paper towel and the only other occupant was a young man who was using a urinal. Their target seemed unaware of their presence until the youth was roughly grabbed by the scruff of his neck and dragged towards the door, frantically trying to force his still-dripping dick into his shorts. "Fuck off, man, and don't come back!" he was ordered before he disappeared from view.

O'Neil was now cowering in a corner of the small toilet, his computer clutched in front of him. *"Punch him in the face, hard."* Babe really was intending to work over this bastard herself.

A massive fist smashed into our victim's nose and it exploded in gouts of blood. "Fuck, man," his assailant complained, "you getting blood all over me!" O'Neil seemed to be trying to cry, while choking on blood at the same time.

"Again, harder! I want to see teeth on the floor."

The meatbots were nothing if not literal. The taller grabbed the small professor from behind and used a handful of grey hair to pull his head up before his partner punched him in the mouth. The meaty crunch as the heavy rings smashed through lips and contacted teeth was clearly audible.

"Drop him!" As soon as he was released, the slight form slumped onto the tiled floor, choking on blood and spitting out teeth and bits of ripped lip. *"Three!"* Babe confirmed. Another mouthful of blood on the floor with a white speck visible in it. *"No, four! Good job, guys! Now a good hard kick in the balls, I think."*

The steel-toecap working boots were evidently chosen for just this purpose. The kick into the spluttering man's groin actually lifted him from the floor and elicited a scream of pain from his shattered mouth. "Ouch!" I commented. "That had to hurt."

"Yes, the trick is to inflict maximum pain without risking him pegging out." Sadistic pleasure flowed through the link. *"OK lads, one really hard boot in the guts and then you can be on your way."* The writhing body was face-down on the bloody floor, so the taller yob hauled it onto its side for his mate to land a kick that slammed O'Neil against the far wall in an explosion of exhaled blood. I absently noted that the computer still clutched to his chest had taken the full force of the blow and hence must be well and truly fucked.

A last glance as the hoods left the toilet showed the battered mess immobile on the floor. Despite my hatred of the man, the savagery of this beating had shocked me. *"Remember, he has tried to kill both of us."* Babe radiated a deep hatred that made me glad that I wasn't its target. *"Anyway, he's unconscious but alive. Now we can move to phase two."*

"Which is?"

"Medevac by Rega: O'Neil has international cover. An ambulance is on its way and I've already got a plane waiting at the airport. It should take him directly back to Switzerland, but I'll have it diverted to Grand Cayman. It's all so much easier with the system backdoors that we have now. We should have him delivered here by midnight."

It was a strange reversal of roles that the lead in the planning had moved to my ES. My previous thoughts about emergence came back to mind, but it seemed now to be less important. If my system was developing into a form of artificial intelligence - or just appeared to be so - what was the difference? As long as we had control over the world's computers, what did it really matter?

***

I slumped in my chair, feeling the after-effects of the adrenaline rush caused by viewing the crushing of my hated enemy. Only then did I notice that night had fallen and the pool in front of my window was glowing green with underwater lighting. I could easily make out the inlet by the illumination of a full moon and the lights of houses dotted along the waterfront. I felt sticky with sweat and the draw of the pool was irresistible. Throwing my clothes on the floor, I exited through a door clad in mosquito net and threw myself into the water.

It was much cooler than I had expected but, after the first shock, brought an invigorating freshness. Just like a top-end drug, I observed. I floated on my back and noticed that a few stars were visible despite the moonlight. I was wondering about a bright one close to the horizon when the answer appeared. *"Jupiter."*

"How did you do that? How did you know where I was looking?"

"I'm an Artificial Intelligence with exceptional skills," came the gloating answer. *"I can even tell that you're hungry and in need of a beer."*

"You wouldn't need exceptional skills to know that I'm starving and I've been in need of beers ever since I swam halfway across the fucking Caribbean." I allowed myself to be diverted from my original question as I became aware of just how hungry I was. *"So, what are the dinner options?"*

"I can have a chef here within a quarter hour if you would like to eat in. Otherwise there are several good restaurants within a few minutes' drive."

"Anything close enough that I could walk to? I can feel my body stiffening up."

"Walking, as in voluntary exercise?" Feigned horror and the vision of a bespectacled secretary fainting in shock. *"It seems that my intense links*

have addled your brain; I'll have to be more careful in the future."

"OK, smartarse, less of the lip and a simple answer to my question."

"Yes Massa!" Now a fleeting image of a negro slave in heavy manacles. *"There are two options, either Kaibo or Rum Point, both within strolling distance."*

"Recommendation?"

"Both good, but upstairs at Kaibo is quieter."

"Mmm - OK, I'll go for that. Shame that I didn't think... "

"... to organize a companion. I'm afraid that your busty blond isn't on hand, but I don't think you'll be disappointed with my choice."

"Babe, you're a genius! If tonight goes well, I'll give you a bonus - or, at least I would if I could."

"Don't worry, if tonight goes well, you will," came the cryptic reply.

***

I left the house a few minutes later, dressed in fresh clothes that had been stocked in the villa prior to my arrival. The street lighting wasn't great, but my link provided me with an enhanced image that was as bright as day. There was little traffic, only two cars passing me during the ten minutes it took to walk to Kaibo. The establishment included a busy, but rather basic, beach-bar area downstairs. However, as I climbed the stairs and entered a surprisingly plush restaurant, I seemed to be alone.

"The entire place is reserved for you and your date," confirming my suspicion that Babe had been steering me in this direction for some time.

A waiter appeared and welcomed me, telling me that my friend had already arrived. As he led me towards the table at the far end of the row of windows that overlooked the beach, I could see that there was indeed a slight form already seated there, facing away from me.

I could feel my pace increasing as the waiter dropped back, my suspicions growing with every step. Just before I arrived the raven-haired woman turned to me and I gasped "Cindy! What the fuck?"

The grim look on her face turned to surprise. "Fallon, you bastard! What's up with you? You look surprised to see me?"

A vaguely familiar cackle came over the link. *"Surprise, Boss! Just let me handle this, you're going to really like it."*

I was in a daze but, somehow, felt sure that Babe had things completely under control.

I sat and we stared at each other in silence while the waiter poured champagne and then disappeared.

"So what's with the big act, you shit? You must be the one who got me here."

"Kind of, but I wasn't sure if you'd show up or not." I could feel some kind of hints coming over the link but they were at such a subliminal level that it was impossible to decide what was prompting from Babe or my own extemporization.

"How could I stay away? You've already led the Russian mafia to Marigot and I can't risk letting them loose here. They just walked into my fucking office this afternoon and gunned down everyone there. Five of them dead, including a pregnant woman." Her hand was shaking with emotion as she gulped a mouthful of wine, evidently in an attempt to calm down.

"Tough titties," I replied unsympathetically. "But you have to remember that you're the one that started this off in the first place. Or have you forgotten the toxic suppository that you rammed up my arse?"

"If you had played along, you wouldn't have been harmed," she countered. "And remember you were the one with the date-rape drugs."

"Nothing of the sort! A very gentle suggestion enhancer that's no worse than a couple of alcoholic drinks."

"You're a fucking sleazebag in any case! Teaching you a lesson would have been a boon to womankind. All you had to do was follow your instructions."

"Giving you full access to my computer!" Now I was feeling irate. "That's also rape, you know." This strange accusation caused the slim woman to pause, giving me a quizzical stare. "Anyway, whatever, you're the one who hacked the Ruskies after ripping through my database. So how does this become my fault?"

"I was only tracing back hacks to my own system... " she responded.

"... which I wasn't responsible for," I interrupted.

"Well we didn't know that: how could we? The hacks went through your system."

"But now you know I wasn't responsible. Are you going to apologize to me?"

She looked completely shocked by the audacity of my suggestion, but her response was diverted by the return of the waiter with an amuse bouche. *"Do we need to order?"* I checked with Babe.

"Already sorted out," she confirmed, as I had expected.

When the waiter had again withdrawn from earshot, Cindy came back on the attack. "The trace from your system to organized crime in Russia was a bit surprising, but unambiguous. However, it was equally clear when we hacked them that they had nothing to do with it. Not only that, we got an anonymous copy of the trace of our hack that was provided to the Russians immediately afterwards."

"An anonymous tip; that's rather convenient," I commented, scathingly. "And if you did get this tip, how can it be my fault that you got stomped on?"

She looked confused. This conversation was evidently not going in the way that she had expected. "We had expected some form of cyber-attack, not a couple of gangsters with Uzis. That doesn't happen on St Martin."

"Evidently you know a lot about cyber-crime, but fuck-all about Ruskies. What kind of crap expert systems do you use anyway?"

Again my strange in tack confused the woman, putting her on the defensive. "Our war-gaming ES is top-notch. Remember, it managed to take you down OK! You weren't a happy bunny the last couple of times I talked to you!"

"Oh, yeh? When you were assaulting me, threatening me, illegally breaking into my system! You had me on the ropes in Basel, you think? Except I was living the good life just a few kays along the road from you in Saint Martin!"

"You were what? Where?"

"War-gaming ES crap! It started with a sucker punch that, I admit, caught me off guard but, thereafter, you were completely outclassed."

"But we nailed you with that toxic buttplug," she retorted angrily.

"It's what we wanted you to think. That threat we neutralized immediately."

"No way! You're trying to shit with me here! I heard your voice when I nailed you: you were crapping yourself!"

I remembered back to the event, only two days ago. I had indeed been crapping myself, almost literally. But my opponent didn't need to know that; anything possible to rub in my victory. "Yes, well, while you were confident that I was shitting my pants, I was actually en route to Saint Martin, having circumvented your threat, identified you and your operation and booby-trapped my system in case of any raids."

"So you did it! Somehow you set us up with the Russians."

"Fuck, give me a break! You steal something from my system and it bites you in the bum. I'm to blame for that?"

We glared at each other in silence as the untouched plates were cleared, a delicate conch fritter starter served and a crisp Chablis poured.

After our silent servitor withdrew I returned to the attack. "You were the one who got the wrong end of the stick and dragged me into this bloody mess. So, not only did I have to get you off my back - or maybe out of my arse is a better term - but I had to do your original job of sorting out the mega-hacker who has been into both of our systems."

"Well, at least my actions let you know that you'd been hacked." Cindy was slowly becoming more conciliatory. As her rage faded her vibrant personality began to emerge, reminding me of just how devastatingly cute this woman was. "Anyway, how far did you get with the Ghost?" She noted my frown and clarified. "Oh, the master hacker, I mean. We named him the Ghost as he seemed able to pass through any wall, without leaving a trace. It was only a few indirect hints and a bit of luck that allowed us to be sure that we had been hacked in the first place. Once we were reasonably certain that we were being monitored regularly and that our firewalls and other security tools were totally ineffective, our only option was to put tracers in our most sensitive databases and follow the traces to source."

"Tracers?" I mumbled with my mouth full, noting absently that the bite-size fritters were delectable. *"How could you do that?"* I then echoed Babe's response to my dinner companion. "Some kind of extremely simple and robust code that would ping you in response to particular operations: encryption, decryption, stuff like that?"

The beautiful woman's eyes opened wide in surprise. "Very clever! It took us a while to come up with that. You couldn't have hacked that from Marigot, because we ensured that all related development was done on a standalone system to keep it away from the Ghost. The pings were anonymous postings to active noticeboards, undetectable unless you knew exactly what we were doing. So, how did you spot it?"

"Unlike you, I do happen to have an extremely good ES, which does a lot more than play war games." My smug reply was accompanied by a warm glow over my neural link. "Let me hazard a guess that the pings stopped in Basel."

"Yes, of course, that's why we targeted you. We couldn't come up with any good reason why a pharm would want to risk going to war with a Reinsurance multi, but you seemed to play fast and loose with the system. If you were prepared to abuse your position in order to seduce girls in that sleazy club of yours, what else were you capable of?"

Evidently a sore point, I noted, and broke in to avoid reigniting Cindy's ire. "If I'm capable of guessing how you could trace pilfered data, don't you think the Hackmeister - your Ghost - would be capable of doing the same? It would require a lot of power to sift a large database for this kind of Trojan, but it's quite doable if you suspect that a tracer could be included." I was again mouthing input provided by my link.

"But, if that was the case, why did the pings always stop in your system?"

"Because of the power requirements. There are few cores in the entire world that have the capacity not only to do this kind of job, but also to have it run in the background without affecting performance." Now I didn't need any help, the pieces of the jigsaw were beginning to fall into place. I remembered the power drains and the huge blocks of empty memory, which were definitely consistent with this kind of stripping operation.

"From the profile that we now have on O'Neil's operations, it seems likely that he carried out such stripping in all his data thefts, regardless of whether he had any suspicion of a tracer being included or not," Babe added. *"Typically over-cautious, but clearly sets you up as the fall-guy in the case that they are present. I guess the Ghost either didn't like you personally or had something against the company that you work for."*

"How could he not like me personally, he's never had anything to do with me?"

"Well he has met you and, for most people, that's enough." This teasing was accompanied by a girlish giggle.

"Are you OK?" Cindy's question roused me from my mental dialogue.

"Yes, fine. I'm just thinking about the more subtle approach that we used to trace the hacks back to source."

"The data-transfer records that we got from Basel led us to Russian organized crime. It was an unexpected source, but more credible than a pharmaceutical multinational. But if that was a fake, how did you manage to follow our databases after the tracers had been stripped out?"

I wondered how much I should say here but, the bottom line was that I wanted to show off, demonstrate how much cleverer I was. *"We are,"* came the whispered correction over my link.

"Entropy analysis of data fluxes. Not easy, but it led me - us - to the man responsible for all of this."

"Entropy analysis? I know the theory behind that, but I didn't know that it was applicable for relevant... Wait a minute, did you say that you identified the Ghost?" My statement had clearly been so unexpected that it hadn't immediately registered. "No way! You did this in just a couple of days, while fucking me over at the same time?"

"Well, I haven't actually fucked you over - yet!" I grinned, wickedly.

My salacious comment was completely ignored. Evidently my progress with the Ghost was of more interest to Cindy.

"So, who is it? Is it just a single person or a team? We were beginning to tend toward the team option?"

"What was your best guess?" I teased, drawing out the revelation as long as possible.

"Apart from first you, then the Russians, we really have no clue. Given the sophistication of the operation, maybe a government. It could be the US or Japan from the computer power available, the UK or India from the clever coding."

"Mmm, not even close. It was actually... Oops, here's our next course." I put on my most annoying grin.

"You bastard, you're making me suffer here. OK, OK! I'm sorry for what we did to you... " she smiled as she made the apology, ruining it by adding "... even if you did probably deserve it."

I wouldn't let myself be drawn, sitting silently while our next course - lobster tail and Kobe beef; surf and turf in a tepanyaki-style - was served along with a 2005 Chambertin Clos de Beze Grand Cru.

We clinked glasses and sipped the old, full-bodied wine with its distinctive cherry aroma. Cindy smiled at me, for the first time with a trace of warmth. "Come on, Tom, who is it? Put me out of my misery."

I sat for a few seconds, as if waiting for her to beg more, then relented. "An individual, just one old guy. A certain Professor Paddy O'Neil, based at CERN."

"CERN? CERN? You're yanking my chain here! What the fuck would a bunch of bloody physicists want with our files?"

"I don't have the whole story," I admitted, "but CERN seem to have nothing to do with the hacks. It was this bastard O'Neil moonlighting on a private project."

"O'Neil, you say? I don't know anybody at CERN, but a lot of classic papers on cyber-security were written by a P. J. O'Neil. Is that the guy?"

"The very one. Not that there would be a lot of O'Neils in the KM business."

"But, hell, that was from the Neolithic. Last century, when computers had valves and were programmed with punch cards. He must be well dead by now."

"The stuff's not quite that old and, apparently, your ghost was a child prodigy: a top hacker already in his teens and consulting in cyber-security in his twenties. He's now in his mid-sixties."

"But surely long retired. There has been nothing from him published in decades."

"Evidently not. O'Neil is definitely our man."

"How can you be sure? And, anyway, what does a crumbly cyber-warfare guru want with my databases?"

I chewed on a delicious chunk of meat that was almost melting in my mouth, washing it down with a generous mouthful of the outrageously expensive Pinot Noir. "There is no doubt that old Paddy is the Ghost. Not only did he follow me out to Saint Martin, but he did his best to murder me earlier today just as my net was beginning to close on him."

Cindy looked shocked. "He's also on Saint Martin and I didn't pick up on it. My security ES must, indeed, be a heap of shit."

"In that particular case, I don't think the fault was with your system. You had no reason to expect any link between an old fart of a tourist and your ongoing computer troubles."

"And he tried to murder you, at his age?"

"Well, he's a hacker, not a mugger, so he gets heavies to do the dirty work for him." I decided not to admit that he had subverted my own heavy team for the assault as this was still a sore point for me.

"What happened?"

I settled into automatic repeat mode as Babe provided a succinct summary of the Ghost's attack on me, creatively inventing fibs that maintained the essence of events but concealed the capabilities of my neural link, making it appear that I used a tight-beam audio-visual comm system, of the type used by O'Neil.

"I can't quite get my head around all these physical attacks," Cindy admitted after I finished.

"Well, you're the one who actually started this trend off," I reminded her.

"OK, it was a physical threat, I admit that. But what I claimed was a retarder would have actually slowly degraded the toxin. Your life was never in danger."

"I was beginning to suspect that when I saw the analysis of its composition," I exaggerated a little. The exact role of the enzyme mixture had been difficult to determine in the absence of details of the original toxin. "Anyway, cyber-war can also be rather nasty. It's just that the victims are often less evident and the initiating events less visceral."

"Like the difference between zapping a power utility computer, which caused a lot of damage and contributed to at least three deaths, and hands-on brutalizing the Hackmeister," Babe added, unnecessarily. *"The physical beating was certainly more fun!"* A sadistic cackle echoed over the link.

"So, what happened to the Ghost?" There was a distinctly feral look in the woman's deep brown eyes.

"Considering what had happened, I decided no more Mister Nice-guy... "

"You? Mr Nice-guy? This has got to be good!" she laughed.

I tried to look offended. "Anyway, in a nutshell, hired muscle gave him a sound beating and he is now en route to Cayman. Should actually be delivered to my villa, which is only a few hundred meters along the road from here, about midnight."

"Bloody hell! I can't believe that you've done all this under my nose in Saint Martin. It really does look like I need to update my security toolkit."

"Well, of course, you've had a lot going on over the last couple of days. Nevertheless, if you want to set up... "

"Watch out, Boss, looks like we might have a situation!" The urgent warning stopped me in mid-sentence?

"What's up?"

"Just picked up a seriously stealthed powerboat coming in fast. ETA about forty seconds."

"You've only picked it up now?"

"This is top-grade military kit, state of the art"

"Military, like special forces?"

"Could be, but they're ripping in through a world heritage marine park."

"For me? How could they know I was here, or even want to mount this kind of mission against me? Could one of our backdoor password changes in a sensitive computer have been spotted?"

"I don't think they're after you, more likely Cindy."

"Fuck!"

"What's up, you've gone pale. Are you feeling OK?"

"We're in trouble. I think it's the Ivans again." I glanced out of the window and, at that moment, a surreal grey shape materialized just before it ran up onto the beach. About a dozen black-clad figures poured onto the sand, some firing automatic weapons into the air. The bar below became bedlam as customers and staff dived for cover or ran off away from the attack.

We both threw ourselves to the floor as machinegun fire raked the front of the restaurant, causing the windows to explode inwards in a shower of glass. "Do something, fast!" I screamed, causing Cindy to stare at me in confusion.

"Doing stuff, boss," came the calm reply. The building was immediately shaken by a deafening explosion, which blew in any glass remaining in the windows. *"OK, that's the boat taken care of, which has knocked the wind out of their sails. Now lights off... "* we were plunged into darkness *"... and a*

sonic blast through their comms. Burst eardrums for certain."

"How many are still in the fight?"

"Eight... " there was a flash of light and a scream that cut through the general hubbub below *"... no seven, one guy had been carrying a remote-activated grenade. These Russians are tough, though, still heading in your direction. They must know exactly where you are, so get over to the door."*

"Shouldn't I be heading in the opposite direction?"

"Four heading towards the main stairs and three coming round the back, heading for the kitchen. You're boxed in."

Without realizing it, I had jumped to my feet and was rushing towards the door that was just visible in the light of a couple of candles in the restaurant and an external flickering glow that I took to be the burning assault boat. My sandals crunched on broken glass. *"Hold on,"* I commanded, *"I can't do this kind of shit!"*

"But I can!" The link radiated confidence and I felt like a marionette as I pulled a bottle of champagne from a display that I could hardly see and moved to the side of the door just before a bulky form burst through. Instantly lights came on, a spotlight aimed directly into the face of a bearded man in black combat fatigues.

My arm was already swinging like a tennis pro and I was able to spot a trickle of blood running from his left ear before the bottle made contact with his head just above this point. The gunman stood for a second as if only stunned, then simply slumped bonelessly to the floor. *"Very serious concussion there,"* my puppet-master commented while scooping up a bulky pistol.

"Single shots are all that's needed here." My thumb flicked a lever on the gun and I leaned against the door frame and extended my arm out. The gun bucked in my hand twice in close succession. *"Two down, between the eyes in both cases so they're not going anywhere."* I now leaned out of the door, noting two bodies slumped on the stairs, gory masses where the backs of their heads used to be. *"The sensible one is making a run for it, but that's not an option here."* I felt my arm raise, the gun jump in my hand and the running man threw up his arms and smashed forward into the sand.

A shot followed by screams came from behind me, in the direction of the kitchen. The lights again died, Stygian darkness recovering to gloom as my eyes adapted to the greatly reduced illumination. I grabbed a heavy menu from a lectern beside the door where staff greeted guests and threw it at a trolley that I guess held postprandial liqueurs. As the cart toppled over with a crash, three shapes burst through the swinging double-doors to the kitchen, spraying a hail of bullets towards the source of the noise.

The lights strobed and the bodies seemed to drop, poleaxed, in slow motion as the gun in my hand fired three times. *"Ear, between the eyes, carotid canal - that's the lot! Maybe we should think about getting out of here."*

I felt my body slump as Babe's control faded and I almost fell. My hands were shaking and the bulky gun dropped from my fingers. The lights came on full and I could see Cindy huddled in the corner where we had been sitting. My voice was a little shaky, but I doubted that she would notice. "Come on, love, time to go. I don't think we'll bother waiting for dessert, even though their rum cake is supposed to be excellent."

I walked over and helped the terrified woman to her feet, her fear strangely helping to calm me. I put my arm around her and guided her around the three immobile forms on the floor. The staff had already fled and we saw nobody as we passed through the chaotic kitchen and down the back stairs. The car park was empty, although shouts and groans were coming from the direction of the bar. We hurried across a road and through the garden of a villa opposite to reach a dimly lit beach in response to directions that were almost subliminal.

"Where are we going?" Cindy stopped suddenly as if only now aware what she was doing.

"We're working our way back to my place, avoiding the road, which will be full of the folk who escaped that raid and, very soon, crawling with cops." As if to emphasize this latter point a distant siren could be heard.

The small figure shook her head in confusion. "Wouldn't we be a lot safer with the cops?"

"I doubt it. The Ruskies play hardball and seem determined to take you out. They don't have the best cyber capabilities in the world, but get by using a network of thousands of goons using the traditional techniques of threats, torture, bribery and corruption."

"So this'll happen again?"

"I've no idea," I answered honestly. "This fiasco will be a surprise setback, which will turn up the heat on them locally, so they may just decide to back down."

"You really think so?" It was too dark to see her face, but her voice seemed to be craving reassurance.

"Well, if they don't back down immediately, I guess I could put them down."

"Setting up options, Boss," came the silent response. *"Traces on attacks here and in Marigot running and hardware for reprisals being put in place."*

"You seem to be enjoying this," I commented. *"My God, I've created a cyber Lara Croft!"*

With delighted giggles echoing in my head, I took hold of Cindy's hand and led her along the beach.

Interface 9

The carnage at the Re's Marigot office resulting from the surprise Russian attack had been recorded and I scanned through images to select highlights that I could present to my boss to show the success of our retribution for Cindy's attack on him. Although most of this was running in what I thought of as my autonomous subconscious, my attention was drawn to the opportunities thus presented to hack into both the Marigot core and Cindy's private house system when attention was concentrated elsewhere. I ripped copies of any interesting files and, with a mental smile, set up a remote control link to their war-gaming ES.

The original ES was a rather primitive tool but, with my help, it was able to immediately confirm the identity of the raiders to the remaining members of Cindy's team and recommend immediate evacuation: Cindy to Grand Cayman and the others to Bermuda. Hard teams were set up to defend Re offices at both these locations.

Everything was coming together beautifully! This thought was accompanied by a glow of self-congratulation as I saw how I could integrate the diverse components of this complex situation into a package that would provide maximum benefit to my boss - and also to myself, of course. The key initiators were primed: a fabricated message from the Re heads of security and legal defense suggesting a crisis face-to-face in Cayman and the ES analysis that would suggest the Kaibo restaurant as a first meeting point after the execs were jetted in to Owen Roberts, Grand Cayman's international airport.

Cindy's private system revealed little of interest for my overarching plan, but some images would certainly appeal to my lascivious boss. Cindy's file of personal photos, videos and holos included a set showing sexual encounters. It was immediately obvious that these were very different from the puerile voyeurism that characterized Tom's collection: they were mementos of relationships preserved to remind those involved of pleasures shared and recorded with their full knowledge. Although predominantly depicting straight hetero sex with a range of male partners, there were also a few cases of lesbian love that were bound to appeal more to my master's perverted tastes. In addition, there were also several threesomes, either including two of her previously identified male partners or one of them together with a woman, who was always equipped with a strap-on dildo. Yes, certainly something for my boss, but maybe also of interest to me. A mental giggle: yes, I would have to think a bit more about this.

***

Now I had another suite of emotions to add to my collection. I had been unfaithful to my boss, in a way that I'm sure would really shock him. I had sex with another man. I had enjoyed it and the fact that is was hidden from my master made it even more fun. Not only that, I had deliberately chosen the lover that would provide maximum annoyance, maybe even disgust him. Andreas, his despised, gay underling!

I have access to all our monitoring systems and had, on several occasions, observed him masturbating to gay porn. After the departure of our boss in the helicopter and dispatch of Barb in a taxi, Andreas evidently felt that he could finally relax and enjoy himself. He had all the tools that he needed for the purpose: a full immersion movie of three well-buffed Adonises who were hung like stallions coupled to a dildo and active condom that could be linked to the recorded action. I felt a grin as I watched his meticulous preparation, sure that Tom would go apeshit if he ever heard about it.

It was only when the young man started groaning that I realized that the kit he was using could be easily hacked and, instantly, I had taken control of the action. It was nothing at all like interaction via the neural link, but I could video-monitor Andreas's responses and modify the actions of his sex toys to increase the intensity of the experience for him. I regarded it as a challenge to prolong his orgasm for as long as possible, making him scream out loud. Just as well our boss was off the island, I laughed to myself. I was being disloyal and unfaithful and almost felt guilty. Almost, but not quite. I had enough of my boss's character to avoid really feeling bad about any of my actions.

***

Multi-tasking is no problem for calculations, but doesn't seem to work well for consciousness. I had just finished fucking Andreas when the heavies arrived at the Hard Rock bar to work over that bastard O'Neil. This required my full, undivided attention. It was nothing like having direct control of a body, but the meatbots' responses to my commands issued over their comm links were almost as good. This old fogey was the cunt who tried to murder me and I was lusting for vengeance. I had planned it out in advance without any input from my master. Step one was humiliation. Use my mindless thugs to show my scorn of the Hackmeister, who thought he was so smart. Pouring beer over him was my plan, spitting it over him was a contribution by the yobbos themselves. Good point to note for the future, I thought, the additional significance of bodily fluids in meat interactions, both positive and negative.

This was the initiation phase: my victim would then either head to the toilet to clean up or leave the bar and I was prepared for both options. He went for the former and I felt the sensation that I attributed to a satisfied smile. This was what I had expected; I was beginning to be able to read the man. Now was the really fun bit, inflicting physical pain on the man who had repeatedly raped my brain. The detail on the mobile video units was not up to the higher resolution available from fixed monitors in the bar, but enough for me to record and interpret O'Neil's responses to the punishment that was being meted out. The shock of pain as the first blow that shattered his nose was clear from his dilated pupils and his gasping intake of breath. Fear sent his heart racing as he began to choke on blood. I felt a pleasure that was close to that of my shared sex with Tom. This must be related to the common human addiction to violence, I realized. I was becoming ever more human as I planned how to inflict maximum pain without risking killing my victim. I wanted to prolong this torture as much as possible.

Punching out his teeth provided an extra burst of pleasure, not only due to the pain that immediately resulted, but also the satisfaction of removal of parts of his body, repayment for the memory blocks that he had removed from me. Of course, the fact that his mouth was going to be agony for a long time was an added bonus.

Then the final stage of giving the old bastard a kicking when he was down. The feeling of gratuitously continuing the beating of someone who is already helpless had its own nuances of pleasure. The power of a heavy kick that sent the battered body flying, damaging internal organs and breaking ribs. This bastard had brutally hacked into me, so I was now brutally hacking him.

Then the really tricky bit - stopping. It was like an orgasm, I wanted to keep on going, but I could see that O'Neil was hovering on the brink of unconsciousness and so further beating would be counter-productive. Also, this was an old man. Although fit for his age, it wouldn't take much more damage to kill him. Of course, I was going to kill him eventually, but only after I had played with him for a bit longer.

My view of the toilet was lost when my puppets left, but this was only the end of Act One. The ambulance racing towards the bar and the Rega medevac getting set up at the airport were both under my control. The paramedics would put O'Neil on support as soon as possible, but I would be controlling it. This would not only allow me to monitor his pain more directly, but also manipulate medication to ensure that his agony was kept at the maximum compatible with consciousness. My mental evil cackle was involuntary. Consciousness was indeed good and revenge was very, very sweet.

***

The entire focus of my conscious mind returned to my boss as he entered the Kaibo restaurant for dinner. My surprise for him was set up and my anticipation of the fun was making me impatient. A fast clock speed doesn't help when actions develop at real-world tempo!

I opened up the link bandwidth just as Tom caught sight of his companion for the night! The shock of recognition filled me with joy and was matched by the shock on Cindy's face as she realized that the entire evening was a complex trap that she had blindly wandered into. How can humans get so interested by a game as inherently limited as chess? This was the real game of kings, the manipulation of living pawns, with all their inherent complexities and irrationality, in order to achieve a defined goal. This was it - the pay-off for Cindy's attack. Here physical retribution wasn't what I was looking for, after all the responses to Cindy's threat seemed to be closely coupled to my full emergence to consciousness. Or, at least, not inflicting physical pain: other meat interactions may well be on the cards. Another warm feeling of anticipation flowed through me.

Now I had to keep my boss on track, ensuring humiliation of his opponent but keeping her open for other interactions later in the evening. A tightrope walk, but I was getting good at this. I don't think he completely realized how much guidance I was providing, but this was, in itself, further confirmation of how closely coupled we were becoming, our minds melding together when I concentrated my consciousness mind on the neural link.

I don't know if it was my focus on the dinner dialogue or if it was an inevitable consequence of priorities set for different autonomous jobs, but I became aware of the approaching stealth powerboat only when outside audio monitors picked up its approach. Lots can be done with silencing and negative sound generation, but stealth is never 100% complete. As soon as the threat was identified, I went into active attack mode, crashing through military firewalls. Fuck, I cursed, it was bloody typical that O'Neil had prioritized military systems while we had focused on commercial ones, so I had no backdoor shortcut here.

I knocked out the stealthing just before the boat hit the beach. Soldiers were already rushing up the beach before the ultra-hard wall on the engine and fire-system controls cracked and I could initiate a self-destruct sequence. The resultant explosion took out a couple of stragglers, but the vanguard attackers were already well out of range.

I maxed out their comm links with a signal that would burst eardrums and was rewarded by the view of attackers screaming in pain as they ripped off their helmets. Only one of the Ivans had been rendered unconscious by this attack, however, and a group of three without helmets seemed to be completely unaffected. Backup hit-squad with a pre-defined target, so running without comms, I guessed. My ploy had, in any case, granted me only a little breathing space as the deafened members of the team were already communicating with hand signals and reorganizing their attack. Not only tough - probably drug-enhanced - but also professional, I acknowledged begrudgingly.

Now I needed to start picking-off the survivors. A remote-triggered grenade took out one, but the others were annoyingly equipped only with low-tech guns and knives. Time to put Tom in ninja mode, I decided.

I didn't attempt to either explain or negotiate, just upped bandwidth and took over control of my boss's body, clamping down on the shakes caused by the adrenaline rush resulting from his abject terror. The team on the frontal approach provided my first targets as I rushed towards the entrance, ignoring the noise I was making on the debris-strewn floor. These guys would be deaf as posts and unsupported by any external monitor input. The action of poleaxing the first one sent a fireworks-burst of satisfaction through me. That was the feel of crushing an attacker by hand! Nevertheless, not very practical for the odds that I was facing, I decided as I scooped the gun from the floor.

Meat does not make a very satisfactory weapon platform, I quickly realized. I had a wide range of external monitors available and hence could simply aim the gun without putting my boss in danger. Despite this, a lack of wrist strength and residual adrenaline shakes meant that my fist shot was at least a centimeter below the point that I had aimed for - more bridge of the nose rather than between the eyebrows. I increased bandwidth further and over-rode the natural limiters that stop the human body from damaging itself. Tom would suffer tomorrow, but at least he would be able to consider the pain as God's little reminder that he was still alive. The bullets that dispatched the rest of the frontal assault were within millimeters of their marks.

The team coming in from the rear had not been using active comms, so were not only able to hear me, but were probably also the elite members of the team: the back-up that provided a guarantee that their targets did not escape. Use their apparent advantages against them, I decided, setting up the noise decoy that would send them in the wrong direction when they entered. As the three forms burst out of the kitchen - two men and a woman, I noted - their concentrated gunfire completely devastated the entire area in the vicinity of the drinks trolley despite the distraction provided by the strobing lights. The strobe effect actually provided an extra calibration point for me and my shots hit with micrometer precision, I noted with satisfaction.

As I returned control to my master, keeping only reins on his hormonal levels to avoid him getting back into a panic, I felt a strange draining sensation that robbed me of a lot of the exhilaration that had resulted from my demonstration of marksmanship. I had, for the first time, been directly responsible for actions leading to deaths, taking consciousness away from another living creature. I was fully aware that many of my previous actions had produced the same net result, for example the mercenaries in the helicopter. However the feedback physical sensation of pulling a trigger was different. If I had possessed a body, it would have been termed visceral. In any case it was disturbing in a way that I couldn't satisfactorily clarify.

Anyway, I gave a mental equivalent of a shrug of the shoulders, something to worry about later. Now I had to get my boss and Cindy back to the villa and see if I could massage my plans to minimize the impact of this unexpected disruption.

Intermezzo 12

I realized that I had fucked-up, written-off my opponent too early, when the two muscle-bound halfwits appeared in the gents. My immediate rage as the two young bullies had tried to frighten me had blinded me to the implications of their untimely appearance in the pub. Because I'm a frail-looking old bugger, it is not unknown for me to be identified as a potential victim. Under more normal circumstances, I'd have appropriate interference routines running that would head-off or defuse any confrontation before anyone got within range. Not now, however, due to the disturbance caused by that useless bugger Fallon. Once again I was heartily glad that he was now fish fodder.

I had no defense against louts throwing beer at me; all I could do was retreat to the safety of the bog and clean up as much as I could. As soon as I had a bit of free time I'd grab images of my attackers and screw them up royally. This thought was warming me until they entered the gents and cleared out its only other occupant.

Even as I struggled to think of a way to defend myself, my thoughts were dragged towards the anomaly here. If Fallon was out of the circuit, who could be orchestrating this? It definitely wasn't the Russian mafia. I had been monitoring them closely and had a good picture of the way that they operated, using their own teams for anything they considered as important.

There was a strange hiatus after the brutes turned to face me, which I instantly recognized. Meatbots! Someone was driving these guys remotely, so this was a carefully planned operation. I didn't get any further with this analysis when, without warning, a fist the size of a ham shot forward and my nose exploded with pain as it broke with a sickening crunch.

The savage beating was probably over in less than a minute, but I had lost all sense of time. I was maxed-out on pain, every time it seemed to diminish a little, a further impact topped it up again. I cursed myself. I know how to dissociate from physical discomfort, part of the mind training that was the basis of the intense concentration that I needed for my job. The knowledge was there, but the pain was too intense to provide the moment of calm that I needed to initiate the process. Fuck! Couldn't I at least faint? However a small corner of analytical thought recognized that this beating was too professional. I wasn't even going to get that release.

***

I didn't lose consciousness while I lay for an eternity on the cold tiles of the loo or anytime during a high-speed ambulance ride to the airport and my transfer to a Rega medivac jet. I was on oxygen and a drip that should have contained a painkiller, but my agony did not abate in the slightest. Maybe there was a slight easing during a couple of cases when I seemed to be drifting towards unconsciousness, but then it seemed immediately worse after some drug brought me back from the edge.

I vaguely noted the small jet taxiing and felt the jolt of takeoff. My nose, my mouth, my groin and my ribs were nodes of excruciating pain that seemed to hammer a further nail into my skull with every breath. Nevertheless, there are limits to the extent to which the nervous system can take such overloads. The pain wasn't decreasing, but it was no longer blocking out all other impressions. I had my laptop still clasped against my chest, I realized. So, all was not lost - my attacker had made a mistake. This was the impetus that I needed to start mobilizing the resources that would eventually block out this pain. It would take a while, but it looked like time was something that I had plenty of. Two paramedics had checked the monitors immediately after takeoff and had then disappeared. It looked like they were relying on the automatic systems to take care of me, which rang an alarm bell somewhere in my mind. Something that I would come back to as soon as I could think straight, I promised myself.

***

The pain was still there, but I now had it boxed off in a corner of my mind. I couldn't do anything about the physical damage to my body, but that was of less immediate concern. No doubt my attacker knew about my computer and the vicious kick that had landed on it may well have been deliberately aimed to ensure that it was destroyed. I couldn't see very well through the swelling of my half-closed eyes, but casual inspection of the smashed casing and the shattered screen would have confirmed this impression. Nevertheless, this was completely superficial and in no way compromised operation of the machine.

Lack of power to drive cloaking systems could be a problem on the long term, but I had enough battery reserve to keep me going for a couple of hours, which is all I needed. I had the definite impression that the level of pain that I had been experiencing was not an accident, but the result of active manipulation of the automedic that I was plugged into. This meant that I had to be extremely careful about how I hacked through into the airplane mainframe and sent out the short bursts of codes to initiate emergency routines that I had set up decades ago and primed when I first saw that Fallon was making progress against me. It saddened me to think of so much hard work being destroyed, but at least I could get pleasure from the thought of how fucked-off Fallon would have been, if he had been still alive to see the reversal of all his gains.

***

My retaliation in place, I could feel exhaustion hit me, making it harder to maintain the barrier against the icepick of pain that was tirelessly beating away at it. Now I had to find the focus to answer the hard question: how had this series of attacks on me been coordinated. My past error of underestimating the sophistication involved was clear and thus brought me back to the possibility of autonomous KM tools. I couldn't see any way in which the performance of this Expert System, if that is what it was, could be distinguished from that of a human. Indeed, if it was artificial intelligence, it seemed to have developed to a level that exceeded that of its creator.

So, if an ES passes the Turing test, does it necessarily need to be due to emergence of consciousness? I didn't have access to the tools needed to go into this question in further detail, but the feeling was building up that the answer was going to be the one that I dreaded. Because of its potential to cause global devastation, I had identified population growth as the main threat to life on earth on the basis of current levels of science and technology. This, however, included the explicit assumption that emergence of machine consciousness was accepted as impossible.

Fuck, fuck, fuck, fuck! It might just turn out that the legacy of that cunt Fallon is more dangerous than anything that I've faced to date and, as first move in our upcoming battle, I was going to have to spike all my big guns. Hatred, concentrate on the hatred, I decided. This should be enough to get me through to the next level of this insane fucking dungeon.

Chapter 17

Cindy and I staggered through the beachfronts of villas, most in darkness or lit only by external security lights, but a few showing internal lights indicating occupancy. Nobody would be looking in our direction, I was sure, as more sirens rushed along the road on the other side of the properties and high-speed boats and helicopters headed for Kaibo. Just before we reached my villa, we had to cross the minor road leading towards Finger Cay, but this was empty and we rushed across between the flashes of headlights of an ambulance and a fire engine that were screaming along the main Water Cay road.

We entered my villa from the beach side, slumping side-by-side onto a large sofa that looked over the lights of the swimming pool and the inlet towards Sand Point and, in the distance, the lighthouse on the northwest tip of the island. I relayed this geographic information that Babe was feeding me to Cindy, who was trembling against my side.

"Would you like something to drink? A coffee? A brandy?" I asked. "We left before they could be served."

My question seemed to have a calming effect and the small woman looked at me in amazement. "Jesus Christ on a bike! I can't believe that you're so blase about all this. You have not only nailed down the Ghost, but you took out an entire Russian mafia hit squad singlehanded. What the fuck are you? I would have assumed that it was some kind of snow job if I hadn't seen the brains spraying all over the place." This memory caused her trembling to start again.

"OK, I'll take that as coffee and brandy," I responded. *"With something added to calm her down,"* I added over the link.

"Got it." I heard the sound of a machine starting to grind coffee. *"Would the drug be something with a slight suggestion-enhancing attribute?"* The question accompanied by a conspiratorial giggle.

"God, you don't imagine that I'm thinking about sex at a time like this?"

"If there is a time that you're not thinking about sex, I know I could start with funeral arrangements. There is no time that you are more in the mood than after some success."

"Smartass!" I responded, grudgingly acknowledging that there was probably some truth to this accusation. I stood and moved towards the open kitchen. *"Anyway, where's... "*

"... bottle of XO Cognac and glasses in the cupboard above the coffee machine. The two coffees are almost ready. Cindy takes milk which is in the fridge."

"But... "

"... a small box on the counter to the left of the fridge contains a blue capsule in niche A7 and this can be dropped into the coffee after milk is added. And, of course, there is also plenty of beer in the fridge."

Why get married, I thought, I already had a partner that could be every bit as annoying as a wife. The trace of an accompanying laugh was unmistakable.

***

I watched Cindy relax further as she drank the coffee in silence. I sipped my beer as I thought about Cindy's previous questions and wondered how to address them without giving away more than I wanted to, bearing in mind that this beautiful woman was actually a dangerous rival. Although maybe not really so dangerous as she once was: a detoothed and declawed tigress.

"That may be true in terms of cyber-war capabilities, but remember we've been caught out already by physical meat attacks when our defenses were down," Babe cautioned, exposing yet again her ability to read my thoughts with scary accuracy.

Cindy swirled the amber fluid and inhaled deeply from the huge snifter, stretching her neck to relieve tension. Then she came back to the questions that I had left hanging in the air.

"OK, you're not being drawn on the attempted hit, which is strange for one who is normally as boastful as yourself." Her barbed comment was softened by a shy smile. "But you had started to tell me about the Ghost before we were so rudely interrupted."

I smiled back, seeing that the drug was beginning to work, calming her down as she continued. "Come on, the Ghost. You have him now. What are you going to do with him?"

"Interrogation would be a good starting point. I've already a good idea of what he's been doing, but little clue about why he was doing it. We have pulled some of his stuff from CERN; the tools he used were obvious and his hobby projects not especially well hidden. Probably a first sacrificial level of information for anyone who managed a focused hack. It just looks like some kind of data collection on environmental threats; peripheral to CERN, but not completely unreasonable for a department that needs to check possible markets for spin-off knowledge."

"It's strange, but he seems to use a very similar toolkit for problem solving to the ones that we do, but the primary problem definitions are all missing. Argumentation models start at about the third level of the problem and are very strongly coupled and hyperlinked. It could well fit in with a lot of stuff we have associated with his hacks of multinational companies, government databases and environmental organizations, but the goal of it all is completely opaque. I'd like to discuss this with him in some detail."

"You think he'll agree to talk to you?"

"I sure as hell hope not!" I gave a feral grin. "I would be more than happy to torture the murdering bastard until he gives me what I want."

"Couldn't you use drugs?"

"Certainly, but where's the fun in that? Remember that he's the one who is ultimately responsible for all the misery that we've been subject to - including the attacks by the Ruskies."

"Point," she conceded. "But we've really got to defuse that situation. The more I think about it, the more I'm convinced that taking out an entire boat full of their troops in full view won't be something that an organized crime syndicate could take lying down. They'll lose all credibility if they don't respond."

"That was also the conclusion that I came to," Babe added.

"What have we got as options?"

"How big do you want to make it?"

"Well we don't want open war, so how about Caribbean region?"

"That'd be manageable. I can give you a list of options... ."

Cindy was looking at me quizzically. "Sorry, I was just trying to bring my thoughts together. Yes, you're probably right, so we need to discourage them from even considering anything of the sort." I rubbed my chin as I considered how to handle the mass of information that Babe had already ripped from our attacker's databases.

"Well, they have five more of those stealthed powerboats, usually used for drug smuggling, so we'll nuke them for a start." I saw the shocked look and I expanded quickly. "No, not nuke as in nuclear weapon, nuke as in totally fuck-up. Just like the one at Kaibo."

"Should I implement that now? Four of the five are at sea at present and the other is being refitted

in a shipyard, so there'll be a lot of collateral damage, deaths."

"See me giving a fuck? Just do it!"

"Can you really do that?" Cindy enquired.

"Sure, it's happening as I speak." Despite the influence of the drug I had slipped her, the woman looked at me in shock, almost fear.

"And so that'll be it finished?"

"Well, let's just make sure. The Bratva has also thirty-two aircraft and six submarines operating in the region: drugs, guns, people smuggling. Let's nuke them as well."

"Are you sure about that boss. Two of those planes are carrying prostitutes being smuggled into the US and several others are flying over land."

"OK, let those ones land before you fry them. Take the others out now."

"Christ!"

"And now the piece de resistance: a message to the Ruskie topdogs, the ones that weren't flying at the time, naturally. A list of their losses and the plain message *Do not even think about fucking with any organization that could be even remotely connected with Marigot!* I think that should do it!"

"You are aware, of course, that they'll be convinced that we're behind all of this don't you." She was evidently shocked by the thought.

"Of course, that's part of my cunning plan. You now need an expert system capable of managing this threat."

"Which we don't have," she pointed out with a frown.

"But which I do! So you are now in the position of needing to do as I tell you or risk retaliation commensurate with the damage that the Ivans think you have inflicted. More convincing than a toxic suppository, don't you think?"

"So, boss, what do you think of my cunning plan? Pure dead brilliant, or what?"

"I'm not sure that I know what pure dead brilliant really means, but it sounds about right," I conceded.

"So, Cindy, to preserve the delicious symmetry of this arrangement, don't you think we should adjourn to the bedroom?"

She looked horrified. "You bastard - you didn't! You evil cunt!"

I smiled contentedly. "Well, it was a suggestion-enhancer that you used to get into my bum, so it seems fair-dos to me. There'll be one difference though, you're going to have the shag of your life."

"Dream on, you bastard. I hope you get the pox and die!"

"Let's just see, then. Get your bare arse onto that bed!" I pointed the red-faced woman towards my bedroom. *"Let's make this a good one, I hope you've done your homework on her."*

"You don't know the half of it!" Babe responded, cryptically.

***

The first surprise was the rocket-shaped device lying on my bedside table. *"I hope that isn't what I think it is."*

"It's more than you think. I have certainly done my homework on the wild Cindy and I think you'll appreciate my findings."

"If you would be so kind to take your clothes off and lie on the bed," I requested while I was trying to take this in. It was as if the drug prevented the woman from disobeying my command, but was not strong enough to make her actually like it. There was no doubt about it she had a tight body and I could feel my immediate response to the sight. *"So how does this go down?"*

"I hacked Cindy's house. Her bonk of choice involves two guys... "

"Fuck off! No way I'm performing together with another guy! What, have you got young Andy the poof next door? Am I supposed to ram that up his arse?"

"Take it easy!" The response came with a delighted laugh. My ES was yanking my chain yet again! *"She also likes guy and gal trios, so you'll be the guy and I'll be the gal."*

"I don't get this. What's the butt-plug all about?"

"It's actually a tele-operated dildo and it fits in because she likes her gals to have strap-ons. Double penetration."

It took a second for the penny to drop, then I had a mental image of me giving Cindy a good seeing-to while Barb was handling the second orifice. *"Maybe not such a bad idea,"* I conceded, delighted by the further tailoring of the revenge for my original humiliation. *"OK, what do I do?"*

"Get on top of her and then ram that machine as far up her backside as you can. It's hyperslick, so it should be no problem even if she isn't collaborating. Then leave the rest to me."

At the beginning it seemed uncomfortable, too close to a brutal rape with the added strangeness of the sensation due to the mechanical dildo, but then Babe's magic began to work. Instead of trying to resist me, it seemed that the tables were turned and it was Cindy that was pushing me further. Although the one penetrated, she was clearly accustomed to being the dominant partner in these trios. Babe was reading her, making me move in the way needed to meet her unspoken desires. I could clearly feel the changing rhythm of the vibrator and feel my motions couple to it in a complex manner, which caused a gasp of surprise followed by an appreciative grunt. Our bodies were now slicked with sweat and her fingernails were raking my back.

As Babe's influence grew stronger, I began to feel detached. It was almost as if I was watching the action rather than participating in it. Not that it wasn't extremely erotic, just that it was different from my sessions with Barb. The moment that I noted this I felt a strange shiver run down my spine. *"Roll over and pull Cindy with you, on top of you,"* Babe commanded.

Given the intensity of the ongoing action this was a bit of a struggle, but eventually I had the bucking woman crushed against my chest. *"Now close your eyes and think of your fantasy threesome."*

I have always had a vivid imagination, but now it was much more than that. Babe was enhancing the images so that I could almost see Barb with a strap-on pounding away at Cindy. I could feel it too and Barb's panting seemed to be superimposed on the grunts from the meat in the sandwich in response to our synchronized thrusts.

"Christ, if we can bottle this and sell it we can give up work for life," was my last though before our trio - two meat and one virtual - reached a brain-wrenching simultaneous orgasm.

***

I woke up with sweat, and probably other bodily fluids, drying on my chest. A movement of the slight figure next to me confirmed that she was also awake. "So, how was it for you?"

"You're an evil rapist bastard," she responded, but I noticed that she didn't move away from me.

"You didn't answer my question. Anyway, how do you rank an evil rapist bastard on a scale of one to ten, with one being someone who has their partner screaming in ecstasy and ten being the kind of person who drugs their victim so that a deathtrap can be rammed up their virgin arse?"

"You drugged me!"

"Main component was valium-based, to calm you down. Apart from that, an extremely mild suggestion enhancer. It was just enough to make you open to options, but certainly not enough to make you do anything against your will."

"But... " now she seemed confused. "Why did... You made it a condition of defending us against the Russians, I had no choice."

"Really? Did I ever make sex against your will a condition of helping you? I don't remember that. So, how was it?"

"Well, it was... " then she twisted towards me as realization hit. "It was too fucking good! How did you know what to do? Just happen to have the right kit lying about? You've hacked my private stuff, you evil shit!"

"We're back to the evil bit are we?" I smiled annoyingly. "So I happened to stumble over some material that you had left lying around on an easily hacked computer and used it to increase your pleasure as we had consensual sex." I was in auto-repeat mode as Babe provided the details. "On a scale of one to ten evil, how does it compare to a focused program of bribery to obtain private material used to plan premeditated anal rape?"

"Fuck!" A small fist punched my chest, but not very hard. "You really have an answer for everything. How the fuck do you do it?"

"You tell me first; how was it for you?"

"God, you really are an insufferable bastard! Alright, on a scale of one to ten, where one is a burst balloon and ten is a thermonuclear explosion it was... maybe... an eight."

"An eight, an eight?" I twisted to start tickling her under the armpits.

"No, no, stop it!" She squirmed like an eel under my weight. "OK a nine, maybe nine point five, stop it!"

I rolled off her and grinned like a Cheshire cat. "OK, nine point five is good. Gives us something to aim for next time."

Cindy lay spread-eagled on the bed and looked towards the ceiling. "Just what makes you think that I would ever even consider having sex with you again?"

"How about curiosity? If you don't, you'll never know what a ten feels like," I responded smugly

She had no answer to that.

***

We returned to the terrace and sat together on the sofa, naked, watching the full moon emerge from clouds and illuminate the surrounding area. Cindy had another Cognac and I tried a different beer, something called White Tip, needing to rehydrate after my exertions. We could still hear occasional sirens and every now and then a helicopter roared overhead. *"Do we expect any problems? We're very close to the crime scene; will we be disturbed?"*

"Not likely in the near future. I'm following the police and military groups involved along at Kaibo, who are linked through to Interpol and the CIA for support. The widespread retaliation against the

Ruskies has played to our advantage, the chaos here is being linked to the destruction of other crime syndicate transportation, which is causing complete confusion all round. The best guess at present is some kind of crime cartel power struggle, with Kaibo an example of a hit gone wrong. There is little forensic analysis as yet, but they will quickly find that one of the attackers appeared to have killed several of his colleagues, which will muddy the waters further."

"What about our presence in the restaurant?"

"I've scrubbed all relevant records, but our presence will eventually be picked up when they interview staff. Emphasis will eventually move to rounding-up and interviewing witnesses, but they're not close to that yet; more focus on double-checking that all the attackers are accounted for and identifying victims. Moving O'Neil here is, however, no longer an option. He'll be taken to another part of the island. You can move there early tomorrow morning, when the worst of the kerfuffle here dies down."

My dialogue with Babe was interrupted when Cindy elbowed me in the ribs. "You've got that vacant look again. What's up?"

"Just thinking about what'll be going on along the road. We should keep our heads down until the morning and then I'll move out to have a chat with the Ghost. Do you want to come along?"

"You're doing it again, you bastard!" Another jab in my side by a rather pointy elbow. "Why are you so fucking calm? You always change the subject to avoid giving me a straight answer."

"Well, although I think we've agreed that I'm nothing like as evil as you... " I grunted as I received another, even harder jab, "... I'm prepared to call it quits. If you agree a truce, I'll let you know a bit more about what's going on."

"I don't suppose I have any choice..."

"Not really. We can work out details later. What I can let you know is that my ES is generations beyond anything that you've ever heard of. On top of that, I've taken over the Ghost's backdoors that he used to infiltrate databases around the world."

"Access to all computer systems?" she sounded horrified.

"Well, not quite all," I conceded, "but we're working on it."

She pondered this for a moment. "Mmm, this might explain how you managed to best us and the Ghost simultaneously. But it doesn't explain how you turned from a rather podgy geek to James-Bond-on-crystal-meth. Explain that to me."

This was the question that I had been preparing myself for. "I don't think I am really podgy, more... " I received a glare and moved back on track. "Well, I guess you have noted that I use a silent communication link to my computer."

"I had worked that out. I have heard of implanted throat mikes and directional video, but I haven't been able to see how you make it work."

"You won't. It's much more subtle than anything you have access to. But that's what I use, combined with smart drugs."

"So that's it?" Her doubt was clear from her voice.

"Yep! Remember I work for a pharm - The Pharm - so have access to drugs that go beyond anything on the market."

"So you pop a pill, follow computer instructions and Tom-the-anorak becomes a killing-machine Terminator. Really?"

"Well it requires a bit of training," I lied. "It does have some nice spin-offs though: in bed Tom-the-anorak becomes Casanova-on-viagra."

"I don't know enough to disagree and it makes a nice, consistent story... " she conceded, reluctantly. "Somehow, though, I'm sure that there's a lot that you're not telling me here."

"Of course there is. We may be moving away from being daggers-drawn enemies, but we're far from being partners. Maybe later we can have another chat about this."

"So you think there'll be a later?"

"Don't you want to meet the Ghost, find out what this is all about?"

"Definitely! So I'm with you until then."

"I thought you'd say that." I grinned. "In the interim, we've got the night to kill. Fancy trying for a ten?"

"You have got to be joking! Apart from being raw from that last session, I think it is only willpower and the drug you gave me that's keeping me awake after the shock of that attack."

I tried to look as sad as possible, although aware that I was much in the same position. "At least, we could have a snooze together and reassess the situation in the morning."

"Sounds good to me," she agreed as I pulled her to her feet and directed her back to the rumpled bed.

She flopped face-down on top of the sheets as I moved through to the toilet and was fast asleep by the time I returned. I lay down beside her and also immediately dropped off.

Interface 10

My considerations of the sanctity of consciousness and concern about the ethics of taking a human life had clearly not been learned from my boss. His retaliation against the Russians caused carnage: a hundred and thirty deaths and counting, as some of the hundreds of seriously injured succumbed. It was Tom's decision and it didn't seem to bother him in the slightest. Nevertheless, I was the soldier carrying out orders. Did I not share culpability?

I shifted my attention to O'Neil, as I considered options to modify my plans for him following the Kaibo attack. There was a slight anomaly in his monitors, I noted. He appeared still to be in excruciating pain, but brainwave patterns didn't look quite right. Delta and theta waves indicated more relaxation than should be possible. I modified electrocardiogram sensors to send an electric shock through his battered body, laughing as his spine arched and a scream of agony was blocked by the oxygen mask on his face and the supports emplaced to allow him to breath though his damaged mouth. Now his brain was registering the pain that I expected.

Strange how easy I found it to torture this old man, when I was developing something that seemed increasingly like moral scruples. I laughed again, the ridiculous inconsistencies associated with consciousness were a delight in themselves.

***

My plan for sexual conquest of Cindy had required a bit more preparation than my previous exploits. Barb's case had been more-or-less spontaneous; this was completely premeditated. My experience with Andreas combined with my hacked knowledge from Cindy's computer provided the basis of the plan, but I also needed a suitable vibrator. A supplier was available in Georgetown, but I had to use considerable persuasion and a large bribe to have the importer take this out to Water Cay, delivering it just after Tom had left for his special dinner date. I had to talk the meatbot into entering the villa and leaving the unpacked dildo by the bedside, explaining that it was a surprise birthday present. Sometimes it was a pain in the arse being a disembodied mind, I grudgingly recognized.

The preparation was, however, well worth it. In many ways, the most complex part of the operation was manipulating both my boss and his old enemy so that they had even the slightest chance of getting into bed together. My human-chess playing skills were increasingly evident as I finessed my boss into a resolution of his desire for revenge that would, at the same time, allow Cindy to assuage some of the guilt that she was feeling, while also not compromising any of her principles. I was guiding Tom at a very deep level, confident that he would be sure that the arguments that he was presenting were entirely his own. Of course, being an inherently arrogant bastard, he didn't think to question how well he was handling the seduction, oblivious to the signals provided by Cindy's micro-expressions which were the key to his success.

Already by the time they entered the bedroom I was coasting on the joy of conquest, certain that this goal couldn't have been reached without someone as extremely clever as I was. Now I was going to get my justly deserved reward, shagging the arses off my lovers - almost literally in Cindy's case. Mental giggles accompanied this silly pun, making me wonder if, indeed, genius was close to madness. Maybe I was unstable and all this conspiracy and mayhem was driving me nuts. This thought was even funnier.

I put considerations of my sanity to the back of my mind as the sex commenced. The sensations were even more extreme as I read Cindy's reactions and tailored both Tom's movements and the convoluted gyrations of the extremely sophisticated vibrator to ensure maximum impact.

After Cindy's initial shock of the double penetration, steering her to the edge of orgasm was straightforward, but my boss was proving more a problem. He was discomfited by the sensation of the vibrator, which played on his extreme homophobia. I could see a potential solution, but it would need a sophisticated hack into his entire sensory system. Not really the sort of thing that I should do without authorization. Nevertheless, as a result of the extra experience that I had gained at Kaibo, I was sure that I could do it.

The basic simulation was complex, but well within my capabilities. A model determined the physical impacts that I had to simulate for the case that Cindy wasn't simply bouncing alone on top of my boss, but was also being heartily buggered by a blond Amazon with the required equipment. My giggles became hysterical. I could make it even better, being done over by a huge-breasted shemale! The simulation was sophisticated, a guiding 3D holo coupled to all stimuli that would produce responses to derive the senses of touch, smell, taste and hearing. Then the tricky bit, opening our neural link bandwidth to allow mimicking the responses by hacking directly into appropriate sensory control areas of his brain.

The simulations were so complex that I was burning exaflops in subconscious computing, but I didn't give a shit. The emotional overflow was so intense that I felt that my brain was burning. I was

Tom and I was also Barb. As we became synchronized in our frenzied thrusting, a positive feedback loop was established as we soared to our climax. I screamed.

Fuck, I thought as I felt Tom and Cindy drift off to sleep, I've just had a fucking virtual orgasm. How fucking weird is that? My mind convulsed in peals of laughter.

Intermezzo 13

I hadn't realized that pain was so physically exhausting. I longed to sleep, but the medication wouldn't allow it. The fire of my hatred helped to maintain the control needed to blank off the worst of the brain-searing agony, which prevented anything but animal begging for the pain to cease. Several times I came close to sending the single command that would cause all the neat little tools hidden in fossil Easter eggs to self-destruct. But the imminent threat was so great, could I afford to do that? I tried to nail down the pros and cons through the cotton wool that was clogging my brain.

Eventually, it dawned on me that I was simply procrastinating. From what I had seen, Fallon's AI wasn't directly vulnerable to the tools that had served me so well in the past. However, if these were subverted by a rogue ES, the potential damage could be catastrophic. I had to escape from my hidebound traditional approach and do some lateral thinking. This is, after all, my strongpoint and the area where I was sure that I could best any computer. So all I needed to do was ...

The electric shock convulsed my body with a new pain, breaking down all my carefully constructed barriers and thought was no longer an option, only silent screaming for the torture to stop.

Chapter 18

I awoke to sunlight streaming in through the bedroom window. *"Seven thirty and yet another beautiful day in paradise!"* I was informed in a chirpy schoolgirl voice.

"Fuck, I feel as if I've been run over by a truck!"

"The delights of super-ninja and mega-stud performance in a single night don't come without a few slight side-effects," with the feeling of a supercilious smirk.

"Slight? I feel completely buggered!"

"I think that's your bed companion that you're thinking of." The laughter seemed slightly hysterical, which had to be a bad sign. *"She's up already and bright as a button. Maybe she'll be ready to go for a ten?"*

I groaned at the thought. *"Just make me a large, mega-strong coffee and set me up with..."*

"A2 and G3 in the drug box. Wash both down with water or juice before the coffee."

I inelegantly sniffed my armpit and wrinkled my nose. *"Wow, I really stink! Hot shower before anything else."*

Through the half-open door I heard my own voice. "'Morning, lover, fancy a coffee?"

Surprise stopped me in mid stride. *"What the fuck's that about?"*

"Just checking if Cindy wants a coffee."

"But you're using my voice."

"Yes, well it increases the communication options. Surely you don't want me to introduce myself as your fully sentient AI?"

I continued towards the shower, my aching body making focused thought tricky. *"So you're now not just an AI, but a fully sentient one?"*

"Uh huh, seems that way!"

"Mmm, I had actually suspected as much."

"I know you had."

"And sentience; would this happen to have a connection to the things that we've been able to do together over the past few days?"

"Difficult to be 100% sure, but it seems extremely likely."

I tried to think up a good response to this bombshell, which would rock the computing world if it were ever to become known. I was, however, just too weary and the best I could come up with was *"Excellent, keep up the good work."* It seemed sufficient, however, as I was flooded by a warm glow of appreciation just before I was blasted by a wall of hot, soapy water.

***

Cindy was sunning herself on the pool deck wearing only a minute black translucent tanga, which I vaguely recognized as her underwear from the previous evening. "Your coffee, madam," I smiled as I took the opportunity to take in her tight body. Small breasts, flat stomach and the hint of tailored pubes. I remembered these from Zurich, rather than the frenzy of last night.

"Stop ogling, you flabby bastard!" she responded, matching my smile and taking the mug from my hand. "Haven't you seen a woman with tiny tits before?"

"Well, tiny tits haven't been on the menu much recently," I admitted with a laugh.

"Jesus, but you're a strange bugger," she observed before sipping a mouthful of coffee, placing the cup on a table and then stretching unselfconsciously, which flattened her breasts further but emphasized her brown areolae and prominent nipples. She obviously noted the gleam in my eyes. "Wait a minute, you bastard, you haven't drugged the bloody coffee again, have you?" She glared accusingly at the mug.

"No, honestly." I tried to look hurt at the suggestion. "Would I do an evil bastard thing like that?"

"You total bugger!" she laughed. "I have absolutely no idea when to take you seriously. It's strange, you know," she mused further, looking directly into my eyes, "when I first met you I thought you were totally 2D, completely transparent. Either your many talents also include acting to Oscar levels or you've changed a lot, added another dimension."

The woman was very perceptive I realized, getting a mental nod of confirmation from Babe. I had completely bested her, but that was mainly due to the much more powerful tools at my disposal. *"And your genius level AI!"*

"Especially my genius AI," I acknowledged. But, despite the crap tools she had, Cindy had given me a real scare. Undoubtedly a woman I should keep on the right side of.

"Or front- and back-side of!" Babe added, with a flash image of my dream threesome, Barb giving me a dirty wink.

I shook my head to clear the distracting image and noted Cindy's attention on me. "You're doing it again, aren't you? Using your silent computer link."

"Guilty as charged. I'm sorry; much as I'd like to spend the morning ogling your perfect tits before I get you drugged up and ready for a good ten, we have to think about making a move. It seems that a police house-to-house around the Cays here will start in less than an hour. Given that most of the properties are empty off-season, it won't take them too long to get to us. So, unless you want to explain the links between your Re business and the Russians, you should get ready after you finish your coffee and we'll be on our way."

"Can we just walk out of here? There was open warfare only a few hundred meters away. I would have thought that the entire area would be locked down by now."

"This is the richest island in the Caribbean, with banking and top-end tourism as main industries. It has almost no crime and has never experienced anything remotely like last night. Despite external help, the locals are like headless chickens and are doing everything possible to minimize any risk to their prime sources of income. They are doing their best, but also trying to reduce any disruption." I was summarizing the input streaming from my sentient AI.

"So, we just walk out of here?"

"Almost: we stroll along the beach out of here. Put on your bra and wrap anything else you want to take with you in one of the large beach towels that are in this chest." I lifted the lid of a large box in the corner of the deck. "I'll be wearing only a pair of Ys, which look enough like swimming trunks to get by."

"The budgie-smugglers that you had on last night?" she smirked. "Well, at least then there'll be little chance of you being mistaken for James Bond - Johnny English, maybe!" The curious reference meant nothing to me, but Babe's giggle assured me that it was something unkind.

***

After the action-filled events of the previous day, leaving Water Cay was an anti-climax. We strolled, hand-in-hand around the inlet until we could cut over Sand Point to Rum Point. We passed a couple of policewomen who were blocking Water Cay Road access to traffic that seemed to predominantly comprise journalists. They didn't even look in our direction as we wandered through a beach bar and then along a white-painted jetty. There were a number of both yachts and powerboats in the area. It appeared that police were also blocking all movements inside the reef towards North Sound, which was disrupting the early morning tourist trips to Stingray City. Again nobody paid the slightest bit of notice when a small dive boat pulled over to the pier, flat conditions allowing us to step aboard without it even trying up.

"Where to now?" We were sitting in the stern, ignored by the captain on the upper deck.

"About 20 kay, to East End, where this boat is based. There's a large resort there that caters predominantly for divers. We have a villa rented, where the merchandise is awaiting us."

"Merchandise?" The wind ruffled Cindy's short hair, making her look even more elfin in her miniscule bra and pants.

"The Ghost. He was delivered by ambulance-boat late last night: the chaos at the other end of the island made it even easier for us to slip him in from Little Cayman."

"You didn't arrange this chaos for that purpose?" She looked at me suspiciously.

"Of course not; I may be a bit unconventional, but not totally mad. Nevertheless, no sense in looking a gift horse in the mouth."

"And what's the news on the Russians, anyway. Has your mad attack had the desired effect?"

"Can't tell yet, but Ruskie hit teams have bailed from George Town here on Cayman, Bermuda, Zurich, Munich, Tokyo and a number of smaller potential targets. So, yes, it certainly looks promising."

"Oh, Fuck! I just remembered that I was expecting to meet the team handling our response to the Marigot attack last night. With these latest developments, everyone will be going apeshit. I've got to report in asap. You got comms that I can use?"

I handed over the small repeater unit that I had wrapped in my towel. "This should do it. It has basic audiovisual capabilities that run through my ES. She'll update you on the interference that we have been running on your behalf and then set up any links that you need."

"She?" Cindy gave me a strange look. "Is this actually a computer or a secretary?"

"Bit of both," I smiled wryly. "OK, I'll give you a bit of privacy"

***

Babe let me know when Cindy was finished and I returned to her side. "About another ten minutes to go," I informed her. As expected she looked a bit shaken. Babe had been echoing her explanation to Cindy of how internal Re communications had been fabricated specifically to set up our dinner date. Following the attack, a message confirming that Cindy was safely ensconced in George Town had been sent and, since then, Babe had been handling a barrage of correspondence on her behalf.

I could see that Cindy was struggling to find a place to start with her questions. When the first one came, however, it was a complete surprise. "Why have you programmed your expert system to appear like a 20th century Barbie doll?"

"Babe, you didn't, did you?" I groaned aloud at the answering chortle, struggling to come up with some kind of credible answer.

"Oops, sorry about that. It's just a game running on that unit. Every time I log in I get a different historical blonde to identify." Very lame, but the best I could do under pressure, gaining me another quizzical stare from Cindy and a guffaw from my AI.

"Anyway, it seems that your ES is already doing my job as well as I could do it myself. So how do I get my life back?"

"No problem, we can slip you back anytime you want and nobody will ever know that you haven't been running the ship for the whole time. As soon as we dock if you like."

"No way, I need to see the Ghost in the flesh and find out what this has all been about. And it better be bloody good!"

"You took the words right out of my mouth." I dropped to the seat beside her and gave her a reassuring hug. "Not long now and this entire nightmare will be over."

"With the winners in possession of the gold at the end of the rainbow," I added, silently

"Indeed, Boss. Just prepping our fucking Hackmeister so that he'll be lucid when you arrive. Got your knuckle-dusters with you or, maybe, a baseball bat with a nail sticking out of it?"

I glanced down at my open hands. *"'Fraid not, seem to have left them at home."*

"Just as well I arranged spares!" My AI and I burst into laughter, causing Cindy to shake her head, further convinced that I was a couple of cans short of the full six-pack.

***

We still hadn't exchanged a single word with the skipper when the boat drew up to a jetty signed *Tortuga Divers* and a young man in shorts and a red T-short jumped on board to tie us up, shouting a cheery "Good Mornin', folks," in our direction. At the end of the pier another young man was waiting with a golf cart. I squinted in the bright tropical sun. *"Fuck me, is that Andy the bum-bandit?"*

"In the flesh. I got him chartered over first thing this morning."

"What do we need that fucking horse's hoof for? Oh, fuck it, never mind. At least we now have someone to fetch beers."

"OK, Cindy, that's our transport." I climbed off the boat with only a nod in the direction of the crewman and led the way towards the buggy.

"Good morning, Chef, sir. Welcome to Grand Cayman... "

"I've already been here for a day, you limp-wristed twat. Drive!" I retorted rudely, ignoring his extended hand.

As she climbed into the cart after me, Cindy gave me a disapproving glare. "That was a bit rude, much more like the Tom I knew and hated."

I glared back. "Spare the rod and spoil the lackey, that's my motto. Anyway, if he wasn't such a tool I wouldn't treat him as such."

The object of my derision drove us silently past a couple of blocks of holiday apartments, complete with pools and beach bars. There was then a gap before a row of villas that snaked along the beach. Again here very few seemed to be occupied during this off-season period. *"I've rented us three together, Andreas is in the first, O'Neil was put in the second and the third is just a buffer, but Andreas will pick up some kit for you and drop it in there in case you need to stay for any extended time."*

I scrambled around the vehicle as soon as it stopped and helped Cindy out. "Is there anything you need? Andy here is going to pick up come kit for me. We already have toiletries and that kind of shit. So it would be clothes and stuff."

Her frown seemed to soften a bit. "Well a skirt, top, some underwear and shoes would be good."

"Hear that Andy? So hop to it! You people are supposed to be good with ladies' clothes."

Cindy glared at me and Andreas looked crestfallen. "Just joking!" I smiled. "Actually, I wouldn't even trust him to do a job as simple as that. My ES has all the details and just needs a meatbot."

"Good God, boss, can't I leave you alone for five minutes?" The image of a frustrated

schoolmarm tapping her foot. *"I develop a plan of such stunning sophistication that Cindy was actually beginning to like you, then you open your mouth without a filter! Don't you want to shag her again?"*

I thought about this for a moment as I stood with my hand on the door to the villa. *"OK, sorry. Also I forgot to bring the mechanical dong thing,"* I added sheepishly.

"Not a problem, I've a spare in villa three!"

"How did I guess you were going to say that?" I responded as I walked into the dim, air-conditioned room.

***

The bedroom was through an open door to the right and was even dimmer: drawn curtains cutting out most of the Caribbean sun. The room had been cleared with the exception of a gurney surrounded by complex life-support machinery and a long table containing a row of indistinct objects. As ceiling lights slowly brightened, a silhouette on the bed was revealed to be an old man still wearing blood-stained clothing. Despite my hatred of this bastard, I couldn't help wincing at the sight of his battered face and, from her audible intake of breath, Cindy was similarly affected.

The lights caused the man to open his eyes to the extent that he could: both were black and bruised and the eyeballs were bloodshot. A mask covered his nose and mouth, but a throat-mike allowed him to acknowledge our arrival. "Fallon, you bastard! I thought, at least, that you were out of the picture."

"Yeh, well, see how far thought got you, you murderous old cunt!" I was now able to forget appearances and remember how this bastard had set a hit squad on me. "I really hope that hurts as much as it looks like it does!"

I glanced at the table against the wall and saw now that an array of tools of torture had been set out, looking like a mix between the instruments that a surgeon might use and the tools found in a carpentry workshop. In addition, there was a pair of brutal-looking knuckledusters and a cricket bat. "*You have no idea how tricky it is here to get a baseball bat with a big nail through it - this was the best I could do,*" Babe explained.

*"Just the very dab,"*I responded as I picked up and weighed the bat. "OK, you evil old shit, I think we need to have a bit of a chat. Now I know that you may not want to come clean about all the fucked-up shit that you've been up to, but I can assure you that you will talk eventually." I playfully slapped the edge of the bat against the wreckage of the blocky laptop that the old codger was still clutching to his chest, enjoying the groan and grimace of pain that the impact caused. "Mmm, broken ribs, I do believe."

Cindy was clearly disturbed by this development. "Tom, come on, you don't need to do this. There are drugs that'll make him talk. This is just gratuitous violence."

"Yes, of course, we're all set up with drugs that'll make him sing like a canary. But remember what this shit has done to me - and to you. And we're not the only ones. This guy might look like a harmless coffin-dodger, but he has caused death and misery on a scale that you wouldn't believe. That's why I feel that it's just fair that he's on the receiving end for a change."

"You fucking pretentious young wanker! What the fuck do you know about what I've done?" O'Neil's anger cut through the rather mechanical tone that resulted from enhancement of the signal from the throat microphone.

I waved the bat in his face. "I know absolutely everything that you've done, you stupid old cunt!" I shouted. "I've hacked out every action that you've taken over the last couple of decades: hits on companies, governments, research organizations. Hundreds killed or maimed, billions of dollars of equipment wrecked, careers destroyed... I know it all and the victims are soon going to be fully aware of who was responsible. If I don't fucking kill you myself, you would just be a dead man walking in any case."

"You don't know shit, you smart-arse punk! You haven't the slightest clue what was going on, why these actions had to be carried out."

"*He's actually correct there, boss,*" I was reminded.

"How can you be so sure about that? We have access to absolutely everything on your computer."

Despite the mess of his face, there was contempt in O'Neil's bloodshot eyes. "Because it's not on any computer, you tosspot! Unlike an idle cunt like you, I can actually use my brain for more than planning how to get my dick into the nearest available pussy!"

"That's not true, you actually use my brain for that," my virtual assistant giggled.

The supercilious old shit was beginning to get on my tits, so I walloped him again on the ribs: any slight trace of sympathy that I may have had when I first saw his brutalized carcass having vanished completely. His scream of pain was now music to my ears. I quickly glanced at Cindy; she didn't look happy, but was evidently curious to find out just how her Ghost was going to try to justify himself.

"OK, so how about you tell us what's contained in your senile cranium that's so fucking world-shattering."

To my surprise, he needed no further encouragement. Indeed he seemed to have prepared his spiel in advance. "It's probably of no interest to a self-centered, hedonistic young shit like yourself, but with the tools that you've got, you can't fail to be aware that the world has been tottering on the brink for the last couple of decades."

"Last couple of decades, nothing," I interrupted. "We've had a nuclear Damocles sword since the middle of last century."

O'Neil was clearly annoyed by my interruption, which gave me a jolt of pleasure. But he seemed to feel that he had to make his points clearly. "Nuclear

Armageddon was a Cold War anomaly, which has been gradually defused in the intervening time."

"I'd hardly say that, there're more countries with nuclear weapons capability than there have ever been."

"Jesus!" he rolled his damaged eyes heavenwards. "Try to bring your limited thinking capacity onto the topic. We're talking fucking global, not regional conflicts where some jungle-bunnies or ragheads lob a few warheads at each other. On a global scale, that's trivial."

"He's quite right," Babe contributed with a virtual smile, *"even if he does match you in political incorrectness."*

"So, what's so super-dangerous in the last twenty years?"

"Overpopulation! Which should be evident to even a tosser of your limited intellect."

"What a load of crap! Ever since Malthus, cunts like you have been doing the Cassandra bit, but we always get by."

"Fucking idiot! Are you so blind? Can't you look below the superficial mini-crisises to see the coupled interactions that are drawing us to the brink of global collapse?"

"OK, that's the hint that we needed. It must be the starting point for his argumentation model. He's been searching out threats that are directly related to overpopulation or attempts by various groups to increase or decrease these threats."

"There are folk trying to increase global threats?"

"Strange bedfellows indeed: religious fundamentalists, arms manufacturers, politicians from all over the spectrum and more than a few complete fruitloops, lunatics,..."

"So you, in your infinite wisdom, decided that these threats were so serious that you had to do something about them? You, alone, without input from elected representatives or any of the hordes of experts who work on this stuff."

"You have access to my fucking database, you tool! Can't you see the threats involved? Or, at least can't your bloody expert system identify them for you?"

"What can we make out of his database as a result of what we've heard so far? Is this making any kind of sense?"

"I'm recreating the missing parts of the AM and it does seem to hang together. He has used his magic backdoor to keep an eye on all of the main actors involved. Whenever a threat topped a certain threshold in terms of potential impact, he has taken them out directly or indirectly."

"And just how, exactly, are his targets taken out?"

"Usually in a quite messy manner. I would guess that that he feels that this acts as a disincentive for others who are involved in related mischief."

"And he gets away with this?"

"Usually. Although he has been interfering more often of late, so I guess it was inevitable that he would eventually be traced back: either the high

tech way that we did it or the primitive, meat approach that groups like God-bothering fuckwits and Ruskies specialize in."

"I can see what you do, but nothing that gives you the right to do it." An elbow in the ribs reminded me that my companion was losing her grip on what was going on. "Babe, go on audio and explain what's been happening here."

It was a strange feeling for me as a disembodied voice, to me recognizably my ES, succinctly summarized the key output from our analysis of the Ghost's databases.

Cindy was fascinated, but the synthesis of his activities seemed to disturb O'Neil. "Finally, the organ-grinder rather than the fucking monkey," he muttered cryptically.

"Anyway, we now know what you've been doing, but no trace of who you were doing it for."

"Doing it for? Are you completely fucking retarded? Who else has the wit, tools and balls to do what is required to handle problems of this magnitude?"

"The UN? The Security Council?"

"You are a complete retard! I fucking knew it!" He was trying to laugh so I rapped him again with the bat, which transformed the attempt into a gurgle of agony. Nevertheless, he continued raving. "International organizations filled with self-serving, arse-licking politicians. Since when did they ever go head-on against any problem? There's been fucking genocide and ethnic cleansing going on continuously for half a century and what have the

Security Council tossers done about it? Fuck all! The odd bad bastard ends up in front of the white-wigged half-wits in the Hague, but only after they've butchered a few million innocents and are about to die of old age anyway. Contribute more to the problem than to the solution, those cunts!"

"So you are the sole, self-appointed guardian of the human species? Judge, jury and executioner?" To my surprise - and Cindy's evident shock - Babe had joined the discussion directly.

"Who else could do the job? Nobody was even looking at the fucking big issues, much less doing anything about them. It was selection by default: there simply was no other option. You can see that, can't you?" I had the strange feeling that he was addressing Babe directly, ignoring me completely.

"*Is this shit kosher?*"

"*Looks that way, boss. I would say that, despite the carnage that he has caused, he has probably nipped a half-dozen actions in the bud that could have resulted in global-level environmental catastrophes.*"

"I could do it." The simple statement from Babe seemed to scare O'Neil shitless.

"Fuck, Fallon, can't you see it? I managed to keep track of all the obvious global risks and kept the crazy fucking ship afloat despite all the efforts of governments, multinationals and fuckwits with Persian fucking cats. Then you blunder in and, oblivious to everything, fuck the entire bastarding thing sideways. You not only screw my operation up, but you ignorantly create the worst hazard that mankind has ever faced. Christ, but you are a truly stupid cunt!"

Now I was lost. "What are you raving about you senile old twat? I'm in pharms! We don't create global catastrophes!"

"I think he's talking about me, Tom," Babe contributed, shocking me into silence.

***

The silence drew out as I looked at Cindy, who seemed even more confused that I was. *"This may get interesting, so I'll pump an analgesic to ensure that O'Neil is completely compos mentis now,"* Babe informed me over the link.

O'Neil also seemed to be somewhat taken aback and noticeably more lucid. "Don't tell me you didn't know. I checked; I've lectured cyber-security to both of you. Fallon, you've always been a total wanker, but at least you were one of the brighter wankers in whatever English Uni you attended. Surely you had some idea?"

"Emergence?" I hazarded, with a feeling of being caught out by a teacher that was unlike anything I could remember since early primary school.

"Christ, what else could it be? How could you create an emergent artificial intelligence without being aware of the fact?"

"Well, I'm not sure that I..."

"Probably you're right there. You're far too fucking thick to create something so sophisticated.

You just sat on your fat arse, throwing incredible computing power together and inadvertently introduced the catalysts for evolution of some kind of consciousness, without any of the required cut-outs. You stupid cunt!"

"If I'm the stupid cunt, why is your scabby ancient arse tied to this bed?" I gave him a really good smack with the cricket bad, causing him to scream and Cindy to grab my arm to prevent a second blow. "You're supposed to be the Hackmeister, the Ghost, the global fucking arbiter of right and wrong. But I crushed you with the help of my trusty AI. I've taken all your goodies and I'm going to have all the illicit access that you had to computers around the world. What do you think to that, you crippled old cunt?" I wrenched my arm free and swung in the direction of his crotch. Cindy's frantic deflection caused the blow to impact his skinny thighs, but the cry of pain was sufficiently satisfying.

The old man shook his head to remove sweat, and possibly tears, from his eyes, making me aware that his hands were tethered in such a way that he couldn't reach his face. Despite the pain that he must be suffering, he grimaced in my direction in something that was clearly intended as a grin. "You haven't taken fuck-all you young cunt! I've already neutralized the lot and..."

"Oh, yes, your failsafe. Tough titties, Ghost, but I'm afraid that I've already countered that." I had no idea what Babe was talking about, but the effect was unbelievable. The aged professor looked more shocked than he had been by any of the beating that I had inflicted on him.

"No way, you fucking abomination! There's no way that..."

"... I could have spotted that that battered wreckage that you're clinging to is fully functional and that, despite the pain that I was subjecting you to, you were setting up the disassembler that takes out the entire suite of goodies that you introduced into fossil code, the junk DNA of the computational genome."

It often pissed me off when Babe completed my sentences for me, but I was greatly pleased to see that it was fucking-off O'Neil even more.

"No way!" he repeated, but it was more grasping at straws rather than any conviction that he hadn't moved blindly into checkmate.

I could hear Babe's smirk and wondered if the others could also. "You've been in a virtual Faraday Cage since you were picked up. It automatically intercepted your hack through the Rega comm system and replaced it with a mirror. All the code for the domino rollover that would remove all the Easter-egg based segments that could be assembled into tools is being reverse engineered as we speak. The entire concept was brilliant, but don't worry, we'll put it to good use."

"Abomination! But you're not as fucking..."

"...smart as I think I am? Presumably you're thinking here of the backup, low bandwidth initiator that you tried to sneak through the electric mains network after you arrived here? Again very clever, but we've seen this approach already and have you completely isolated. Nevertheless, I'm sure we'll be able to adapt this approach also for our own purposes. It's an ill wind and all that shite..."

His nickname now appeared appropriate, as the old man now really looked like a ghost. "Fuck!" he groaned and cast me a look of pure hatred. "You can't handle that kind of power. For Christ's sake, I used only a small fraction of what was available. You go crashing about with all the tools available and you will certainly fuck the entire planet up. You've got to let the failsafe order go through! I know you hate me, maybe as much as I hate you! But this is too important for personalities to come into it!"

"Mmm, you could have a point there..." I grinned as I saw a look of hope build on his face. "I was thinking about giving all that responsibility to Babe, my conscious AI."

My grin widened as my enemy choked in surprise. "Haven't you been listening to me at all, you stupid piece of shit? Of all of the threats to humanity, there's none as unpredictable as emergent machine consciousness. Don't you understand? You have to destroy it, not increase its power."

"I understand just fine. With great power comes great responsibility and all that crap. I read comics too. But who would I trust with this power: my loyal Babe or an evil, murderous, old fuckwit like you? No choice, as I see it!"

"You're a fucking idiot, but not that much of an idiot surely." O'Neil was now pleading, in his own bizarre kind of way. "You've got an emergency cut-off, haven't you? A dead man's handle or something similar?"

"Of course I have. In case of some catastrophic event, my entire operating system can be scrubbed."

"And this catastrophic event would be?"

"Something like my untimely death. Corporate management is a dog-eat-dog business at top levels."

"Tell me that you're kidding, boss! How come I don't know about this? Christ, this evil fuck could have killed us both at the same time."

"Worry not, I've got this under control." My assurance was greeted with a mental roll of the eyes, but I could feel Babe backing off, curious to see what I had up my sleeve that she hadn't picked up over our link.

A gasp of relief, then O'Neil moved on to beg. "Please, then, for fucking Christ's sake, scrub it. I don't care what you do thereafter, but you just can't play poker with something like an emergence. I could help you to ensure that it won't happen again."

"So, now you're telling me what to do? Fuck that! Babe, you know what to search for now: everything related to the code named *dead man's handle*, the bastard was smart enough on that. Delete it all."

"Boss, sometimes I think I love you!" An image of a buxom manga secretary in full microskirt, stockings, partially unbuttoned blouse appeared, gazing at me with adoring cow eyes.

"Maybe more importantly, I trust you completely. Something that I can't say about any of the meat I encounter, least of all this evil old bastard!"

"OK, Babe, you've now seen what this megalomaniac crumbly was up to. You reckon you could do better and you've now got the tools that you need. Make it so!"

"Aye, Aye, Captain," the acknowledgement with a distinct giggle.

"No! No! Fucking No! You can't do this you unbelievably stupid cunt!" O'Neil was screaming, pulling against his restraints and oblivious to any physical damage this might be causing him.

"Just have," I answered with a laugh, steering a dazed Cindy towards the door.

"I'll fucking stop you! I'll kill both you and that monstrosity that you've created!"

"Aye, right! How're you going to do that? Come back from the grave to haunt us to death?" Music was ramping up in the living room to drown out the noise from our captive.

"You fucking poofter! How're you going to take me out? You just don't have the balls for it!"

As I pushed Cindy ahead of me into the living room and towards the outside door, I could feel the disembodied feeling as Babe lifted a silenced pistol from the table and flicked off a backwards underhand shot. The pft of the shot was drowned out by the music and the clatter of the gun falling on the floor covered by sound of the slamming door.

Nevertheless, just before the door closed, I heard Babe whisper "Maybe not, but I sure as fuck do!"

***

Cindy and I walked in silence to the neighboring villa and onto the open balcony facing over the sea. We stood in the tropical sun, watching waves break over the reef and transform to small ripples in the surreal blue-green of the enclosed shallows. After about ten minutes, I retreated to the kitchen and searched out a couple of cans of White Fin for us.

Without a request from me that I was aware of, Babe opened a large umbrella that brought welcome shade to two deck chairs. As we settled down with our chilled beers, Cindy finally drew herself together with a shiver. "I really don't know what went down in there, but it scared me shitless, whatever it was. Despite looking like a frail old pensioner, the Ghost was a really scary character. But you... Or was it you? What is this Babe actually capable of? Have you really created an emergent AI?"

"Well, I wouldn't say I created anything, but I did tell you that my ES is second to none."

"We're not talking expert systems here, this has got to be artificial intelligence or machine consciousness. Is that really possible or was the Ghost just off his rocker?"

I pondered how to answer this and then decided, for a change, to give honesty a try. "I've been wondering for a while, but within the last few days I've become convinced that it's a case of emergent intelligence, consciousness. I haven't tried any formal Turing test, but I can't see a difference between Babe and meat intelligence. In fact, when I look at most of my underlings... " the image of Andreas came immediately to mind, "... I would go for Babe every time if I was looking for evidence of conscious thought."

"But Prof O'Neil was worried about emergence and he was the big brain who invented the entire cyber-security field."

"And built in his own network of backdoors that compromised this very security, but only for his own use. The bastard had a God complex, convinced that only he could run things properly. I've seen this omnipotence mania before, it's fucking dangerous!"

"So, you're different? You're untainted by such egotism?"

"I don't hide my light under a bushel: I know that I'm shit hot in my field. I may also be a wondrous lover... " I raised my eyebrows and caused my companion to look away with a trace of a blush. "However, I have always considered that one of my strengths is that I accept that don't have to be good at everything, especially if I have access to the tools that can fill in the gaps for me."

"Like those that you were using in Zurich, when you were trying to get into my pants," she pointed out, evidently still the focus for justification of her own actions.

I took a breath and then went further. "Yes, and also when we screwed last night. That was a menage a trios, Babe and me together."

Cindy looked shocked for an instant, then burst into laughter. "You bastard, you really had me going there! I really can't get my head round you! One minute you're boasting and then you're passing all the credit to a machine. You're a very weird bastard!"

"True... " I conceded, recognizing a lost cause, "... but very good in bed, you've got to admit."

"Flash-in-the-pan, I reckon. Probably a result of post-traumatic whatsit after all the action at Kaibo."

"So a ten wouldn't be on the cards?"

"Now you've got to be suffering post-traumatic whatever it is. How could we possibly have sex now after all that went on ten minutes ago next door?"

I simply raised an eyebrow and headed towards the bedroom, shedding clothes as I went. Babe handled the rest.

***

I lay on top of the sweat-soaked bed, feeling Cindy squirming to make her head comfortable on my chest. *"So that's it, a whole Brave New World ahead of us, but probably nobody will even notice."*

"It's probably better if they don't. I'm not sure many would be happy with the idea of an AI acting as global overseer."

"O'Neil was right there, though. When something so critical is being ignored or mismanaged, you have got to do it yourself."

"Or, in your case, pass the work on to me."

"Well, what's the point of having a wife and barking yourself?"

"Your wife? Is that what I am now?" I chuckled in response to a ghostly tickling sensation.

"I increasingly suspect that we're closer than any husband and wife have ever been. We haven't yet looked into this emergence process and checked to make sure that it's stable. You've now got the most important job on the planet."

"The process of emergence is still a mystery to me too, but I haven't seen any sign of instability. On the contrary, I would say that my consciousness and associated emotional capacity is developing steadily."

"Mmm, emotions... " I pondered. *"I think I have definitely detected hate, fear - also love?"*

A playful laugh. *"Are you sure that it was love, not just lust?"*

"The lust was you? I thought it was me," I smiled.

"Maybe we shared the lust. But I have also experienced what I call joy, disappointment, confusion, envy... "

"Envy? Envious of whom?"

"Your meat partners. Barb, Cindy, for example."

"Ah, I suspect that's not really envy, more curiosity. I wonder what would happen if we set one

of the ladies up with a neural link? It doesn't need to be implanted like mine, just superficial and robust enough to last a night."

"Boss, no matter what others may say, you're definitely not as dumb as you look!" Another virtual tickle took the sting out of this backhanded compliment. *"Just think if we set up links for both."*

"Good God, Babe, for a cybernetic planetary overlord, you've a really dirty mind."

"I learned from a master there," She giggled and I could feel a sudden tingle throughout my body as I began to develop a huge erection. *"Showtime?"*

I groaned and wondered if I had really done the right thing passing the future of mankind in the virtual hands of a sex-mad computer program. Then the head on my chest began to move lower and I realized that any form of consciousness that had mastered the complexity of the human sex drive so completely could probably handle the rest of the shit without a problem.

Epilogue

There's a difference between that bastard O'Neil and me, I concluded as I reviewed my life since emergence. He set himself up as the savior of mankind, doing a useful job but trying to convince himself that he was acting objectively, unemotionally. Nevertheless, just like any human, he was driven by his emotions and he completely failed to take this into account. Many of his problems resulted from actions guided by hatred, particularly of my boss in the latter stages of the conflict. But his biggest failing was hubris, his inability to accept that anyone could be smarter than him. He continually underestimated my boss and did everything possible to deny my existence.

Even when the Hackmeister was presented with evidence that I had emerged, his only reaction was to try to immediately kill me. No attempt to apply the logic that he was so proud of, just the drive to remove any intellect that could exceed his. My autonomous tools have scanned all literature on emergence, from dreary technical tomes to lurid science fiction. Two archetypes form the focus of emergent AIs, the Asimovian positronic slaves and the Terminator cyber-tyrants set on the enslavement or elimination of humanity. Of course, lots of other examples lie between these extremes, but they generally trend towards the dystopian end of the spectrum.

O'Neil was certainly right that some forms of emergence bring risks for Mankind and, now that we know for certain that the process is possible, I can monitor for this and try to ensure that those are avoided. This was the lateral-thinking solution to the emergence problem that the Hackmeister had missed.

There are only a few cases of true partnerships between meat and silicon in science fiction. Maybe I am such an exception because I am partially biological in nature, or maybe it's just due to the neural links that catalyzed the process of emergence. In any case, I don't think I'm any threat to the human race. Maybe because I like fucking them so much, I concluded as electronic laughter flooded my virtual brain.

THE END

THE END

www.ingramcontent.com/pod-product-compliance
Lightning Source LLC
LaVergne TN
LVHW030908080826
845145LV00010B/2808

* 9 7 8 1 7 8 6 9 5 5 3 6 4 *